NOTHING LASTS FOREVER

Books by Sidney Sheldon

NOTHING LASTS FOREVER
THE STARS SHINE DOWN
THE DOOMSDAY CONSPIRACY
MEMORIES OF MIDNIGHT
THE SANDS OF TIME
WINDMILLS OF THE GODS
IF TOMORROW COMES
MASTER OF THE GAME
RAGE OF ANGELS
BLOODLINE
A STRANGER IN THE MIRROR
THE OTHER SIDE OF MIDNIGHT
THE NAKED FACE

SIDNEY SHELDON

NOTHING LASTS FOREVER

William Morrow and Company, Inc.
New York

This Large Print Book carries the Seal of Approval of N.A.V.H.

Library of Congress Cataloging-in-Publication Data

Sheldon, Sidney.
    Nothing lasts forever / by Sidney Sheldon.
       p. cm.
    ISBN 0-688-13874-8
    1. Women physicians—United States—Fiction. 2. Hospitals—United States—Fiction. I. Title.
  PS3569.H3927N67   1994
  813'.54—dc20
                                           94-5437
                                             CIP

Printed in the United States of America

First Edition

1 2 3 4 5 6 7 8 9 10

TO ANASTASIA AND
RODERICK MANN, WITH LOVE

The author wishes to express his deep
appreciation to the many doctors, nurses,
and medical technicians who were
generous enough to share their expertise
with him.

What cannot be cured with medicaments is cured by the knife, what the knife cannot cure is cured with the searing iron, and whatever this cannot cure must be considered incurable.
—HIPPOCRATES, CIRCA 480 B.C.

There are three classes of human beings: men, women, and women physicians.
—SIR WILLIAM OSLER

NOTHING
LASTS
FOREVER

Prologue

San Francisco
Spring 1995

District Attorney Carl Andrews was in a fury. "What the hell is going on here?" he demanded. "We have three doctors living together and working at the same hospital. One of them almost gets an entire hospital closed down, the second one kills a patient for a million dollars, and the third one is murdered."

Andrews stopped to take a deep breath. "And they're all women! Three goddam women doctors! The media is treating them like celebrities. They're all over the tube. *60 Minutes* did a segment on them. Barbara Walters did a special on them. I can't pick up a newspaper or magazine without seeing their pictures, or reading about them. Two to one,

15

Hollywood is going to make a movie about them, and they'll turn the bitches into some kind of heroines! I wouldn't be surprised if the government put their faces on postage stamps, like Presley. Well, by God, I won't have it!" He slammed a fist down against the photograph of a woman on the cover of *Time* magazine. The caption read: "Dr. Paige Taylor—Angel of Mercy or the Devil's Disciple?"

"Dr. Paige Taylor." The district attorney's voice was filled with disgust. He turned to Gus Venable, his chief prosecuting attorney. "I'm handing this trial over to you, Gus. I want a conviction. Murder One. The gas chamber."

"Don't worry," Gus Venable said quietly. "I'll see to it."

Sitting in the courtroom watching Dr. Paige Taylor, Gus Venable thought: *She's jury-proof.* Then he smiled to himself. *No one is jury-proof.* She was tall and slender, with eyes that were a startling dark brown in her pale face. A disinterested observer would have dismissed her as an attractive woman. A more observant one would have noticed something else—that all the different phases of her life coexisted in her. There was the happy excitement of the child, superimposed onto the shy uncertainty of the adolescent and the wisdom and pain of the woman. There was a look of innocence about her. *She's the kind of girl,* Gus Venable thought cynically, *a man would be proud to take home to his mother. If his mother had a taste for cold-blooded killers.*

There was an almost eerie sense of remoteness in her eyes, a look that said that Dr. Paige Taylor had retreated deep inside herself to a different place, a different time, far from the cold, sterile courtroom where she was trapped.

The trial was taking place in the venerable old San Francisco Hall of Justice on Bryant Street. The building, which housed the Superior Court and County Jail, was a forbidding-looking edifice, seven stories high, made of square gray stone. Visitors arriving at the courthouse were funneled through electronic security checkpoints. Upstairs, on the third floor, was the Superior Court. In Courtroom 121, where murder trials were held, the judge's bench stood against the rear wall, with an American flag behind it. To the left of the bench was the jury box, and in the center were two tables separated by an aisle, one for the prosecuting attorney, the other for the defense attorney.

The courtroom was packed with reporters

and the type of spectators attracted to fatal highway accidents and murder trials. As murder trials went, this one was spectacular. Gus Venable, the prosecuting attorney, was a show in himself. He was a burly man, larger than life, with a mane of gray hair, a goatee, and the courtly manner of a Southern plantation owner. He had never been to the South. He had an air of vague bewilderment and the brain of a computer. His trademark, summer and winter, was a white suit, with an old-fashioned stiff-collar shirt.

Paige Taylor's attorney, Alan Penn, was Venable's opposite, a compact, energetic shark, who had built a reputation for racking up acquittals for his clients.

The two men had faced each other before, and their relationship was one of grudging respect and total mistrust. To Venable's surprise, Alan Penn had come to see him the week before the trial was to begin.

"I came here to do you a favor, Gus."

Beware of defense attorneys bearing gifts. "What did you have in mind, Alan?"

"Now understand—I haven't discussed this with my client yet, but suppose—just suppose—I could persuade her to plead guilty to a reduced charge and save the State the cost of a trial?"

"Are you asking me to plea-bargain?"

"Yes."

Gus Venable reached down to his desk, searching for something. "I can't find my damn calendar. Do you know what the date is?"

"June first. Why?"

"For a minute there, I thought it must be Christmas already, or you wouldn't be asking for a present like that."

"Gus . . ."

Venable leaned forward in his chair. "You know, Alan, ordinarily, I'd be inclined to go along with you. Tell you the truth, I'd like to be in Alaska fishing right now. But the answer is no. You're defending a cold-blooded killer who murdered a helpless patient for his money. I'm demanding the death penalty."

"I think she's innocent, and I—"

Venable gave a short, explosive laugh. "No, you don't. And neither does anyone else. It's an open-and-shut case. Your client is as guilty as Cain."

"Not until the jury says so, Gus."

"They will." He paused. "They will."

After Alan Penn left, Gus Venable sat there thinking about their conversation. Penn's coming to him was a sign of weakness. Penn knew there was no chance he could win the trial. Gus Venable thought about the irrefutable evidence he had, and the witnesses he was going to call, and he was satisfied.

There was no question about it. Dr. Paige Taylor was going to the gas chamber.

It had not been easy to impanel a jury. The case had occupied the headlines for months. The cold-bloodedness of the murder had created a tidal wave of anger.

The presiding judge was Vanessa Young, a tough, brilliant black jurist rumored to be the next nominee for the United States Supreme Court. She was not known for being patient with lawyers, and she had a quick temper. There was an adage among San Francisco trial lawyers: *If your client is guilty, and you're looking for mercy, stay away from Judge Young's courtroom.*

The day before the start of the trial, Judge Young had summoned the two attorneys to her chambers.

"We're going to set some ground rules, gentlemen. Because of the serious nature of this trial, I'm willing to make certain allowances to make sure that the defendant gets a fair trial. But I'm warning both of you not to try to take advantage of that. Is that clear?"

"Yes, your honor."

"Yes, your honor."

* * *

Gus Venable was finishing his opening statement. "And so, ladies and gentlemen of the jury, the State will prove—yes, prove beyond a reasonable doubt—that Dr. Paige Taylor killed her patient, John Cronin. And not only did she commit murder, she did it for money . . . a lot of money. She killed John Cronin for one million dollars.

"Believe me, after you've heard all the evidence, you will have no trouble in finding Dr. Paige Taylor guilty of murder in the first degree. Thank you."

The jury sat in silence, unmoved but expectant.

Gus Venable turned to the judge. "If it please your honor, I would like to call Gary Williams as the State's first witness."

When the witness was sworn in, Gus Venable said, "You're an orderly at Embarcadero County Hospital?"

"Yes, that's right."

"Were you working in Ward Three when John Cronin was brought in last year?"

"Yes."

"Can you tell us who the doctor in charge of his case was?"

"Dr. Taylor."

21

"How would you characterize the relationship between Dr. Taylor and John Cronin?"

"Objection!" Alan Penn was on his feet. "He's calling for a conclusion from the witness."

"Sustained."

"Let me phrase it another way. Did you ever hear any conversations between Dr. Taylor and John Cronin?"

"Oh, sure. I couldn't help it. I worked that ward all the time."

"Would you describe those conversations as friendly?"

"No, sir."

"Really? Why do you say that?"

"Well, I remember the first day Mr. Cronin was brought in, and Dr. Taylor started to examine him, he said to keep her . . ." He hesitated. "I don't know if I can repeat his language."

"Go ahead, Mr. Williams. I don't think there are any children in this courtroom."

"Well, he told her to keep her fucking hands off him."

"He said *that* to Dr. Taylor?"

"Yes, sir."

"Please tell the court what else you may have seen or heard."

"Well, he always called her 'that bitch.' He

22

didn't want her to go near him. Whenever she came into his room, he would say things like 'Here comes that bitch again!' and 'Tell that bitch to leave me alone' and 'Why don't they get me a *real* doctor?' "

Gus Venable paused to look over to where Dr. Taylor was seated. The jurors' eyes followed him. Venable shook his head, as though saddened, then turned back to the witness. "Did Mr. Cronin seem to you to be a man who wanted to give a million dollars to Dr. Taylor?"

Alan Penn was on his feet again. "Objection! He's calling for an opinion again."

Judge Young said, "Overruled. The witness may answer the question."

Alan Penn looked at Paige Taylor and sank back in his seat.

"Hell, no. He hated her guts."

Dr. Arthur Kane was in the witness box.

Gus Venable said, "Dr. Kane, you were the staff doctor in charge when it was discovered that John Cronin was mur—" He looked at Judge Young. ". . . killed by insulin being introduced into his IV. Is that correct?"

"It is."

"And you subsequently discovered that Dr. Taylor was responsible."

"That's correct."

"Dr. Kane, I'm going to show you the official hospital death form signed by Dr. Taylor." He picked up a paper and handed it to Kane. "Would you read it aloud, please?"

Kane began to read. " 'John Cronin. Cause of Death: Respiratory arrest occurred as a complication of myocardial infarction occurring as a complication of pulmonary embolus.' "

"And in layman's language?"

"The report says that the patient died of a heart attack."

"And that paper is signed by Dr. Taylor?"

"Yes."

"Dr. Kane, was that the true cause of John Cronin's death?"

"No. The insulin injection caused his death."

"So, Dr. Taylor administered a fatal dose of insulin and then falsified the report?"

"Yes."

"And you reported it to Dr. Wallace, the hospital administrator, who then reported it to the authorities?"

"Yes. I felt it was my duty." His voice rang with righteous indignation. "I'm a doctor. I don't believe in taking the life of another human being under any circumstances."

*   *   *

The next witness called was John Cronin's widow. Hazel Cronin was in her late thirties, with flaming red hair, and a voluptuous figure that her plain black dress failed to conceal.

Gus Venable said, "I know how painful this is for you, Mrs. Cronin, but I must ask you to describe to the jury your relationship with your late husband."

The widow Cronin dabbed at her eyes with a large lace handkerchief. "John and I had a loving marriage. He was a wonderful man. He often told me I had brought him the only real happiness he had ever known."

"How long were you married to John Cronin?"

"Two years, but John always said it was like two years in heaven."

"Mrs. Cronin, did your husband ever discuss Dr. Taylor with you? Tell you what a great doctor he thought she was? Or how helpful she had been to him? Or how much he liked her?"

"He never mentioned her."

"Never?"

"Never."

"Did John ever discuss cutting you and your brothers out of his will?"

"Absolutely not. He was the most generous man in the world. He always told me that there was nothing I couldn't have, and that when he died . . ." Her voice broke. ". . . that when he died, I would be a wealthy woman, and . . ." She could not go on.

Judge Young said, "We'll have a fifteen-minute recess."

Seated in the back of the courtroom, Jason Curtis was filled with anger. He could not believe what the witnesses were saying about Paige. *This is the woman I love*, he thought. *The woman I'm going to marry.*

Immediately after Paige's arrest, Jason Curtis had gone to visit her in jail.

"We'll fight this," he assured her. "I'll get you the best criminal lawyer in the country." A name immediately sprang to mind. *Alan Penn.* Jason had gone to see him.

"I've been following the case in the papers," Penn said. "The press has already tried and convicted her of murdering John Cronin for a bundle. What's more, she admits she killed him."

"I know her," Jason Curtis told him. "Believe me, there's no way Paige could have done what she did for money."

"Since she admits she killed him," Penn said, "what we're dealing with here then is euthanasia. Mercy killings are against the law in California, as in most states, but there are a lot of mixed feelings about them. I can make a pretty good case for Florence Nightingale listening to a Higher Voice and all that shit, but the problem is that your lady love killed a patient who left her a million dollars in his will. Which came first, the chicken or the egg? Did she know about the million before she killed him, or after?"

"Paige didn't know a thing about the money," Jason said firmly.

Penn's tone was noncommittal. "Right. It was just a happy coincidence. The DA is calling for Murder One, and he wants the death penalty."

"Will you take the case?"

Penn hesitated. It was obvious that Jason Curtis believed in Dr. Taylor. *The way Samson believed in Delilah.* He looked at Jason and thought: *I wonder if the poor son of a bitch had a haircut and doesn't know it.*

Jason was waiting for an answer.

"I'll take the case, as long as you know it's all uphill. It's going to be a tough one to win."

Alan Penn's statement turned out to be overly optimistic.

* * *

When the trial resumed the following morning, Gus Venable called a string of new witnesses.

A nurse was on the stand. "I heard John Cronin say, 'I know I'll die on the operating table. You're going to kill me. I hope they get you for murder.'"

An attorney, Roderick Pelham, was on the stand. Gus Venable said, "When you told Dr. Taylor about the million dollars from John Cronin's estate, what did she say?"

"She said something like 'It seems unethical. He was my patient.'"

"She admitted it was unethical?"

"Yes."

"But she agreed to take the money?"

"Oh, yes. Absolutely."

Alan Penn was cross-examining.

"Mr. Pelham, was Dr. Taylor expecting your visit?"

"Why, no, I . . ."

"You didn't call her and say, 'John Cronin left you one million dollars'?"

"No. I . . ."

"So when you told her, you were actually face-to-face with her?"

"Yes."

"In a position to see her reaction to the news?"

"Yes."

"And when you told her about the money, how did she react?"

"Well—she—she seemed surprised, but . . ."

"Thank you, Mr. Pelham. That's all."

The trial was now in its fourth week. The spectators and press had found the prosecuting attorney and defense attorney fascinating to watch. Gus Venable was dressed in white and Alan Penn in black, and the two of them had moved around the courtroom like players in a deadly, choreographed game of chess, with Paige Taylor the sacrificial pawn.

Gus Venable was tying up the loose ends.

"If the court please, I would like to call Alma Rogers to the witness stand."

When his witness was sworn in, Venable said, "Mrs. Rogers, what is your occupation?"

"It's *Miss* Rogers."

"I do beg your pardon."

"I work at the Corniche Travel Agency."

"Your agency books tours to various countries and makes hotel reservations and handles other accommodations for your clients?"

"Yes, sir."

"I want you to take a look at the defendant. Have you ever seen her before?"

"Oh, yes. She came into our travel agency two or three years ago."

"And what did she want?"

"She said she was interested in a trip to London and Paris and, I believe, Venice."

"Did she ask about package tours?"

"Oh, no. She said she wanted everything first class—plane, hotel. And I believe she was interested in chartering a yacht."

The courtroom was hushed. Gus Venable walked over to the prosecutor's table and held up some folders. "The police found these brochures in Dr. Taylor's apartment. These are travel itineraries to Paris and London and Venice, brochures for expensive hotels and airlines, and one listing the cost of chartering a private yacht."

There was a loud murmur from the courtroom.

The prosecutor had opened one of the brochures.

"Here are some of the yachts listed for charter," he read aloud. "The *Christina O* . . . twenty-six thousand dollars a week plus ship's expenses . . . the *Resolute Time*, twenty-four thousand five hundred dollars a week . . . the *Lucky Dream,* twenty-seven thousand three

30

hundred dollars a week." He looked up. "There's a check mark after the *Lucky Dream*. Paige Taylor had already selected the twenty-seven-thousand-three-hundred-a-week yacht. She just hadn't selected her victim yet.

"We'd like to have these marked Exhibit A." Venable turned to Alan Penn and smiled. Alan Penn looked at Paige. She was staring down at the table, her face pale. "Your witness."

Penn rose to his feet, stalling, thinking fast.

"How is the travel business these days, Miss Rogers?"

"I beg your pardon?"

"I asked how business was. Is Corniche a large travel agency?"

"It's quite large, yes."

"I imagine a lot of people come in to inquire about trips."

"Oh, yes."

"Would you say five or six people a day?"

"Oh, no!" Her voice was indignant. "We talk to as many as fifty people a day about travel arrangements."

"Fifty people a day?" He sounded impressed. "And the day we're talking about was two or three years ago. If you multiply fifty by nine hundred days, that's roughly forty-five thousand people."

"I suppose so."

"And yet, out of all those people, you remembered Dr. Taylor. Why is that?"

"Well, she and her two friends were so excited about taking a trip to Europe. I thought it was lovely. They were like schoolgirls. Oh, yes. I remember them very clearly, particularly because they didn't look like they could afford a yacht."

"I see. I suppose everyone who comes in and asks for a brochure goes away on a trip?"

"Well, of course not. But—"

"Dr. Taylor didn't actually *book* a trip, did she?"

"Well, no. Not with us. She—"

"Nor with anyone else. She merely asked to see some brochures."

"Yes. She—"

"That's not the same as *going* to Paris or London, is it?"

"Well, no, but—"

"Thank you. You may step down."

Venable turned to Judge Young. "I would like to call Dr. Benjamin Wallace to the stand. . . ."

* * *

"Dr. Wallace, you're in charge of administration at Embarcadero County Hospital?"

"Yes."

"So, of course, you're familiar with Dr. Taylor and her work?"

"Yes, I am."

"Were you surprised to learn that Dr. Taylor was indicted for murder?"

Penn was on his feet. "Objection, your honor. Dr. Wallace's answer would be irrelevant."

"If I may explain," interrupted Venable. "It could be very relevant if you'll just let me . . ."

"Well, let's see what develops," said Judge Young. "But no nonsense, Mr. Venable."

"Let me approach the question differently," continued Venable. "Dr. Wallace, every physician is required to take the Hippocratic Oath, is that not so?"

"Yes."

"And part of that oath is"—the prosecutor read from a paper in his hand—" 'that I shall abstain from every act of mischief or corruption'?"

"Yes."

"Was there anything Dr. Taylor did in the past that made you believe she was capable of breaking her Hippocratic Oath?"

"Objection."

"Overruled."

"Yes, there was."

"Please explain what it was."

"We had a patient who Dr. Taylor decided needed a blood transfusion. His family refused to grant permission."

"And what happened?"

"Dr. Taylor went ahead and gave the patient the transfusion anyway."

"Is that legal?"

"Absolutely not. Not without a court order."

"And then what did Dr. Taylor do?"

"She obtained the court order afterward, and changed the date on it."

"So she performed an illegal act, and falsified the hospital records to cover it up?"

"That is correct."

Alan Penn glanced over at Paige, furious. *What the hell else has she kept from me?* he wondered.

If the spectators were searching for any telltale sign of emotion on Paige Taylor's face, they were disappointed.

Cold as ice, the foreman of the jury was thinking.

* * *

Gus Venable turned to the bench. "Your honor, as you know, one of the witnesses I had hoped to call is Dr. Lawrence Barker. Unfortunately, he is still suffering from the effects of a stroke and is unable to be in this courtroom to testify. Instead I will now question some of the hospital staff who have worked with Dr. Barker."

Penn stood up. "I object. I don't see the relevance. Dr. Barker is not here, nor is Dr. Barker on trial here. If . . ."

Venable interrupted. "Your honor, I assure you that my line of questioning is very relevant to the testimony we have just heard. It also has to do with the defendant's competency as a doctor."

Judge Young said skeptically, "We'll see. This is a courtroom, not a river. I won't stand for any fishing expeditions. You may call your witnesses."

"Thank you."

Gus Venable turned to the bailiff. "I would like to call Dr. Mathew Peterson."

An elegant-looking man in his sixties approached the witness box. He was sworn in, and when he took his seat, Gus Venable said, "Dr. Peterson, how long have you worked at Embarcadero County Hospital?"

"Eight years."

"And what is your specialty?"

"I'm a cardiac surgeon."

"And during the years you've been at Embarcadero County Hospital, did you ever have occasion to work with Dr. Lawrence Barker?"

"Oh, yes. Many times."

"What was your opinion of him?"

"The same as everyone else's. Aside, possibly, from DeBakey and Cooley, Dr. Barker is the best heart surgeon in the world."

"Were you present in the operating room on the morning that Dr. Taylor operated on a patient named . . ." He pretended to consult a slip of paper. ". . . Lance Kelly?"

The witness's tone changed. "Yes, I was there."

"Would you describe what happened that morning?"

Dr. Peterson said reluctantly, "Well, things started to go wrong. We began losing the patient."

"When you say 'losing the patient . . .' "

"His heart stopped. We were trying to bring him back, and . . ."

"Had Dr. Barker been sent for?"

"Yes."

"And did he come into the operating room while the operation was going on?"

"Toward the end. Yes. But it was too late

to do anything. We were unable to revive the patient."

"And did Dr. Barker say anything to Dr. Taylor at that time?"

"Well, we were all pretty upset, and . . ."

"I asked you if Dr. Barker said anything to Dr. Taylor."

"Yes."

"And what did Dr. Barker say?"

There was a pause, and in the middle of the pause, there was a crack of thunder outside, like the voice of God. A moment later, the storm broke, nailing raindrops to the roof of the courthouse.

"Dr. Barker said, 'You killed him.' "

The spectators were in an uproar. Judge Young slammed her gavel down. "That's enough! Do you people live in caves? One more outburst like that and you'll all be standing outside in the rain."

Gus Venable waited for the noise to die down. In the hushed silence he said, "Are you sure that's what Dr. Barker said to Dr. Taylor? 'You killed him'?"

"Yes."

"And you have testified that Dr. Barker was a man whose medical opinion was valued?"

"Oh, yes."

"Thank you. That's all, doctor." He turned to Alan Penn. "Your witness."

Penn rose and approached the witness box.

"Dr. Peterson, I've never watched an operation, but I imagine there's enormous tension, especially when it's something as serious as a heart operation."

"There's a great deal of tension."

"At a time like that, how many people are in the room? Three or four?"

"Oh, no. Always half a dozen or more."

"Really?"

"Yes. There are usually two surgeons, one assisting, sometimes two anesthesiologists, a scrub nurse, and at least one circulating nurse."

"I see. Then there must be a lot of noise and excitement going on. People calling out instructions and so on."

"Yes."

"And I understand that it's a common practice for music to be playing during an operation."

"It is."

"When Dr. Barker came in and saw that Lance Kelly was dying, that probably added to the confusion."

"Well, everybody was pretty busy trying to save the patient."

"Making a lot of noise?"

"There was plenty of noise, yes."

"And yet, in all that confusion and noise, and over the music, you could hear Dr. Barker say that Dr. Taylor had killed the patient. With all that excitement, you could have been wrong, couldn't you?"

"No, sir. I could not be wrong."

"What makes you so sure?"

Dr. Peterson sighed. "Because I was standing right next to Dr. Barker when he said it."

There was no graceful way out.

"No more questions."

The case was falling apart, and there was nothing he could do about it. It was about to get worse.

Denise Berry took the witness stand.

"You're a nurse at Embarcadero County Hospital?"

"Yes."

"How long have you worked there?"

"Five years."

"During that time, did you ever hear any conversations between Dr. Taylor and Dr. Barker?"

"Sure. Lots of times."

"Can you repeat some of them?"

Nurse Berry looked at Dr. Taylor and hesitated. "Well, Dr. Barker could be very sharp . . ."

"I didn't ask you that, Nurse Berry. I asked you to tell us some specific things you heard him say to Dr. Taylor."

There was a long pause. "Well, one time he said she was incompetent, and . . ."

Gus Venable put on a show of surprise. "You heard Dr. Barker say that Dr. Taylor was incompetent?"

"Yes, sir. But he was always . . ."

"What other comments did you hear him make about Dr. Taylor?"

The witness was reluctant to speak. "I really can't remember."

"Miss Berry, you're under oath."

"Well, once I heard him say . . ." The rest of the sentence was a mumble.

"We can't hear you. Speak up, please. You heard him say what?"

"He said he . . . he wouldn't let Dr. Taylor operate on his dog."

There was a collective gasp from the courtroom.

"But I'm sure he only meant . . ."

"I think we can all assume that Dr. Barker meant what he said."

All eyes were fixed on Paige Taylor.

*   *   *

The prosecutor's case against Paige seemed overwhelming. Yet Alan Penn had the reputation of being a master magician in the courtroom. Now it was his turn to present the defendant's case. Could he pull another rabbit out of his hat?

Paige Taylor was on the witness stand, being questioned by Alan Penn. This was the moment everyone had been waiting for.

"John Cronin was a patient of yours, Dr. Taylor?"

"Yes, he was."

"And what were your feelings toward him?"

"I liked him. He knew how ill he was, but he was very courageous. He had surgery for a cardiac tumor."

"You performed the heart surgery?"

"Yes."

"And what did you find during the operation?"

"When we opened up his chest, we found that he had melanoma that had metastasized."

"In other words, cancer that had spread throughout his body."

"Yes. It had metastasized throughout the lymph glands."

"Meaning that there was no hope for him? No heroic measures that could bring him back to health?"

"None."

"John Cronin was put on life-support systems?"

"That's correct."

"Dr. Taylor, did you deliberately administer a fatal dose of insulin to end John Cronin's life?"

"I did."

There was a sudden buzz in the courtroom.

She's really a cool one, Gus Venable thought. *She makes it sound as though she gave him a cup of tea.*

"Would you tell the jury why you ended John Cronin's life?"

"Because he asked me to. He begged me to. He sent for me in the middle of the night, in terrible pain. The medications we were giving him were no longer working." Her voice was steady. "He said he didn't want to suffer anymore. His death was only a few days away. He pleaded with me to end it for him. I did."

"Doctor, did you have any reluctance to let him die? Any feelings of guilt?"

Dr. Paige Taylor shook her head. "No. If

42

you could have seen . . . There was simply no point to letting him go on suffering."

"How did you administer the insulin?"

"I injected it into his IV."

"And did that cause him any additional pain?"

"No. He simply drifted off to sleep."

Gus Venable was on his feet. "Objection! I think the defendant means he drifted off to his death! I—"

Judge Young slammed down her gavel. "Mr. Venable, you're out of order. You'll have your chance to cross-examine the witness. Sit down."

The prosecutor looked over at the jury, shook his head, and took his seat.

"Dr. Taylor, when you administered the insulin to John Cronin, were you aware that he had put you in his will for one million dollars?"

"No. I was stunned when I learned about it."

Her nose should be growing, Gus Venable thought.

"You never discussed money or gifts at any time, or asked John Cronin for anything?"

A faint flush came to her cheeks. "Never!"

"But you were on friendly terms with him?"

"Yes. When a patient is that ill, the

doctor-patient relationship changes. We discussed his business problems and his family problems."

"But you had no reason to expect anything from him?"

"No."

"He left that money to you because he had grown to respect you and trust you. Thank you, Dr. Taylor." Penn turned to Gus Venable. "Your witness."

As Penn returned to the defense table, Paige Taylor glanced toward the back of the courtroom. Jason was seated there, trying to look encouraging. Next to him was Honey. A stranger was sitting next to Honey in the seat that Kat should have occupied. *If she were still alive. But Kat is dead,* Paige thought. *I killed her, too.*

Gus Venable rose and slowly shuffled over to the witness box. He glanced at the rows of press. Every seat was filled, and the reporters were all busily scribbling. *I'm going to give you something to write about,* Venable thought.

He stood in front of the defendant for a long moment, studying her. Then he said casually, "Dr. Taylor . . . was John Cronin the first patient you murdered at Embarcadero County Hospital?"

Alan Penn was on his feet, furious. "Your honor, I—!"

Judge Young had already slammed her gavel down. "Objection sustained!" She turned to the two attorneys. "There will be a fifteen-minute recess. I want to see counsel in my chambers."

When the two attorneys were in her chambers, Judge Young turned to Gus Venable. "You *did* go to law school, didn't you, Gus?"

"I'm sorry, your honor. I—"

"Did you see a tent out there?"

"I beg your pardon?"

Her voice was a whiplash. "My courtroom is not a circus, and I don't intend to let you turn it into one. How dare you ask an inflammatory question like that!"

"I apologize, your honor. I'll rephrase the question and—"

"You'll do more than that!" Judge Young snapped. "You'll rephrase your attitude. I'm warning you, you pull one more stunt like that and I'll declare a mistrial."

"Yes, your honor."

* * *

When they returned to the courtroom, Judge Young said to the jury, "The jury will completely disregard the prosecutor's last question." She turned to the prosecutor. "You may go on."

Gus Venable walked back to the witness box. "Dr. Taylor, you must have been very surprised when you were informed that the man you murdered left you one million dollars."

Alan Penn was on his feet. "Objection!"

"Sustained." Judge Young turned to Venable. "You're trying my patience."

"I apologize, your honor." He turned back to the witness. "You must have been on *very* friendly terms with your patient. I mean, it isn't every day that an almost complete stranger leaves us a million dollars, is it?"

Paige Taylor flushed slightly. "Our friendship was in the context of a doctor-patient relationship."

"Wasn't it a little more than that? A man doesn't cut his beloved wife and family out of his will and leave a million dollars to a stranger without some kind of persuasion. Those talks you claimed to have had with him about his business problems . . ."

Judge Young leaned forward and said warningly, "Mr. Venable . . ." The prosecutor raised his hands in a gesture of surrender. He turned back to the defendant. "So you and

John Cronin had a friendly chat. He told you
personal things about himself, and he liked
you and respected you. Would you say that's
a fair summation, doctor?"

"Yes."

"And for doing that he gave you a million
dollars?"

Paige looked out at the courtroom. She
said nothing. She had no answer.

Venable started to walk back toward the
prosecutor's table, then suddenly turned to
face the defendant again.

"Dr. Taylor, you testified earlier that you
had no idea that John Cronin was going to
leave you any money, or that he was going to
cut his family out of his will."

"That's correct."

"How much does a resident doctor make
at Embarcadero County Hospital?"

Alan Penn was on his feet. "Objection! I
don't see—"

"It's a proper question. The witness may
answer."

"Thirty-eight thousand dollars a year."

Venable said sympathetically, "That's not
very much these days, is it? And out of that,
there are deductions and taxes and living expenses. That wouldn't leave enough to take a
luxury vacation trip, say, to London or Paris
or Venice, would it?"

"I suppose not."

"No. So you didn't plan to take a vacation like that, because you knew you couldn't afford it."

"That's correct."

Alan Penn was on his feet again. "Your honor . . ."

Judge Young turned to the prosecutor. "Where is this leading, Mr. Venable?"

"I just want to establish that the defendant could not plan a luxury trip without getting the money from someone."

"She's already answered the question."

Alan Penn knew he had to do something. His heart wasn't in it, but he approached the witness box with all the good cheer of a man who had just won the lottery.

"Dr. Taylor, do you remember picking up these travel brochures?"

"Yes."

"Were you planning to go to Europe or to charter a yacht?"

"Of course not. It was all sort of a joke, an impossible dream. My friends and I thought it would lift our spirits. We were very tired, and . . . it seemed like a good idea at the time." Her voice trailed off.

Alan Penn glanced covertly at the jury. Their faces registered pure disbelief.

Gus Venable was questioning the defendant on reexamination. "Dr. Taylor, are you acquainted with Dr. Lawrence Barker?"

She had a sudden memory flash. *I'm going to kill Lawrence Barker. I'll do it slowly. I'll let him suffer first . . . then I'll kill him.* "Yes. I know Dr. Barker."

"In what connection?"

"Dr. Barker and I have often worked together during the past two years."

"Would you say that he's a competent doctor?"

Alan Penn jumped up from his chair. "I object, your honor. The witness . . ."

But before he could finish or Judge Young could rule, Paige answered, "He's more than competent. He's brilliant."

Penn sank back in his chair, too stunned to speak.

"Would you care to elaborate on that?"

"Dr. Barker is one of the most renowned cardiovascular surgeons in the world. He has a large private practice, but he donates three days a week to Embarcadero County Hospital."

"So you have a high regard for his judgment in medical matters?"

"Yes."

"And do you feel he would be capable of judging another doctor's competence?"

Penn willed Paige to say *I don't know.*

She hesitated. "Yes."

Gus Venable turned to the jury, "You've heard the defendant testify that she had a high regard for Dr. Barker's medical judgment. I hope she listened carefully to Dr. Barker's judgment about her competence . . . or the lack of it."

Alan Penn was on his feet, furious. "Objection!"

"Sustained."

But it was too late. The damage had been done.

During the next recess, Alan Penn pulled Jason into the men's room.

"What the hell have you gotten me into?" Penn demanded angrily. "John Cronin hated her, Barker hated her. I insist on my clients telling me the truth, and the whole truth. That's the only way I can help them. Well, I can't help *her.* Your lady friend has given me a snow job so deep I need skis. Every time she opens her mouth she puts a nail in her coffin. The fucking case is in free fall!"

That afternoon, Jason Curtis went to see Paige.

"You have a visitor, Dr. Taylor."

Jason walked into Paige's cell.

"Paige . . ."

She turned to him, and she was fighting back tears. "It looks pretty bad, doesn't it?"

Jason forced a smile. "You know what the man said—'It's not over till it's over.' "

"Jason, you don't believe that I killed John Cronin for his money, do you? What I did, I did only to help him."

"I believe you," Jason said quietly. "I love you."

He took her into his arms. *I don't want to lose her,* Jason thought. *I can't. She's the best thing in my life.* "Everything is going to be all right. I promised you we would be together forever."

Paige held him close and thought, *Nothing lasts forever. Nothing. How could everything have gone so wrong . . . so wrong . . . so wrong . . .*

BOOK I

Chapter One

San Francisco
July 1990

"**H**unter, Kate."

"Here."

"Taft, Betty Lou."

"I'm here."

"Taylor, Paige."

"Here."

They were the only women among the large group of incoming first-year residents gathered in the large, drab auditorium at Embarcadero County Hospital.

Embarcadero County was the oldest hospital in San Francisco, and one of the oldest in the country. During the earthquake of 1989, God had played a joke on the residents of San Francisco and left the hospital standing. It was an ugly complex, occupying more than three square blocks, with buildings of brick and stone, gray with years of accumulated grime.

Inside the front entrance of the main building was a large waiting room, with hard wooden benches for patients and visitors. The walls were flaking from too many decades of coats of paint, and the corridors were worn and uneven from too many thousands of patients in wheelchairs and on crutches and walkers. The entire complex was coated with the stale patina of time.

Embarcadero County Hospital was a city within a city. There were over nine thousand people employed at the hospital, including four hundred staff physicians, one hundred and fifty part-time voluntary physicians, eight hundred residents, and three thousand nurses, plus the technicians, unit aides, and other technical personnel. The upper floors contained a complex of twelve operating rooms, central supply, a bone bank, central scheduling, three emergency wards, an AIDS ward, and over two thousand beds.

Now, on the first day of the arrival of the new residents in July, Dr. Benjamin Wallace, the hospital administrator, rose to address them. Wallace was the quintessential politician, a tall, impressive-looking man with small skills and enough charm to have ingratiated his way up to his present position.

"I want to welcome all of you new resident doctors this morning. For the first two years of medical school, you worked with cadavers. In the last two years, you have worked with hospital patients under the supervision of senior doctors. Now, it's *you* who are going to be responsible for your patients. It's an awesome responsibility, and it takes dedication and skill."

His eyes scanned the auditorium. "Some of you are planning to go into surgery. Others of you will be going into internal medicine. Each group will be assigned to a senior resident who will explain the daily routine to you. From now on, everything you do could be a matter of life or death."

They were listening intently, hanging on every word.

"Embarcadero is a county hospital. That means we admit anyone who comes to our door. Most of the patients are indigent. They come here because they can't afford a private hospital. Our emergency rooms are busy twenty-four hours a day. You're going to be overworked and underpaid. In a private hospital, your first year would consist of routine scut work. In the second year, you would be allowed to hand a scalpel to the surgeon, and in your third year, you would be permitted to do some supervised minor surgery. Well, you can forget all that. Our motto here is 'Watch one, do one, teach one.'

"We're badly understaffed, and the quicker we can get you into the operating rooms, the better. Are there any questions?"

There were a million questions the new residents wanted to ask.

"None? Good. Your first day officially begins tomorrow. You will report to the main reception desk at five-thirty tomorrow morning. Good luck!"

The briefing was over. There was a general exodus toward the doors and the low buzz of excited conversations. The three women found themselves standing together.

"Where are all the other women?"

"I think we're it."

"It's a lot like medical school, huh? The boys' club. I have a feeling this place belongs to the Dark Ages."

The person talking was a flawlessly beautiful black woman, nearly six feet tall, large-boned, but intensely graceful. Everything about her, her walk, her carriage, the cool, quizzical look she carried in her eyes, sent out a message of aloofness. "I'm Kate Hunter. They call me Kat."

"Paige Taylor." Young and friendly, intelligent-looking, self-assured.

They turned to the third woman.

"Betty Lou Taft. They call me Honey." She spoke with a soft Southern accent. She had an open, guileless face, soft gray eyes, and a warm smile.

"Where are you from?" Kat asked.

"Memphis, Tennessee."

They looked at Paige. She decided to give them the simple answer. "Boston."

"Minneapolis," Kat said. *That's close enough,* she thought.

Paige said, "It looks like we're all a long way from home. Where are you staying?"

"I'm at a fleabag hotel," Kat said. "I haven't had a chance to look for a place to live."

Honey said, "Neither have I."

Paige brightened. "I looked at some apartments this morning. One of them was terrific, but I can't afford it. It has three bedrooms . . ."

They stared at one another.

"If the three of us shared . . ." Kat said.

The apartment was in the Marina district, on Filbert Street. It was perfect for them. 3Br/2Ba, nu cpts, lndry, prkg, utils pd. It was furnished in early Sears Roebuck, but it was neat and clean.

When the three women were through inspecting it, Honey said, "I think it's lovely."

"So do I!" Kat agreed.

They looked at Paige.

"Let's take it."

They moved into the apartment that afternoon. The janitor helped them carry their luggage upstairs.

"So you're gonna work at the hospital," he said. "Nurses, huh?"

"Doctors," Kat corrected him.

He looked at her skeptically. "Doctors? You mean, like *real* doctors?"

"Yes, like real doctors," Paige told him.

He grunted. "Tell you the truth, if I needed medical attention, I don't think I'd want a woman examining my body."

"We'll keep that in mind."

"Where's the television set?" Kat asked. "I don't see one."

"If you want one, you'll have to buy it. Enjoy the apartment, ladies—er, doctors." He chuckled.

They watched him leave.

Kat said, imitating his voice, "Nurses, eh?" She snorted. "Male chauvinist. Well, let's pick out our bedrooms."

"Any one of them is fine with me," Honey said softly.

They examined the three bedrooms. The

master bedroom was larger than the other two.

Kat said, "Why don't you take it, Paige? You found this place."

Paige nodded. "All right."

They went to their respective rooms and began to unpack. From her suitcase, Paige carefully removed a framed photograph of a man in his early thirties. He was attractive, wearing black-framed glasses that gave him a scholarly look. Paige put the photograph at her bedside, next to a bundle of letters.

Kat and Honey wandered in. "How about going out and getting some dinner?"

"I'm ready," Paige said.

Kat saw the photograph. "Who's that?"

Paige smiled. "That's the man I'm going to marry. He's a doctor who works for the World Health Organization. His name is Alfred Turner. He's working in Africa right now, but he's coming to San Francisco so we can be together."

"Lucky you," Honey said wistfully. "He looks nice."

Paige looked at her. "Are you involved with anyone?"

"No. I'm afraid I don't have much luck with men."

Kat said, "Maybe your luck will change at Embarcadero."

* * *

The three of them had dinner at Tarantino's, not far from their apartment building. During dinner they chatted about their backgrounds and lives, but there was a restraint to their conversation, a holding back. They were three strangers, probing, cautiously getting to know one another.

Honey spoke very little. *There's a shyness about her,* Paige thought. *She's vulnerable. Some man in Memphis probably broke her heart.*

Paige looked at Kat. *Self-confident. Great dignity. I like the way she speaks. You can tell she came from a good family.*

Meanwhile, Kat was studying Paige. *A rich girl who never had to work for anything in her life. She's gotten by on her looks.*

Honey was looking at the two of them. *They're so confident, so sure of themselves. They're going to have an easy time of it.*

They were all mistaken.

When they returned to their apartment, Paige was too excited to sleep. She lay in bed, thinking about the future. Outside her window, in the street, there was the sound of a car crash, and then people shouting, and in

Paige's mind it dissolved into the memory of African natives yelling and chanting, and guns being fired. She was transported back in time, to the small jungle village in East Africa, caught in the middle of a deadly tribal war.

Paige was terrified. "They're going to kill us!"

Her father took her in his arms. "They won't harm us, darling. We're here to help them. They know we're their friends."

And without warning, the chief of one of the tribes had burst into their hut. . . .

Honey lay in bed thinking, *This is sure a long way from Memphis, Tennessee, Betty Lou. I guess I can never go back there. Never again.* She could hear the sheriff's voice saying to her, "Out of respect for his family, we're going to list the death of the Reverend Douglas Lipton as a 'suicide for reasons unknown,' but I would suggest that you get the fuck out of this town fast, and stay out. . . ."

Kat was staring out the window of her bedroom, listening to the sounds of the city. She could hear the raindrops whispering, *You made it . . . you made it . . . I showed them all they were wrong. You want to be a doctor? A black woman doctor? And the rejections from medical schools. "Thank you for sending us your application. Unfortunately our enrollment is complete at this time."*

"In view of your background, perhaps we might suggest that you would be happier at a smaller university."

She had top grades, but out of twenty-five schools she had applied to, only one had accepted her. The dean of the school had said, "In these days, it's nice to see someone who comes from a normal, decent background."

If he had only known the terrible truth.

Chapter Two

At five-thirty the following morning, when the new residents checked in, members of the hospital staff were standing by to guide them to their various assignments. Even at that early hour, the bedlam had begun.

The patients had been coming in all night, arriving in ambulances, and police cars, and on foot. The staff called them the "F and J's"— the flotsam and jetsam that streamed into the emergency rooms, broken and bleeding, victims of shootings and stabbings and automobile accidents, the wounded in flesh and spirit, the homeless and the unwanted, the ebb and flow of humanity that streamed through the dark sewers of every large city.

There was a pervasive feeling of organized chaos, frenetic movements and shrill sounds and dozens of unexpected crises that all had to be attended to at once.

The new residents stood in a protective huddle, getting attuned to their new environment, listening to the arcane sounds around them.

Paige, Kat, and Honey were waiting in the corridor when a senior resident approached them. "Which one of you is Dr. Taft?"

Honey looked up and said, "I am."

The resident smiled and held out his hand. "It's an honor to meet you. I've been asked to look out for you. Our chief of staff says that you have the highest medical school grades this hospital has ever seen. We're delighted to have you here."

Honey smiled, embarrassed. "Thank you."

Kat and Paige looked at Honey in astonishment. *I wouldn't have guessed she was that brilliant*, Paige thought.

"You're planning to go into internal medicine, Dr. Taft?"

"Yes."

The resident turned to Kat. "Dr. Hunter?"

"Yes."

"You're interested in neurosurgery."

"I am."

He consulted a list. "You'll be assigned to Dr. Lewis."

The resident looked over at Paige. "Dr. Taylor?"

"Yes."

"You're going into cardiac surgery."

"That's right."

"Fine. We'll assign you and Dr. Hunter to surgical rounds. You can report to the head nurse's office. Margaret Spencer. Down the hall."

"Thank you."

Paige looked at the others and took a deep breath. "Here I go! I wish us all luck!"

The head nurse, Margaret Spencer, was more a battleship than a woman, heavyset and stern-looking, with a brusque manner. She was busy behind the nurses' station when Paige approached.

"Excuse me . . ."

Nurse Spencer looked up. "Yes?"

"I was told to report here. I'm Dr. Taylor."

Nurse Spencer consulted a sheet. "Just a moment." She walked through a door and returned a minute later with some scrubs and white coats.

"Here you are. The scrubs are to wear in the operating theater and on rounds. When you're doing rounds, you put a white coat over the scrubs."

"Thanks."

"Oh. And here." She reached down and handed Paige a metal tag that read "Paige Taylor, M.D." "Here's your name tag, doctor."

Paige held it in her hand and looked at it for a long time. *Paige Taylor, M.D.* She felt as though she had been handed the Medal of Honor. All the long hard years of work and study were summed up in those brief words. *Paige Taylor, M.D.*

Nurse Spencer was watching her. "Are you all right?"

"I'm fine." Paige smiled. "I'm just fine, thank you. Where do I . . . ?"

"Doctors' dressing room is down the corridor to the left. You'll be making rounds, so you'll want to change."

"Thank you."

Paige walked down the corridor, amazed at the amount of activity around her. The corridor was crowded with doctors, nurses, technicians, and patients, hurrying to various destinations. The insistent chatter of the public address system added to the din.

"Dr. Keenan . . . OR Three. . . . Dr. Keenan . . . OR Three."

"Dr. Talbot . . . Emergency Room One. Stat. . . . Dr. Talbot . . . Emergency Room One. Stat."

"Dr. Engel . . . Room 212. . . . Dr. Engel . . . Room 212."

Paige approached a door marked DOCTORS' DRESSING ROOM and opened it. Inside there were a dozen doctors in various stages of undress. Two of them were totally naked. They turned to stare at Paige as the door opened.

"Oh! I . . . I'm sorry," Paige mumbled, and quickly closed the door. She stood there, uncertain about what to do. A few feet down the corridor, she saw a door marked NURSES' DRESSING ROOM. Paige walked over to it and opened the door. Inside, several nurses were changing into their uniforms.

One of them looked up. "Hello. Are you one of the new nurses?"

"No," Paige said tightly. "I'm not." She closed the door and walked back to the doctors' dressing room. She stood there a moment, then took a deep breath and entered. The conversation came to a stop.

One of the men said, "Sorry, honey. This room is for doctors."

"I'm a doctor," Paige said.

They turned to look at one another. "Oh? Well, er . . . welcome."

"Thank you." She hesitated a moment, then walked over to an empty locker. The men watched as she put her hospital clothes into the locker. She looked at the men for a moment, then slowly started to unbutton her blouse.

The doctors stood there, not sure what to do. One of them said, "Maybe we should—er—give the little lady some privacy, gentlemen."

The little lady! "Thank you," Paige said. She stood there, waiting, as the doctors finished dressing and left the room. *Am I going to have to go through this every day?* she wondered.

In hospital rounds, there is a traditional formation that never varies. The attending physician is always in the lead, followed by the senior resident, then the other residents, and one or two medical students. The attending physician Paige had been assigned to was Dr. William Radnor. Paige and five other residents were gathered in the hallway, waiting to meet him.

In the group was a young Chinese doctor. He held out his hand. "Tom Chang," he said. "I hope you're all as nervous as I am."

Paige liked him immediately.

A man was approaching the group. "Good

morning," he said. "I'm Dr. Radnor." He was soft-spoken, with sparkling blue eyes. Each resident introduced himself.

"This is your first day of rounds. I want you to pay close attention to everything you see and hear, but at the same time, it's important to appear relaxed."

Paige made a mental note. *Pay close attention, but appear to be relaxed.*

"If the patients see that you're tense, *they're* going to be tense, and they'll probably think they're dying of some disease you aren't telling them about."

Don't make patients tense.

"Remember, from now on, you're going to be responsible for the lives of other human beings."

Now responsible for other lives. Oh, my God!

The longer Dr. Radnor talked, the more nervous Paige became, and by the time he was finished, her self-confidence had completely vanished. *I'm not ready for this!* she thought. *I don't know what I'm doing. Who ever said I could be a doctor? What if I kill somebody?*

Dr. Radnor was going on, "I will expect detailed notes on each one of your patients— lab work, blood, electrolytes, everything. Is that clear?"

There were murmurs of "Yes, doctor."

71

"There are always thirty to forty surgical patients here at one time. It's your job to make sure that everything is properly organized for them. We'll start the morning rounds now. In the afternoon, we'll make the same rounds again."

It had all seemed so easy at medical school. Paige thought about the four years she had spent there. There had been one hundred and fifty students, and only fifteen women. She would never forget the first day of Gross Anatomy class. The students had walked into a large white tiled room with twenty tables lined up in rows, each table covered with a yellow sheet. Five students were assigned to each table.

The professor had said, "All right, pull back the sheets." And there, in front of Paige, was her first cadaver. She had been afraid that she would faint or be sick, but she felt strangely calm. The cadaver had been preserved, which somehow removed it one step from humanity.

In the beginning the students had been hushed and respectful in the anatomy laboratory. But, incredibly to Paige, within a week, they were eating sandwiches during the dissections, and making rude jokes. It was a form of self-defense, a denial of their own mortality. They gave the corpses names, and treated them like old friends. Paige tried to force herself to act as casually as the other students, but she found it difficult. She looked at the cadaver she was working on, and thought: *Here was a man with a home and a family. He went to an office every day, and once a year he took a vacation with his wife and children. He probably loved sports and enjoyed movies and plays, and he laughed and cried, and he watched his children grow up and he shared their joys and their sorrows, and he had big, wonderful dreams. I hope they all came true.* . . . A bittersweet sadness engulfed her because he was dead and *she* was alive.

In time, even to Paige, the dissections became routine. *Open the chest, examine the ribs, lungs, pericardial sac covering the heart, the veins, arteries, and nerves.*

Much of the first two years of medical school was spent memorizing long lists that the students referred to as the Organ Recital. First the cranial nerves: olfactory, optic, oculomotor, trochlear, trigeminal, abducens, facial, auditory, glossopharyngeal, vagus, spinal, and hypoglossal.

The students used mnemonics to help them remember. The classic one was "*On old Olympus's towering tops, a French and*

73

German *vended* some *hops*." The modern male version was "*Oh, oh, oh, to touch and feel a girl's vagina—such heaven*."

The last two years of medical school were more interesting, with courses in internal medicine, surgery, pediatrics, and obstetrics, and they worked at the local hospital. *I remember the time . . .* Paige was thinking.

"Dr. Taylor . . ." The senior resident was staring at her.

Paige came to with a start. The others were already halfway down the corridor.

"Coming," she said hastily.

The first stop was at a large, rectangular ward, with rows of beds on both sides of the room, with a small stand next to each bed. Paige had expected to see curtains separating the beds, but here there was no privacy.

The first patient was an elderly man with a sallow complexion. He was sound asleep, breathing heavily. Dr. Radnor walked over to the foot of the bed, studied the chart there, then went to the patient's side and gently touched his shoulder. "Mr. Potter?"

The patient opened his eyes. "Huh?"

"Good morning. I'm Dr. Radnor. I'm just checking to see how you're doing. Did you have a comfortable night?"

"It was okay."

"Do you have any pain?"

"Yeah. My chest hurts."

"Let me take a look at it."

When he finished the examination, he said, "You're doing fine. I'll have the nurse give you something for the pain."

"Thanks, doctor."

"We'll be back to see you this afternoon."

They moved away from the bed. Dr. Radnor turned to the residents. "Always try to ask questions that have a yes or no answer so the patient doesn't tire himself out. And reassure him about his progress. I want you to study his chart and make notes. We'll come back here this afternoon to see how he's doing. Keep a running record of every patient's chief complaint, present illness, past illnesses, family history, and social history. Does he drink, smoke, etc.? When we make the rounds again, I'll expect a report on the progress of each patient."

They moved on to the bed of the next patient, a man in his forties.

"Good morning, Mr. Rawlings."

"Good morning, doctor."

"Are you feeling better this morning?"

"Not so good. I was up a lot last night. My stomach's hurting."

Dr. Radnor turned to the senior resident.

"What did the proctoscopy show?"

"No sign of any problem."

"Give him a barium enema and an upper GI, stat."

The senior resident made a note.

The resident standing next to Paige whispered in her ear, "I guess you know what stat stands for. 'Shake that ass, tootsie!' "

Dr. Radnor heard. " 'Stat' comes from the Latin, *statim*. Immediately."

In the years ahead, Paige was to hear it often.

The next patient was an elderly woman who had had a bypass operation.

"Good morning, Mrs. Turkel."

"How long are you going to keep me in here?"

"Not very long. The procedure was a success. You'll be going home soon."

And they moved on to the next patient.

The routine was repeated over and over, and the morning went by swiftly. They saw thirty patients. After each patient, the residents frantically scribbled notes, praying that they would be able to decipher them later.

One patient was a puzzle to Paige. She seemed to be in perfect health.

When they had moved away from her, Paige asked, "What's her problem, doctor?"

Dr. Radnor sighed. "She has no problem.

She's a gomer. And for those of you who forgot what you were taught in medical school, gomer is an acronym for 'Get out of my emergency room!' Gomers are people who *enjoy* poor health. That's their hobby. I've admitted her six times in the last year."

They moved on to the last patient, an old woman on a respirator, who was in a coma.

"She's had a massive heart attack," Dr. Radnor explained to the residents. "She's been in a coma for six weeks. Her vital signs are failing. There's nothing more we can do for her. We'll pull the plug this afternoon."

Paige looked at him in shock. "Pull the plug?"

Dr. Radnor said gently, "The hospital ethics committee made the decision this morning. She's a vegetable. She's eighty-seven years old, and she's brain-dead. It's cruel to keep her alive, and it's breaking her family financially. I'll see you all at rounds this afternoon."

They watched him walk away. Paige turned to look at the patient again. She was alive. *In a few hours she will be dead. We'll pull the plug this afternoon.*

That's murder! Paige thought.

Chapter Three

That afternoon, when the rounds were finished, the new residents gathered in the small upstairs lounge. The room held eight tables, an ancient black-and-white television set, and two vending machines that dispensed stale sandwiches and bitter coffee.

The conversations at each table were almost identical.

One of the residents said, "Take a look at my throat, will you? Does it look raw to you?"

"I think I have a fever. I feel lousy."

"My abdomen is swollen and tender. I know I have appendicitis."

"I've got this crushing pain in my chest. I

hope to God I'm not having a heart attack!"

Kat sat down at a table with Paige and Honey. "How did it go?" she asked.

Honey said, "I think it went all right."

They both looked at Paige. "I was tense, but I was relaxed. I was nervous, but I stayed calm." She sighed. "It's been a long day. I'll be glad to get out of here and have some fun tonight."

"Me, too," Kat agreed. "Why don't we have dinner and then go see a movie?"

"Sounds great."

An orderly approached their table. "Dr. Taylor?"

Paige looked up. "I'm Dr. Taylor."

"Dr. Wallace would like to see you in his office."

The hospital administrator! *What have I done?* Paige wondered.

The orderly was waiting. "Dr. Taylor . . ."

"I'm coming." She took a deep breath and got to her feet. "I'll see you later."

"This way, doctor."

Paige followed the orderly into an elevator and rode up to the fifth floor, where Dr. Wallace's office was located.

Benjamin Wallace was seated behind his desk. He glanced up as Paige walked in. "Good afternoon, Dr. Taylor."

"Good afternoon."

Wallace cleared his throat. "Well! Your first day and you've already made quite an impression!"

Paige looked at him, puzzled. "I . . . I don't understand."

"I hear you had a little problem in the doctors' dressing room this morning."

"Oh." *So, that's what this is all about!*

Wallace looked at her and smiled. "I suppose I'll have to make some arrangements for you and the other girls."

"We're . . ." *We're not girls,* Paige started to say. "We would appreciate that."

"Meanwhile, if you don't want to dress with the nurses . . ."

"I'm not a nurse," Paige said firmly. "I'm a doctor."

"Of course, of course. Well, we'll do something about accommodations for you, doctor."

"Thank you."

He handed Paige a sheet of paper. "Meanwhile, this is your schedule. You'll be on call for the next twenty-four hours, starting at six o'clock." He looked at his watch. "That's thirty minutes from now."

Paige was looking at him in astonishment. Her day had started at five-thirty that morning. *"Twenty-four hours?"*

"Well, thirty-six, actually. Because you'll be starting rounds again in the morning."

Thirty-six hours! I wonder if I can handle this.

She was soon to find out.

Paige went to look for Kat and Honey.

"I'm going to have to forget about dinner and a movie," Paige said. "I'm on a thirty-six-hour call."

Kat nodded. "We just got our bad news. I go on it tomorrow, and Honey goes on Wednesday."

"It won't be so bad," Paige said cheerfully. "I understand there's an on-call room to sleep in. I'm going to enjoy this."

She was wrong.

An orderly was leading Paige down a long corridor.

"Dr. Wallace told me that I'll be on call for thirty-six hours," Paige said. "Do all the residents work those hours?"

"Only for the first three years," the orderly assured her.

Great!

"But you'll have plenty of chance to rest, doctor."

"I will?"

"In here. This is the on-call room." He opened the door, and Paige stepped inside. The room resembled a monk's cell in some poverty-stricken monastery. It contained nothing but a cot with a lumpy mattress, a cracked wash basin, and a bedside stand with a telephone on it. "You can sleep here between calls."

"Thanks."

The calls began as Paige was in the coffee shop, just starting to have her dinner.

"Dr. Taylor . . . ER Three. . . . Dr. Taylor . . . ER Three."

"We have a patient with a fractured rib. . . ."

"Mr. Henegan is complaining of chest pains. . . ."

"The patient in Ward Two has a headache. Is it all right to give him an acetaminophen . . . ?"

At midnight, Paige had just managed to fall asleep when she was awakened by the telephone.

"Report to ER One." It was a knife wound, and by the time Paige had taken care of it, it was one-thirty in the morning. At two-fifteen she was awakened again.

"Dr. Taylor . . . Emergency Room Two. Stat."

Paige said, groggily, "Right." *What did he say it meant? Shake that ass, tootsie.* She forced herself up and moved down the corridor to the emergency room. A patient had been brought in with a broken leg. He was screaming with pain.

"Get an X-ray," Paige ordered. "And give him Demerol, fifty milligrams." She put her hand on the patient's arm. "You're going to be fine. Try to relax."

Over the PA system, a metallic disembodied voice said, "Dr. Taylor . . . Ward Three. Stat."

Paige looked at the moaning patient, reluctant to leave him.

The voice came on again, "Dr. Taylor . . . Ward Three. Stat."

"Coming," Paige mumbled. She hurried out the door and down the corridor to Ward Three. A patient had vomited, aspirated, and was choking.

"He can't breathe," the nurse said.

"Suction him," Paige ordered. As she watched the patient begin to catch his breath, she heard her name again on the PA system. "Dr. Taylor . . . Ward Four. Ward Four." Paige shook her head and ran down to Ward Four, to a screaming patient with abdominal spasms. Paige gave him a quick examination. "It could be intestinal dysfunction. Get an ultrasound," Paige said.

By the time she returned to the patient with the broken leg, the pain reliever had taken effect. She had him moved to the operating room and set the leg. As she was finishing, she heard her name again. "Dr. Taylor, report to Emergency Room Two. Stat."

"The stomach ulcer in Ward Four is having a pain. . . ."

At 3:30 A.M.: "Dr. Taylor, the patient in Room 310 is hemorrhaging. . . ."

There was a heart attack in one of the wards, and Paige was nervously listening to the patient's heartbeat when she heard her name called over the PA system: "Dr. Taylor . . . ER Two. Stat. . . . Dr. Taylor . . . ER Two. Stat."

I must not panic, Paige thought. *I've got to remain calm and cool.* She panicked. Who was more important, the patient she was examining, or the next patient? "You stay here," she said inanely. "I'll be right back."

As Paige hurried toward ER Two, she heard her name called again. "Dr. Taylor . . . ER One. Stat. . . . Dr. Taylor . . . ER One. Stat."

Oh, my God! Paige thought. She felt as though she were caught up in the middle of some endless terrifying nightmare.

During what was left of the night, Paige was awakened to attend to a case of food poisoning, a broken arm, a hiatal hernia, and a fractured rib. By the time she stumbled back into the on-call room, she was so exhausted that she could hardly move. She crawled onto the little cot and had just started to doze off when the telephone rang again.

She reached out for it with her eyes closed. "H'lo . . ."

"Dr. Taylor, we're waiting for you."

"Wha'?" She lay there, trying to remember where she was.

"Your rounds are starting, doctor."

"My rounds?" *This is some kind of bad joke*, Paige thought. *It's inhuman. They can't work anyone like this!* But they were waiting for her.

Ten minutes later, Paige was making the rounds again, half asleep. She stumbled against Dr. Radnor. "Excuse me," she mumbled, "but I haven't had any sleep . . ."

He patted her on the shoulder sympathetically. "You'll get used to it."

When Paige finally got off duty, she slept for fourteen straight hours.

The intense pressure and punishing hours proved to be too much for some of the residents, and they simply disappeared from the hospital. *That's not going to happen to me,* Paige vowed.

The pressure was unrelenting. At the end of one of Paige's shifts, thirty-six grueling hours, she was so exhausted that she had no idea where she was. She stumbled to the elevator and stood there, her mind numb.

Tom Chang came up to her. "Are you all right?"

"Fine," Paige mumbled.

He grinned. "You look like hell."

"Thanks. Why do they do this to us?" Paige asked.

Chang shrugged. "The theory is that it keeps us in touch with our patients. If we go home and leave them, we don't know what's happening to them while we're gone."

Paige nodded. "That makes sense." It made no sense at all. "How can we take care of them if we're asleep on our feet?"

Chang shrugged again. "I don't make the rules. It's the way all hospitals operate." He looked at Paige more closely. "Are you going to be able to make it home?"

Paige looked at him and said haughtily, "Of course."

"Take care." Chang disappeared down the corridor.

Paige waited for the elevator to arrive. When it finally came, she was standing there, sound asleep.

Two days later, Paige was having breakfast with Kat.

"Do you want to hear a terrible confession?" Paige asked. "Sometimes when they wake me up at four o'clock in the morning to give somebody an aspirin, and I'm stumbling down the hall, half conscious, and I pass the rooms where all the patients are tucked in and having a good night's sleep, I feel like banging on all the doors and yelling, 'Everybody wake up!' "

Kat held out her hand. "Join the club."

The patients came in all shapes, sizes, ages, and colors. They were frightened, brave, gentle, arrogant, demanding, considerate. They were human beings in pain.

Most of the doctors were dedicated people.

As in any profession, there were good doctors and bad doctors. They were young and old, clumsy and adept, pleasant and nasty. A few of them, at one time or another, made sexual advances to Paige. Some were subtle and some were crude.

"Don't you ever feel lonely at night? I know that I do. I was wondering . . ."

"These hours are murder, aren't they? Do you know what I find gives me energy? Good sex. Why don't we . . . ?"

"My wife is out of town for a few days. I have a cabin near Carmel. This weekend we could . . ."

And the patients.

"So you're my doctor, eh? You know what would cure me . . . ?"

"Come closer to the bed, baby. I want to see if those are real. . . ."

Paige gritted her teeth and ignored them all. *When Alfred and I are married, this will stop.* And just the thought of Alfred gave her a glow. He would be returning from Africa soon. *Soon.*

At breakfast one morning before rounds, Paige and Kat talked about the sexual harassment they were experiencing.

"Most of the doctors behave like perfect

gentlemen, but a few of them seem to think we're perks that go with the territory, and that we're there to service them," Kat said. "I don't think a week goes by but what one of the doctors hits on me. 'Why don't you come over to my place for a drink? I've got some great CDs.' Or in the OR, when I'm assisting, the surgeon will brush his arm across my breast. One moron said to me, 'You know, whenever I order chicken, I like the dark meat.' "

Paige sighed. "They think they're flattering us by treating us as sex objects. I'd rather they treated us as doctors."

"A lot of them don't even want us around. They either want to fuck us or they want to fuck us. You know, it's not fair. Women are judged inferior until we prove ourselves, and men are judged superior until they prove what assholes they are."

"It's the old boys' network," Paige said. "If there were more of us, we could start a new girls' network."

Paige had heard of Arthur Kane. He was the subject of constant gossip around the hospital. His nickname was Dr. 007—licensed to kill. His solution to every problem was to operate, and he had a higher rate of operations than any other doctor at the hospital. He also had a higher mortality rate.

He was bald, short, hawk-nosed, with tobacco-stained teeth, and was grossly overweight. Incredibly, he fancied himself a ladies' man. He liked to refer to the new nurses and female residents as "fresh meat."

Paige Taylor was fresh meat. He saw her in the upstairs lounge and sat down at her table, uninvited.

"I've been keeping an eye on you."

Paige looked up, startled. "I beg your pardon?"

"I'm Dr. Kane. My friends call me Arthur." There was a leer in his voice.

Paige wondered how many friends he had.

"How are you getting along here?"

The question caught Paige off-guard. "I . . . all right, I think."

He leaned forward. "This is a big hospital. It's easy to get lost here. Do you know what I mean?"

Paige said warily, "Not exactly."

"You're too pretty to be just another face in the crowd. If you want to get somewhere here, you need someone to help you. Someone who knows the ropes."

The conversation was getting more unpleasant by the minute.

"And you'd like to help me."

"Right." He bared his tobacco-stained teeth. "Why don't we discuss it at dinner?"

"There's nothing to discuss," Paige said. "I'm not interested."

Arthur Kane watched Paige get up and walk away, and there was a baleful expression on his face.

First-year surgical residents were on a two-month rotation schedule, alternating among obstetrics, orthopedics, urology, and surgery.

Paige learned that it was dangerous to go into a training hospital in the summer for any serious illness, because many of the staff doctors were on vacation and the patients were at the mercy of the inexperienced young residents.

Nearly all surgeons liked to have music in the operating room. One of the doctors was nicknamed Mozart and another Axl Rose because of their tastes in music.

For some reason, operations always seemed to make everyone hungry. They constantly discussed food. A surgeon would be in the middle of removing a gangrenous gall bladder from a patient and say, "I had a great dinner last night at Bardelli's. Best Italian food in all of San Francisco."

"Have you eaten the crab cakes at the Cypress Club . . . ?"

"If you like good beef, try the House of Prime Rib over on Van Ness."

And meanwhile, a nurse would be mopping up the patient's blood and guts.

When they weren't talking about food, the doctors talked about baseball or football scores.

"Did you see the 49ers play last Sunday? I bet they miss Joe Montana. He always came through for them in the last two minutes of a game."

And out would come a ruptured appendix.

Kafka, Paige thought. *Kafka would have loved this.*

At three in the morning, when Paige was asleep in the on-call room, she was awakened by the telephone.

A raspy voice said, "Dr. Taylor—Room 419—a heart attack patient. You'll have to hurry!" The line went dead.

Paige sat on the edge of the bed, fighting sleep, and stumbled to her feet. *You have to hurry!* She went into the corridor, but there was no time to wait for an elevator. She rushed up the stairs and ran down the fourth-floor corridor to Room 419, her heart pounding. She flung open the door and stood there, staring.

Room 419 was a storage room.

Kat Hunter was making her rounds with Dr. Richard Hutton. He was in his forties, brusque and fast. He spent no more than two or three minutes with each patient, scanning their charts, then snapping out orders to the surgical residents in a machine-gun, staccato fashion.

"Check her hemoglobin and schedule surgery for tomorrow. . . ."

"Keep a close eye on his temperature chart. . . ."

"Cross-match four units of blood. . . ."

"Remove these stitches. . . ."

"Get some chest films. . . ."

Kat and the other residents were busily making notes on everything, trying hard to keep up with him.

They approached a patient who had been in the hospital a week and had had a battery of tests for a high fever, with no results.

When they were out in the corridor, Kat asked, "What's the matter with him?"

"It's a GOK," a resident said. "A God only knows. We've done X-rays, CAT scans, MRIs, spinal taps, liver biopsy. Everything. We don't know what's wrong with him."

They moved into a ward where a young patient, his head bandaged after an operation, was sleeping. As Dr. Hutton started to unwrap the head dressing, the patient woke up, startled. "What . . . what's going on?"

"Sit up," Dr. Hutton said curtly. The young man was trembling.

I'll never treat my patients that way, Kat vowed.

The next patient was a healthy-looking man in his seventies. As soon as Dr. Hutton approached the bed, the patient yelled, "*Gonzo!* I'm going to sue you, you dirty son of a bitch."

"Now, Mr. Sparolini . . ."

"Don't Mr. Sparolini me! You turned me into a fucking eunuch."

That's an oxymoron, Kat thought.

"Mr. Sparolini, you agreed to have the vasectomy, and—"

"It was my wife's idea. Damn bitch! Just wait till I get home."

They left him muttering to himself.

"What's his problem?" one of the residents asked.

"His problem is that he's a horny old goat.

His young wife has six kids and she doesn't want any more."

The next patient was a little girl, ten years old. Dr. Hutton looked at her chart. "We're going to give you a shot to make the bad bugs go away."

A nurse filled a syringe and moved toward the little girl.

"No!" she screamed. "You're going to hurt me!"

"This won't hurt, baby," the nurse assured her.

The words were a dark echo in Kat's mind.

This won't hurt, baby. . . . It was the voice of her stepfather whispering to her in the scary dark.

"This will feel good. Spread your legs. Come on, you little bitch!" And he had pushed her legs apart and forced his male hardness into her and put his hand over her mouth to keep her from screaming with the pain. She was thirteen years old. After that night, his visits became a terrifying nightly ritual. "You're lucky you got a man like me to teach you how to fuck," he would tell her. "Do you know what a Kat is? A little pussy. And I want some." And he would fall on top of her and grab her, and no amount of crying or pleading would make him stop.

Kat had never known her father. Her mother was a cleaning woman who worked nights at an office building near their tiny apartment in Gary, Indiana. Kat's stepfather was a huge man who had been injured in an accident at a steel mill, and he stayed home most of the time, drinking. At night, when Kat's mother left for work, he would go into Kat's room. "You say anything to your mother or brother, and I'll kill him," he told Kat. *I can't let him hurt Mike*, Kat thought. Her brother was five years younger than she, and Kat adored him. She mothered him and protected him and fought his battles for him. He was the only bright spot in Kat's life.

One morning, terrified as Kat was by her stepfather's threats, she decided she had to tell her mother what was happening. Her mother would put a stop to it, would protect her.

"Mama, your husband comes to my bed at night when you're away, and forces himself on me."

Her mother stared at her a moment, then

slapped Kat hard across the face.

"Don't you dare make up lies like that, you little slut!"

Kat never discussed it again. The only reason she stayed at home was because of Mike. *He'd be lost without me,* Kat thought. But the day she learned she was pregnant, she ran away to live with an aunt in Minneapolis.

The day Kat ran away from home, her life completely changed.

"You don't have to tell me what happened," her Aunt Sophie had said. "But from now on, you're going to stop running away. You know that song they sing on *Sesame Street*? 'It's Not Easy Being Green'? Well, honey, it's not easy being black, either. You have two choices. You can keep running and hiding and blaming the world for your problems, or you can stand up for yourself and decide to be somebody important."

"How do I do that?"

"By *knowing* that you're important. First, you get an image in your mind of who you want to be, child, and what you want to be. And then you go to work, *becoming* that person."

I'm not going to have his baby, Kat decided. *I want an abortion.*

It was arranged quietly, during a weekend, and it was performed by a midwife who was a friend of Kat's aunt. When it was over, Kat thought fiercely, *I'm never going to let a man touch me again. Never!*

Minneapolis was a fairyland for Kat. Within a few blocks of almost every home were lakes and streams and rivers. And there were over eight thousand acres of landscaped parks. She went sailing on the city lakes and took boat rides on the Mississippi.

She visited the Great Zoo with Aunt Sophie and spent Sundays at the Valleyfair Amusement Park. She went on the hay rides at Cedar Creek Farm, and watched knights in armor jousting at the Shakopee Renaissance Festival.

Aunt Sophie watched Kat and thought, *The girl has never had a childhood.*

Kat was learning to enjoy herself, but Aunt Sophie sensed that deep inside her niece was a place that no one could reach, a barrier she had set up to keep her from being hurt again.

She made friends at school. But never with boys. Her girlfriends were all dating, but Kat was a loner, and too proud to tell anyone why. She looked up to her aunt, whom she loved very much.

Kat had taken little interest in school, or in reading books, but Aunt Sophie changed all that. Her home was filled with books, and Sophie's excitement about them was contagious.

"There are wonderful worlds in there," she told the young girl. "Read, and you'll learn where you came from and where you're going. I've got a feeling that you're going to be famous one day, baby. But you have to get an education first. This is America. You can become anybody you want to be. You may be black and poor, but so were some of our congresswomen, and movie stars, and scientists, and sports legends. One day we're going to have a black president. You can be anything you want to be. It's up to you."

It was the beginning.

Kat became the top student in her class. She was an avid reader. In the school library one day, she happened to pick up a copy of Sinclair Lewis's *Arrowsmith,* and she was fascinated by the story of the dedicated young doctor. She read Agnes Cooper's *Promises to Keep,* and *Woman Surgeon* by Dr. Else Roe, and it opened up a whole new world for Kat. She discovered that there were people on this earth who devoted themselves to helping others, to saving lives. When Kat came home from school one day, she said to Aunt Sophie, "I'm going to be a doctor. A famous one."

Chapter Four

On Monday morning, three of Paige's patients' charts were missing, and Paige was blamed.

On Wednesday, Paige was awakened at 4:00 A.M. in the on-call room. Sleepily, she picked up the telephone. "Dr. Taylor."

Silence.

"Hello . . . hello."

She could hear breathing at the other end of the line. And then there was a click.

Paige lay awake for the rest of the night.

In the morning, Paige said to Kat, "I'm either becoming paranoid or someone hates me." She told Kat what had happened.

"Patients sometimes get grudges against

doctors," Kat said. "Can you think of anyone who . . . ?"

Paige sighed. "Dozens."

"I'm sure there's nothing to worry about."

Paige wished that she could believe it.

In the late summer, the magic telegram arrived. It was waiting for Paige when she returned to the apartment late at night. It read: "Arriving San Francisco noon Sunday. Can't wait to see you. Love, Alfred."

He was finally on his way back to her! Paige read the telegram again and again, her excitement growing each time. *Alfred!* His name conjured up a tumbling kaleidoscope of exciting memories . . .

Paige and Alfred had grown up together. Their fathers were part of a medical cadre of WHO that traveled to Third World countries, fighting exotic and virulent diseases. Paige and her mother accompanied Dr. Taylor, who headed the team.

Paige and Alfred had had a fantasy childhood. In India, Paige learned to speak Hindi. At the age of two, she knew that the name for the bamboo hut they lived in was *basha*. Her father was *gorasahib*, a white man, and she was *nani*, a little sister. They addressed Paige's father as *abadhan*, the leader, or *baba*, father.

When Paige's parents were not around, she drank *bhanga*, an intoxicating drink made with hashish leaves, and ate *chapati* with *ghi*.

And then they were on their way to Africa. Off to another adventure!

Paige and Alfred became used to swimming and bathing in rivers that had crocodiles and hippopotamuses. Their pets were baby zebras and cheetahs and snakes. They grew up in windowless round huts made of wattle and daub, with packed dirt floors and conical thatched roofs. *Someday*, Paige vowed to herself, *I'm going to live in a real house, a beautiful cottage with a green lawn and a white picket fence.*

To the doctors and nurses, it was a difficult, frustrating life. But to the two children, it was a constant adventure, living in the land of lions, giraffes, and elephants. They went to primitive cinder-block schoolhouses, and when none was available, they had tutors.

Paige was a bright child, and her mind was a sponge, absorbing everything. Alfred adored her.

"I'm going to marry you one day, Paige," he said when she was twelve, he fourteen.

"I'm going to marry you, too, Alfred."

They were two serious children, determined to spend the rest of their lives together.

The doctors from WHO were selfless, dedicated men and women who devoted their lives to their work. They often worked under nearly impossible circumstances. In Africa, they had to compete with *wogesha*—the native medical practitioners whose primitive remedies were passed on from father to son, and often had deadly effects. The Masai's traditional remedy for flesh wounds was *olkilorite*, a mixture of cattle blood, raw meat, and essence of a mysterious root.

The Kikuyu remedy for smallpox was to have children drive out the sickness with sticks.

"You must stop that," Dr. Taylor would tell them. "It doesn't help."

"Better than having you stick sharp needles in our skin," they would reply.

The dispensaries were tables lined up under the trees, for surgery. The doctors saw hundreds of patients a day, and there was always a long line waiting to see them—lepers, natives with tubercular lungs, whooping cough, smallpox, dysentery.

Paige and Alfred were inseparable. As they grew older, they would walk to the market together, to a village miles away. And they would talk about their plans for the future.

Medicine was a part of Paige's early life. She learned to care for patients, to give shots and dispense medications, and she anticipated ways to help her father.

Paige loved her father. Curt Taylor was the most caring, selfless man she had ever known. He genuinely liked people, dedicating his life to helping those who needed him, and he instilled that passion in Paige. In spite of the long hours he worked, he managed to find time to spend with his daughter. He made the discomfort of the primitive places they lived in fun.

Paige's relationship with her mother was something else. Her mother was a beauty from a wealthy social background. Her cool aloofness kept Paige at a distance. Marrying a doctor who was going to work in far-off exotic places had seemed romantic to her, but the harsh reality had embittered her. She was not a warm, loving woman, and she seemed to Paige always to be complaining.

"Why did we ever have to come to this godforsaken place, Curt?"

"The people here live like animals. We're going to catch some of their awful diseases."

"Why can't you practice medicine in the United States and make money like other doctors?"

And on and on it went.

The more her mother criticized him, the more Paige adored her father.

When Paige was fifteen years old, her mother disappeared with the owner of a large cocoa plantation in Brazil.

"She's not coming back, is she?" Paige asked.

"No, darling. I'm sorry."

"I'm glad!" She had not meant to say that. She was hurt that her mother had cared so little for her and her father that she had abandoned them.

The experience made Paige draw even closer to Alfred Turner. They played games together and went on expeditions together, and shared their dreams.

"I'm going to be a doctor, too, when I grow up," Alfred confided. "We'll get married, and we'll work together."

"And we'll have lots of children!"

"Sure. If you like."

On the night of Paige's sixteenth birthday, their lifelong emotional intimacy exploded into a new dimension. At a little village in East Africa, the doctors had been called away on an emergency, because of an epidemic, and Paige, Alfred, and a cook were the only ones left in camp.

They had had dinner and gone to bed. But in the middle of the night Paige had been awakened in her tent by the faraway thunder of stampeding animals. She lay there, and as the minutes went by and the sound of the stampede came closer, she began to grow afraid. Her breath quickened. There was no telling when her father and the others would return.

She got up. Alfred's tent was only a few feet away. Terrified, Paige got up, raised the flap of the tent, and ran to Alfred's tent.

He was asleep.

"Alfred!"

He sat up, instantly awake. "Paige? Is anything wrong?"

"I'm frightened. Could I get into bed with you for a while?"

"Sure." They lay there, listening to the animals charging through the brush.

In a few minutes, the sounds began to die away.

Alfred became conscious of Paige's warm body lying next to him.

"Paige, I think you'd better go back to your tent."

Paige could feel his male hardness pressing against her.

All the physical needs that had been building up within them came boiling to the surface.

"Alfred."

"Yes?" His voice was husky.

"We're getting married, aren't we?"

"Yes."

"Then it's all right."

And the sounds of the jungle around them disappeared, and they began to explore and discover a world no one had ever possessed but themselves. They were the first lovers in the world, and they gloried in the wonderful miracle of it.

At dawn, Paige crept back to her tent and she thought, happily, *I'm a woman now.*

From time to time, Curt Taylor suggested to Paige that she return to the United States to live with his brother in his beautiful home in Deerfield, north of Chicago.

"Why?" Paige would ask.

"So that you can grow up to be a proper young lady."

"I *am* a proper young lady."

"Proper young ladies don't tease wild monkeys and try to ride baby zebras."

Her answer was always the same. "I won't leave you."

When Paige was seventeen, the WHO team went to a jungle village in South Africa to fight a typhoid epidemic. Making the situation even more perilous was the fact that shortly after the doctors arrived, war broke out between two local tribes. Curt Taylor was warned to leave.

"I can't, for God's sake. I have patients who will die if I desert them."

Four days later, the village came under attack. Paige and her father huddled in their little hut, listening to the yelling and the sounds of gunfire outside.

Paige was terrified. "They're going to kill us!"

Her father had taken her in his arms. "They won't harm us, darling. We're here to help them. They know we're their friends."

And he had been right.

The chief of one of the tribes had burst into the hut with some of his warriors. "Do not worry. We guard you." And they had.

The fighting and shooting finally stopped, but in the morning Curt Taylor made a decision.

He sent a message to his brother. *Sending Paige out on next plane. Will wire details. Please meet her at airport.*

Paige was furious when she heard the news. She was taken, sobbing wildly, to the

111

dusty little airport where a Piper Cub was waiting to fly her to a town where she could catch a plane to Johannesburg.

"You're sending me away because you want to get rid of me!" she cried.

Her father held her close in his arms. "I love you more than anything in the world, baby. I'll miss you every minute. But I'll be going back to the States soon, and we'll be together again."

"Promise?"

"Promise."

Alfred was there to see Paige off.

"Don't worry," Alfred told Paige. "I'll come and get you as soon as I can. Will you wait for me?"

It was a pretty silly question, after all those years.

"Of course I will."

Three days later, when Paige's plane arrived at O'Hare Airport in Chicago, Paige's Uncle Richard was there to greet her. Paige had never met him. All she knew about him was that he was a very wealthy businessman whose wife had died several years earlier. "He's the successful one in the family," Paige's father always said.

Paige's uncle's first words stunned her.

"I'm sorry to tell you this, Paige, but I just received word that your father was killed in a native uprising."

Her whole world had been shattered in an instant. The ache was so strong that she did not think she could bear it. *I won't let my uncle see me cry*, Paige vowed. *I won't. I never should have left. I'm going back there.*

Driving from the airport, Paige stared out the window, looking at the heavy traffic.

"I hate Chicago."

"Why, Paige?"

"It's a jungle."

Richard would not permit Paige to return to Africa for her father's funeral, and that infuriated her.

He tried to reason with her. "Paige, they've already buried your father. There's no point in your going back."

But there was a point: *Alfred was there.*

A few days after Paige arrived, her uncle sat down with her to discuss her future.

"There's nothing to discuss," Paige informed him. "I'm going to be a doctor."

At twenty-one, when Paige finished college, she applied to ten medical schools and was accepted by all of them. She chose a school in Boston.

It took two days to reach Alfred by telephone in Zaire, where he was working part-time with a WHO unit.

When Paige told him the news, he said, "That's wonderful, darling. I'm nearly finished with my medical courses. I'll stay with WHO for a while, but in a few years we'll be practicing together."

Together. The magical word.

"Paige, I'm desperate to see you. If I can get out for a few days, could you meet me in Hawaii?"

There wasn't the slightest hesitation. "Yes."

And they had both managed it. Later, Paige could only imagine how difficult it must have been for Alfred to make the long journey, but he never mentioned it.

They spent three incredible days at a small hotel in Hawaii, called Sunny Cove, and it was as though they had never been apart. Paige wanted so much to ask Alfred to go back to Boston with her, but she knew how selfish that would have been. The work that he was doing was far more important.

On their last day together, as they were getting dressed, Paige asked, "Where will they be sending you, Alfred?"

"Gambia, or maybe Bangladesh."

To save lives, to help those who so desperately need him. She held him tightly and closed her eyes. She never wanted to let him go.

As though reading her thoughts, he said, "I'll never let you get away."

Paige started medical school, and she and Alfred corresponded regularly. No matter in what part of the world he was, Alfred managed to telephone Paige on her birthday and at Christmas. Just before New Year's Eve, when Paige was in her second year of school, Alfred telephoned.

"Paige?"

"Darling! Where are you?"

"I'm in Senegal. I figured out it's only eighty-eight hundred miles from the Sunny Cove hotel."

It took a minute for it to sink in.

"Do you mean . . . ?"

"Can you meet me in Hawaii for New Year's Eve?"

"Oh, yes! Yes!"

Alfred traveled nearly halfway around the world to meet her, and this time the magic was even stronger. Time had stood still for both of them.

"Next year I'll be in charge of my own cadre at WHO," Alfred said. "When you finish school, I want us to get married. . . ."

They were able to get together once more, and when they weren't able to meet, their letters spanned time and space.

All those years he had worked as a doctor in Third World countries, like his father and Paige's father, doing the wonderful work that they did. And now, at last, he was coming home to her.

As Paige read Alfred's telegram for the fifth time, she thought, *He's coming to San Francisco!*

Kat and Honey were in their bedrooms, asleep. Paige shook them awake. "Alfred's coming! He's coming! He'll be here Sunday!"

"Wonderful," Kat mumbled. "Why don't you wake me up Sunday? I just got to bed."

Honey was more responsive. She sat up and said, "That's great! I'm dying to meet him. How long since you've seen him?"

"Two years," Paige said, "but we've always stayed in touch."

"You're a lucky girl," Kat sighed. "Well, we're all awake now. I'll put on some coffee."

The three of them sat around the kitchen table.

"Why don't we give Alfred a party?" Honey suggested. "Kind of a 'Welcome to the Groom' party."

"That's a good idea," Kat agreed.

"We'll make it a real celebration—a cake, balloons—the works!"

"We'll cook dinner for him here," Honey said.

Kat shook her head. "I've tasted your cooking. Let's send out for food."

Sunday was four days away, and they spent all their spare time discussing Alfred's arrival. By some miracle, the three of them were off duty on Sunday.

Saturday, Paige managed to get to a beauty salon. She went shopping and splurged on a new dress.

"Do I look all right? Do you think he'll like it?"

"You look sensational!" Honey assured her. "I hope he deserves you."

Paige smiled. "I hope I deserve *him*. You'll love him. He's fantastic!"

On The Sunday, an elaborate lunch they had ordered was laid out on the dining-room table, with a bottle of iced champagne. The women stood around, nervously waiting for Alfred's arrival.

At two o'clock, the doorbell rang, and Paige ran to the door to open it. There was Alfred. A bit tired-looking, a little thinner. But he was her Alfred. Standing next to him was a brunette who appeared to be in her thirties.

"Paige!" Alfred exclaimed.

Paige threw her arms around him. Then she turned to Honey and Kat and said proudly, "This is Alfred Turner. Alfred, these are my roommates, Honey Taft and Kat Hunter."

"Pleased to meet you," Alfred said. He turned to the woman at his side. "And this is Karen Turner. My wife."

The three women stood there, frozen.

Paige said slowly, "Your wife?"

"Yes." He frowned. "Didn't . . . didn't you get my letter?"

"Letter?"

"Yes. I sent it several weeks ago."

"No . . ."

"Oh. I . . . I'm terribly sorry. I explained it all in my . . . but of course, if you didn't get the . . ." His voice trailed off . . . "I'm really sorry, Paige. You and I have been apart so long, that I . . . and then I met Karen . . . and you know how it is . . ."

"I know how it is," Paige said numbly. She turned to Karen and forced a smile. "I . . . I hope you and Alfred will be very happy."

"Thank you."

There was an awkward silence.

Karen said, "I think we had better go, darling."

"Yes. I think you had," Kat said.

Alfred ran his fingers through his hair. "I'm really sorry, Paige. I . . . well . . . goodbye."

"Goodbye, Alfred."

The three women stood there, watching the departing newlyweds.

"That bastard!" Kat said. "What a lousy thing to do."

Paige's eyes were brimming with tears. "I . . . he didn't mean to . . . I mean . . . he must have explained everything in his letter."

Honey put her arms around Paige. "There ought to be a law that all men should be castrated."

"I'll drink to that," Kat said.

"Excuse me," Paige said. She hurried to her bedroom and closed the door behind her.

She did not come out for the rest of the day.

Chapter Five

During the next few months, Paige saw very little of Kat and Honey. They would have a hurried breakfast in the cafeteria and occasionally pass one another in the corridors. They communicated mainly by leaving notes in the apartment.

"Dinner is in the fridge."

"The microwave is out."

"Sorry, I didn't have time to clean up."

"What about the three of us having dinner out Saturday night?"

The impossible hours continued to be a punishment, testing the limits of endurance for all the residents.

Paige welcomed the pressure. It gave her no time to think about Alfred and the wonderful future they had planned together. And yet, she could not get him out of her mind. What he had done filled her with a deep pain that refused to go away. She tortured herself with the futile game of "what if?"

What if I had stayed with Alfred in Africa?

What if he had come to Chicago with me?

What if he had not met Karen?

What if . . . ?

On a Friday when Paige went into the change room to put on her scrubs, the word "bitch" had been written on them with a black marker pen.

The following day when Paige went to look for her scut book, it was gone. All her notes had disappeared. *Maybe I misplaced it*, Paige thought.

But she couldn't make herself believe it.

The world outside the hospital ceased to exist. Paige was aware that Iraq was pillaging Kuwait, but that was overshadowed by the needs of a fifteen-year-old patient who was dying of leukemia. The day East and West Germany became united, Paige was busy trying to save the life of a diabetic patient. Margaret Thatcher resigned as prime minister of England, but more important, the patient in 214 was able to walk again.

What made it bearable was the doctors Paige worked with. With few exceptions, they had dedicated themselves to healing others, relieving pain, and saving lives. Paige watched the miracles they performed every day, and it filled her with a sense of pride.

The greatest stress was working in the ER. The emergency room was constantly overcrowded with people suffering every form of trauma imaginable.

The long hours at the hospital and the pressures placed an enormous strain on the doctors and nurses who worked there. The divorce rate among the doctors was extraordinarily high, and extramarital affairs were common.

Tom Chang was one of those having a problem. He told Paige about it over coffee.

"I can handle the hours," Chang confided, "but my wife can't. She complains that she never sees me anymore and that I'm a stranger to our little girl. She's right. I don't know what to do about it."

"Has your wife visited the hospital?"

"No."

"Why don't you invite her here for lunch, Tom? Let her see what you're doing here and how important it is."

Chang brightened. "That's a good idea. Thanks, Paige. I will. I would like you to meet her. Will you join us for lunch?"

"I'd love to."

Chang's wife, Sye, turned out to be a lovely young woman with a classic, timeless beauty. Chang showed her around the hospital, and afterward they had lunch in the cafeteria with Paige.

Chang had told Paige that Sye had been born and raised in Hong Kong.

"How do you like San Francisco?" Paige asked.

There was a small silence. "It's an interesting city," Sye said politely, "but I feel as though I am a stranger here. It is too big, too noisy."

"But I understand Hong Kong is also big and noisy."

"I come from a small village an hour away from Hong Kong. There, there is no noise and no automobiles, and everyone knows his neighbors." She looked at her husband. "Tom and I and our little daughter were very happy there. It is very beautiful on the island of

Llama. It has white beaches and small farms, and nearby is a little fishing village, Sak Kwu Wan. It is so peaceful."

Her voice was filled with a wistful nostalgia. "My husband and I were together much of the time, as a family should be. Here, I never see him."

Paige said, "Mrs. Chang, I know it's difficult for you right now, but in a few years, Tom will be able to set up his own practice, and then his hours will be much easier."

Tom Chang took his wife's hand. "You see? Everything will be fine, Sye. You must be patient."

"I understand," she said. There was no conviction in her voice.

As they talked, a man walked into the cafeteria, and as he stood at the door, Paige could see only the back of his head. Her heart started to race. He turned around. It was a complete stranger.

Chang was watching Paige. "Are you all right?"

"Yes," Paige lied. *I've got to forget him. It's over.* And yet, the memories of all those wonderful years, the fun, the excitement, the love they had for each other . . . *How do I forget all that? I wonder if I could persuade any of the doctors here to do a lobotomy on me.*

*   *   *

Paige ran into Honey in the corridor. Honey was out of breath and looked worried.

"Is everything all right?" Paige asked.

Honey smiled uneasily. "Yes. Fine." She hurried on.

Honey had been assigned to an attending physician named Charles Isler, who was known around the hospital as a martinet.

On Honey's first day of rounds, he had said, "I've been looking forward to working with you, Dr. Taft. Dr. Wallace has told me about your outstanding record at medical school. I understand you're going to practice internal medicine."

"Yes."

"Good. So, we'll have you here for three more years."

They began their rounds.

The first patient was a young Mexican boy. Dr. Isler ignored the other residents and turned to Honey. "I think you'll find this an interesting case, Dr. Taft. The patient has all the classic signs and symptoms: anorexia, weight loss, metallic taste, fatigue, anemia, hyperirritability, and uncoordination. How would you diagnose it?" He smiled expectantly.

Honey looked at him a moment. "Well, it

could be several things, couldn't it?"

Dr. Isler was watching her, puzzled. "It's a clear-cut case of—"

One of the other residents broke in, "Lead poisoning?"

"That's right," Dr. Isler said.

Honey smiled. "Of course. Lead poisoning."

Dr. Isler turned to Honey again. "How would you treat it?"

Honey said evasively, "Well, there are several different methods of treatment, aren't there?"

A second resident spoke up. "If the patient has had long-term exposure, he should be treated as a potential case of encephalopathy."

Dr. Isler nodded. "Right. That's what we're doing. We're correcting the dehydration and electrolyte disturbances, and giving him chelation therapy."

He looked at Honey. She nodded in agreement.

The next patient was a man in his eighties. His eyes were red and his eyelids were stuck together.

"We'll have your eyes taken care of in a moment," Dr. Isler assured him. "How are you feeling?"

"Oh, not too bad for an old man."

Dr. Isler pulled aside the blanket to reveal the patient's swollen knee and ankle. There were lesions on the soles of his feet.

Dr. Isler turned to the residents. "The swelling is caused by arthritis." He looked at Honey. "Combined with the lesions and the conjunctivitis, I'm sure you know what the diagnosis is."

Honey said slowly, "Well, it could be . . . you know . . ."

"It's Reiter's syndrome," one of the residents spoke up. "The cause is unknown. It's usually accompanied by low-grade fever."

Dr. Isler nodded. "That's right." He looked at Honey. "What is the prognosis?"

"The prognosis?"

The other resident replied. "The prognosis is unclear. It can be treated with anti-inflammation drugs."

"Very good," Dr. Isler said.

They made the rounds of a dozen more patients, and when they were finished, Honey said to Dr. Isler, "Could I see you for a moment alone, Dr. Isler?"

"Yes. Come into my office."

When they were seated in his office, Honey said, "I know you're disappointed in me."

"I must admit that I was a little surprised that you—"

Honey interrupted. "I know, Dr. Isler. I didn't close my eyes last night. To tell you the truth, I was so excited about working with you that I . . . I just couldn't sleep."

He looked at her in surprise. "Oh. I see. I knew there had to be a reason for . . . I mean, your medical school record was so fantastic. What made you decide to become a doctor?"

Honey looked down for a moment, then said softly, "I had a younger brother who was injured in an accident. The doctors did everything they could to try to save him . . . but I watched him die. It took a long time, and I felt so helpless. I decided then that I was going to spend my life helping other people get well." Her eyes welled up with tears.

She's so vulnerable, Isler thought. "I'm glad we had this little talk."

Honey looked at him and thought, *He believed me.*

Chapter Six

Across town, in another part of the city, reporters and TV crews were waiting in the street for Lou Dinetto as he left the courtroom, smiling and waving, the greeting of royalty to the peasants. There were two bodyguards at his side, a tall, thin man known as the Shadow, and a heavyset man called Rhino. Lou Dinetto was, as always, dressed elegantly and expensively, in a gray silk suit with a white shirt, blue tie, and alligator shoes. His clothes had to be carefully tailored to make him look trim, because he was short and stout, with bandy legs. He always had a smile and a ready quip for the press, and they enjoyed quoting him. Dinetto had been indicted and tried three times on charges

131

ranging from arson to racketeering to murder, and each time had gone free.

Now as he left the courtroom, one of the reporters yelled out, "Did you know you were going to be acquitted, Mr. Dinetto?"

Dinetto laughed. "Of course I did. I'm an innocent businessman. The government has got nothing better to do than to persecute me. That's one of the reasons our taxes are so high."

A TV camera was aimed at him. Lou Dinetto stopped to smile into it.

"Mr. Dinetto, can you explain why two witnesses who were scheduled to testify against you in your murder trial failed to appear?"

"Certainly I can explain it," Dinetto said. "They were honest citizens who decided not to perjure themselves."

"The government claims that you're the head of the West Coast mob, and that it was you who arranged for—"

"The only thing I arrange for is where people sit at my restaurant. I want everybody to be comfortable." He grinned at the milling crowd of reporters. "By the way, you're all invited to the restaurant tonight for a free dinner and drinks."

He was moving toward the curb, where a black stretch limousine was waiting for him.

"Mr. Dinetto . . ."

"Mr. Dinetto . . ."

"Mr. Dinetto . . ."

"I'll see you at my restaurant tonight, boys and girls. You all know where it is."

And Lou Dinetto was in the car, waving and smiling. Rhino closed the door of the limousine and got into the front seat. The Shadow slipped behind the wheel.

"That was great, boss!" Rhino said. "You sure know how to handle them bums."

"Where to?" the Shadow asked.

"Home. I can use a hot bath and a good steak."

The car started off.

"I don't like that question about the witnesses," Dinetto said. "You sure they'll never . . . ?"

"Not unless they can talk underwater, boss."

Dinetto nodded. "Good."

The car was speeding along Fillmore Street. Dinetto said, "Did you see the look on the DA's face when the judge dismissed . . . ?"

A small dog appeared out of nowhere, directly in front of the limousine. The Shadow swung the wheel hard to avoid hitting it and jammed on the brakes. The car jumped the curb and crashed into a lamppost. Rhino's head flew forward into the windshield.

"What the *fuck* are you doing?" Dinetto screamed. "You trying to kill me?"

The Shadow was trembling. "Sorry, boss. A dog ran in front of the car . . ."

"And you decided his life was more important than mine? You stupid asshole!"

Rhino was moaning. He turned around, and Dinetto saw blood pouring from a large cut in his forehead.

"For Christ's sake!" Dinetto screamed. "Look what you've done!"

"I'm all right," Rhino mumbled.

"The hell you are!" Dinetto turned to the Shadow. "Get him to a hospital."

The Shadow backed the limousine off the curb.

"The Embarcadero is only a couple of blocks down. We'll take him to the emergency ward there."

"Right, boss."

Dinetto sank back in his seat. "A dog," he said disgustedly. "Jesus!"

Kat was in the emergency ward when Dinetto, the Shadow, and Rhino walked in. Rhino was bleeding heavily.

Dinetto called out to Kat, "Hey, you!"

Kat looked up. "Are you talking to me?"

"Who the hell do you think I'm talking to?

This man is bleeding. Get him fixed up right away."

"There are half a dozen others ahead of him," Kat said quietly. "He'll have to wait his turn."

"He's not waiting for anything," Dinetto told her. "You'll take care of him now."

Kat stepped over to Rhino and examined him. She took a piece of cotton and pressed it against the cut. "Hold it there. I'll be back."

"I said to take care of him *now*," Dinetto snapped.

Kat turned to Dinetto. "This is an emergency hospital ward. I'm the doctor in charge. So either keep quiet or get out."

The Shadow said, "Lady, you don't know who you're talking to. You better do what the man says. This is Mr. Lou Dinetto."

"Now that the introductions are over," Dinetto said impatiently, "take care of my man."

"You have a hearing problem," Kat said. "I'll tell you once more. Keep quiet or get out of here. I have work to do."

Rhino said, "You can't talk to—"

Dinetto turned to him. "Shut up!" He looked at Kat again, and his tone changed. "I would appreciate it if you could get to him as soon as possible."

"I'll do my best." Kat sat Rhino down on a cot. "Lie down. I'll be back in a few minutes."

She looked at Dinetto. "There are some chairs over there in the corner."

Dinetto and the Shadow watched her walk to the other end of the ward to take care of the waiting patients.

"Jesus," the Shadow said. "She has no idea who you are."

"I don't think it would make any difference. She's got balls."

Fifteen minutes later, Kat returned to Rhino and examined him. "No concussion," she announced. "You're lucky. That's a nasty cut."

Dinetto stood watching as Kat skillfully put stitches in Rhino's forehead.

When Kat was finished, she said, "That should heal nicely. Come back in five days, and I'll take out the stitches."

Dinetto walked over and examined Rhino's forehead. "That's a damn good job."

"Thanks," Kat said. "Now, if you'll excuse me . . ."

"Wait a minute," Dinetto called. He turned to the Shadow. "Give her a C-note."

The Shadow took a hundred-dollar bill out of his pocket. "Here."

"The cashier's office is outside."

"This isn't for the hospital. It's for you."

"No, thanks."

Dinetto stared as Kat walked away and began working on another patient.

The Shadow said, "Maybe it wasn't enough, boss."

Dinetto shook his head. "She's an independent broad. I like that." He was silent for a moment. "Doc Evans is retiring, right?"

"Yeah."

"Okay. I want you to find out everything you can about this doctor."

"What for?"

"Leverage. I think she might come in very handy."

Chapter Seven

Hospitals are run by nurses. Margaret Spencer, the chief nurse, had worked at Embarcadero County Hospital for twenty years and knew where all the bodies—literally and figuratively—were buried. Nurse Spencer was in charge of the hospital, and doctors who did not recognize it were in trouble. She knew which doctors were on drugs or addicted to alcohol, which doctors were incompetent, and which doctors deserved her support. In her charge were all the student nurses, registered nurses, and operating room nurses. It was Margaret Spencer who decided which of them would be assigned to the various surgeries, and since the nurses ranged from indispensable to incompetent, it paid the doctors to get along with her. She had the power to assign an inept scrub nurse to assist on a complicated kidney removal, or, if she liked the doctor, to send her most competent nurse to help him with a simple tonsillectomy. Among Margaret Spencer's many prejudices was an antipathy to women doctors and to blacks.

Kat Hunter was a black woman doctor.

Kat was having a hard time. Nothing was overtly said or done, and yet prejudice was at work in ways too subtle to pin down. The nurses she asked for were unavailable, those assigned to her were close to incompetent. Kat found herself frequently being sent to examine male clinic patients with venereal diseases. She accepted the first few cases as routine, but when she was given half a dozen to examine in one day, she became suspicious.

At a lunch break she said to Paige, "Have you examined many men with venereal disease?"

Paige thought for a moment. "One last week. An orderly."

I'm going to have to do something about this, Kat thought.

*   *   *

Nurse Spencer had planned to get rid of Dr. Hunter by making her life so miserable that she would be forced to quit, but she had not counted on Kat's dedication or her ability. Little by little, Kat was winning over the people she worked with. She had a natural skill that impressed her fellow workers as well as her patients. But the real breakthrough happened because of what came to be known around the hospital as the famous pig blood caper.

On morning rounds one day, Kat was working with a senior resident named Dundas. They were at the bedside of a patient who was unconscious.

"Mr. Levy was in an automobile accident," Dundas informed the younger residents. "He's lost a great deal of blood, and he needs an immediate transfusion. The hospital is short of blood right now. This man has a family, and they refuse to donate any blood to him. It's infuriating."

Kat asked, "Where is his family?"

"In the visitors' waiting room," Dr. Dundas said.

"Do you mind if I talk to them?" Kat asked.

"It won't do any good. I've already spoken to them. They've made up their minds."

When the rounds were over, Kat went

into the visitors' waiting room. The man's wife and grown son and daughter were there. The son wore a yarmulke and ritual tallis.

"Mrs. Levy?" Kat asked the woman.

She stood up. "How is my husband? Is the doctor going to operate?"

"Yes," Kat said.

"Well, don't ask us to give any of our blood. It's much too dangerous these days, with AIDS and all."

"Mrs. Levy," Kat said, "you can't get AIDS by donating blood. It's not poss—"

"Don't tell me! I read the papers. I know what's what."

Kat studied her a moment. "I can see that. Well, it's all right, Mrs. Levy. The hospital is short of blood right now, but we've solved the problem."

"Good."

"We're going to give your husband pig's blood."

The mother and son were staring at Kat, shocked.

"*What?*"

"Pig's blood," Kat said cheerfully. "It probably won't do him any harm." She turned to leave.

"Wait a minute!" Mrs. Levy cried.

Kat stopped. "Yes?"

"I, uh . . . just give us a minute, will you?"

"Certainly."

Fifteen minutes later, Kat went up to Dr. Dundas. "You don't have to worry about Mr. Levy's family anymore. They're all happy to make a blood donation."

The story became an instant legend around the hospital. Doctors and nurses who had ignored Kat before made a point of speaking to her.

A few days later, Kat went into the private room of Tom Leonard, an ulcer patient. He was eating an enormous lunch that he had had brought in from a nearby delicatessen.

Kat walked up to his bed. "What are you doing?"

He looked up and smiled. "Having a decent lunch for a change. Want to join me? There's plenty here."

Kat rang for a nurse.

"Yes, doctor?"

"Get this food out of here. Mr. Leonard is on a strict hospital diet. Didn't you read his chart?"

"Yes, but he insisted on—"

"Remove it, please."

"Hey! Wait a minute!" Leonard protested. "I can't eat the pap this hospital is giving me!"

"You'll eat it if you want to get rid of your

ulcer." Kat looked at the nurse. "Take it out."

Thirty minutes later, Kat was summoned to the office of the administrator.

"You wanted to see me, Dr. Wallace?"

"Yes. Sit down. Tom Leonard is one of your patients, isn't he?"

"That's right. I found him eating a hot pastrami sandwich with pickles and potato salad for lunch today, full of spices and—"

"And you took it away from him."

"Of course."

Wallace leaned forward in his chair. "Doctor, you probably were not aware that Tom Leonard is on the hospital's supervisory board. We want to keep him happy. Do you get my meaning?"

Kat looked at him and said stubbornly, "No, sir."

He blinked. "What?"

"It seems to me that the way to keep Tom Leonard happy is to get him healthy. He's not going to be cured if he tears his stomach apart."

Benjamin Wallace forced a smile. "Why don't we let him make that decision?"

Kat stood up. "Because *I'm* his doctor. Is there anything else?"

"I . . . er . . . no. That's all."

Kat walked out of the office.

Benjamin Wallace sat there stunned. *Women doctors!*

Kat was on night duty when she received a call. "Dr. Hunter, I think you had better come up to 320."

"Right away."

The patient in Room 320 was Mrs. Molloy, a cancer patient in her eighties, with a poor prognosis. As Kat neared the door she heard voices inside, raised in argument. Kat stepped inside the room.

Mrs. Molloy was in bed, heavily sedated, but conscious. Her son and two daughters were in the room.

The son was saying, "I say we split the estate up three ways."

"No!" one of the daughters said. "Laurie and I are the ones who have been taking care of Mama. Who's been doing the cooking and cleaning for her? We have! Well, we're entitled to her money and—"

"I'm as much her flesh and blood as you are!" the man yelled.

Mrs. Molloy lay in bed, helpless, listening.

Kat was furious. "Excuse me," she said.

One of the women glanced at her. "Come back later, nurse. We're busy."

145

Kat said angrily, "This is my patient. I'm giving you all ten seconds to get out of this room. You can wait in the visitors' waiting room. Now get out before I call security and have you thrown out."

The man started to say something, but the look in Kat's eyes stopped him. He turned to his sisters and shrugged. "We can talk outside."

Kat watched the three of them leave the room. She turned to Mrs. Molloy in bed and stroked her head. "They didn't mean anything by it," Kat said softly. She sat at the bedside, holding the old woman's hand, and watched her drop off to sleep.

We're all dying, Kat thought. *Forget what Dylan Thomas said. The real trick is to go gentle into that good night.*

Kat was in the middle of treating a patient when an orderly came into the ward. "There's an urgent call for you at the desk, doctor."

Kat frowned. "Thank you." She turned to the patient, who was in a full body cast, with his legs suspended on a pulley. "I'll be right back."

In the corridor, at the nurses' station, Kat picked up the desk telephone. "Hello?"

"Hi, sis."

"Mike!" She was excited to hear from him, but her excitement immediately turned to concern. "Mike, I told you never to call me here. You have the number at the apartment if—"

"Hey, I'm sorry. This couldn't wait. I have a little problem."

Kat knew what was coming.

"I borrowed some money from a fellow to invest in a business . . ."

Kat didn't bother asking what kind of business. "And it failed."

"Yeah. And now he wants his money."

"How much, Mike?"

"Well, if you could send five thousand . . ."

"What?"

The desk nurse was looking at Kat curiously.

Five thousand dollars. Kat lowered her voice. "I don't have that much. I . . . I can send you half now and the rest in a few weeks. Will that be all right?"

"I guess so. I hate to bother you, sis, but you know how it is."

Kat knew exactly how it was. Her brother was twenty-two years old and was always involved in mysterious deals. He ran with gangs, and God only knew what they were up to, but Kat felt a deep responsibility toward him. *It's all my fault*, Kat thought. *If I hadn't run away from home and deserted him . . .* "Stay out of trouble, Mike. I love you."

"I love you, too, Kat."

I'll have to get him that money, somehow, Kat thought. *Mike's all I have in the world.*

Dr. Isler had been looking forward to working with Honey Taft again. He had forgiven her inept performance and, in fact, was flattered that she was in such awe of him. But now, on rounds with her once more, Honey stayed behind the other residents and never volunteered an answer to his questions.

Thirty minutes after rounds, Dr. Isler was seated in Benjamin Wallace's office.

"What's the problem?" Wallace asked.

"It's Dr. Taft."

Wallace looked at him in genuine surprise. "Dr. Taft? She has the best recommendations I've ever seen."

"That's what puzzles me," Dr. Isler said. "I've been getting reports from some of the other residents. She's misdiagnosing cases and making serious mistakes. I'd like to know what the hell is going on."

"I don't understand. She went to a fine medical school."

"Maybe you should give the dean of the

school a call," Dr. Isler suggested.

"That's Jim Pearson. He's a good man. I'll call him."

A few minutes later, Wallace had Jim Pearson on the telephone. They exchanged pleasantries, and then Wallace said, "I'm calling about Betty Lou Taft."

There was a brief silence. "Yes?"

"We seem to be having a few problems with her, Jim. She was admitted here with your wonderful recommendation."

"Right."

"In fact, I have your report in front of me. It says she was one of the brightest students you ever had."

"That's right."

"And that she was going to be a credit to the medical profession."

"Yes."

"Was there any doubt about . . . ?"

"None," Dr. Pearson said firmly. "None at all. She's probably a little nervous. She's high-strung, but if you just give her a chance, I'm sure she'll be fine."

"Well, I appreciate your telling me. We'll certainly give her every chance. Thank you."

"Not at all." The line went dead.

Jim Pearson sat there, hating himself for what he had done.

But my wife and children come first.

Chapter Eight

Honey Taft had the bad fortune to have been born into a family of overachievers. Her handsome father was the founder and president of a large computer company in Memphis, Tennessee, her lovely mother was a genetic scientist, and Honey's older twin sisters were as attractive, as brainy, and as ambitious as their parents. The Tafts were among the most prominent families in Memphis.

Honey had inconveniently come along when her sisters were six years old.

"Honey was our little accident," her mother would tell their friends. "I wanted to have an abortion, but Fred was against it. Now he's sorry."

Where Honey's sisters were stunning, Honey was plain. Where they were brilliant, Honey was average. Her sisters had started talking at nine months. Honey had not uttered a word until she was almost two.

"We call her 'the dummy,'" her father would laugh. "Honey is the ugly duckling of the Taft family. Only I don't think she's going to turn into a swan."

It was not that Honey was ugly, but neither was she pretty. She was ordinary-looking, with a thin, pinched face, mousy blond hair, and an unenviable figure. What Honey *did* have was an extraordinarily sweet, sunny disposition, a quality not particularly prized in a family of competitive overachievers.

From the earliest time Honey could remember, her greatest desire was to please her parents and sisters and make them love her. It was a futile effort. Her parents were busy with their careers, and her sisters were busy winning beauty contests and scholarships. To add to Honey's misery, she was inordinately shy. Consciously or unconsciously, her family had implanted in her a feeling of deep inferiority.

In high school, Honey was known as the Wallflower. She attended school dances and parties by herself, and smiled and tried not to show how miserable she was, because she did not want to spoil anyone's fun. She would watch her sisters picked up at the house by the most popular boys at school, and then she would go up to her lonely room to struggle with her homework.

And try not to cry.

On weekends and during the summer holidays, Honey made pocket money by babysitting. She loved taking care of children, and the children adored her.

When Honey was not working, she would go off and explore Memphis by herself. She visited Graceland, where Elvis Presley had lived, and walked down Beale Street, where the blues started. She wandered through the Pink Palace Museum, and the Planetarium, with its roaring, stomping dinosaur. She went to the aquarium.

And Honey was always alone.

She was unaware that her life was about to change drastically.

Honey knew that many of her classmates were having love affairs. They discussed it constantly at school.

"Have you gone to bed with Ricky yet? He's the best . . . !"

"Joe is really into orgasms . . ."

"I was out with Tony last night. I'm exhausted. What an animal! I'm seeing him again tonight . . ."

Honey stood there listening to their conversations, and she was filled with a bittersweet envy, and a feeling that she would never know what sex was like. *Who would want me?* Honey wondered.

One Friday night, there was a school prom. Honey had no intention of going, but her father said, "You know, I'm concerned. Your sisters tell me that you're a wallflower, and that you're not going to the prom because you can't get a date."

Honey blushed. "That's not true," she said. "I do have a date, and I *am* going." *Don't let him ask who my date is*, Honey prayed.

He didn't.

Now Honey found herself at the prom, seated in her usual corner, watching the others dancing and having a wonderful time.

And that was when the miracle occurred.

Roger Merton, the captain of the football team and the most popular boy at school, was on the dance floor, having a fight with his girlfriend. He had been drinking.

"You're a no-good, selfish bastard!" she said.

"And you're a dumb bitch!"

"You can go screw yourself."

"I don't have to screw myself, Sally. I can screw somebody else. Anyone I want to."

"Go ahead!" She stormed off the dance floor.

Honey could not help but overhear.

Merton saw her looking at him. "What the hell are you staring at?" He was slurring his words.

"Nothing," Honey said.

"I'll show the bitch! You think I won't show her?"

"I . . . yes."

"Damn right. Let's have a li'l drink."

Honey hesitated. Merton was obviously drunk. "Well, I don't . . ."

"Great. I have a bottle in the car."

"I really don't think I . . ."

And he had Honey's arm and was steering her out of the room. She went along because she did not want to make a scene and embarrass him.

Outside, Honey tried to pull away. "Roger, I don't think this is a good idea. I . . ."

"What the hell are you—chicken?"

"No, I . . ."

"Okay, then. Come on."

He led her to his car and opened the door. Honey stood there a moment.

"Get in."

"I can only stay a moment," Honey said.

She got in the car because she did not want to upset Roger. He climbed in beside her.

"We're going to show that dumb broad, aren't we?" He held out a bottle of bourbon. "Here."

Honey had had only one drink of alcohol before and she had hated it. But she did not want to hurt Roger's feelings. She looked at him and reluctantly took a small sip.

"You're okay," he said. "You're new at school, huh?"

Honey was in three of his classes. "No," Honey said. I . . ."

He leaned over and began to play with her breasts.

Startled, Honey pulled away.

"Hey! Come on. Don't you want to please me?" he said.

And that was the magic phrase. Honey wanted to please everybody, and if this was the way to do it . . .

In the uncomfortable backseat of Merton's car, Honey had sex for the first time, and it opened an incredible new world to her. She did not particularly enjoy the sex, but that was not important. The important thing was that Merton enjoyed it. In fact, Honey was amazed by how *much* he enjoyed it. It seemed to make him ecstatic. She had never seen anyone enjoy anything so much. *So this is how to please a man*, Honey thought.

It was an epiphany.

Honey was unable to get the miracle of what had occurred out of her mind. She lay in bed, remembering Merton's hard maleness inside her, thrusting faster and faster, and then his moans, "Oh, yes, yes . . . Jesus, you're fantastic, Sally . . ."

And Honey had not even minded that. She had pleased the captain of the football team! The most popular boy in school! *And I really didn't even know what I was doing*, Honey thought. *If I truly learned how to please a man . . .*

And that was when Honey had her second epiphany.

The following morning, Honey went to the Pleasure Chest, a porno bookstore on Poplar Street, and bought half a dozen books on eroticism. She smuggled them home and read them in the privacy of her room. She was astounded by what she was reading.

She raced through the pages of *The Perfumed Garden* and the *Kama Sutra*, the *Tibetan Arts of Love*, the *Alchemy of Ecstasy*, and then went back for more. She read the words of Gedun Chopel and the arcane accounts by Kanchinatha.

She studied the exciting photographs of the thirty-seven positions of lovemaking, and she learned the meaning of the Half Moon and the Circle, the Lotus Petal, and the Pieces of Cloud, and the way of churning.

Honey became an expert on the eight types of oral sex, and the paths of the sixteen pleasures, and the ecstasy of the string of marbles. She knew how to teach a man to perform *karuna*, to intensify his pleasure. In theory, at least.

Honey felt she was now ready to put her knowledge into practice.

The *Kama Sutra* had several chapters on aphrodisiacs to arouse a man, but since Honey had no idea where she could obtain *Hedysarum gangeticum*, the *kshirika* plant, or the *Xanthochymus pictorius*, she figured out her own substitutes.

When Honey saw Roger Merton in class the following week, she walked up to him and said, "I really enjoyed the other night. Can we do it again?"

It took him a moment to remember who

Honey was. "Oh. Sure. Why not? My folks are out tonight. Why don't you come by about eight o'clock?"

When Honey arrived at Merton's house that night, she had a small jar of maple syrup with her.

"What's that for?" Merton asked.

"I'm going to show you," Honey said.

She showed him.

The next day, Merton was telling his buddies at school about Honey.

"She's incredible," he said. "You wouldn't believe what she can do with a little warm syrup!"

That afternoon, half a dozen boys were asking Honey for dates. From that time on, she started going out every night. The boys were very happy, and that made Honey very happy.

Honey's parents were delighted by their daughter's sudden popularity.

"It took our girl a little while to bloom," her father said proudly, "but now she's turned into a real Taft!"

Honey had always had poor grades in mathematics, and she knew she had failed badly on her final test. Her mathematics teacher, Mr. Janson, was a bachelor and lived near the school. Honey paid him a visit one evening. He opened the door and looked at her in surprise.

"Honey! What are you doing here?"

"I need your help," Honey said. "My father will kill me if I fail your course. I brought some math problems, and I wonder if you would mind going over them with me."

He hesitated a moment. "This is unusual, but . . . very well."

Mr. Janson liked Honey. She was not like the other girls in his class. They were raucous and indifferent, while Honey was sensitive and caring, always eager to please. He wished that she had more of an aptitude for mathematics.

Mr. Janson sat next to Honey on the couch and began to explain the arcane intricacies of logarithms.

Honey was not interested in logarithms. As Mr. Janson talked, Honey moved closer and closer to him. She started breathing on his neck and into his ear, and before he knew what was happening, Mr. Janson found that his pants were unzipped.

He was looking at Honey in astonishment. "What are you doing?"

"I've wanted you since the first time I saw you," Honey said. She opened her purse and took out a small can of whipped cream.

"What's that?"

"Let me show you . . ."

Honey received an A in math.

It was not only the accessories Honey used that made her so popular. It was the knowledge she had gleaned from all the ancient books on erotica she had read. She delighted her partners with techniques they had never even dreamed of, that were thousands of years old, and long forgotten. She brought a new meaning to the word "ecstasy."

Honey's grades improved dramatically, and she was suddenly even more popular than her sisters had been in their high school days. Honey was dined at the Private Eye and the Bombay Bicycle Club, and taken to the Ice Capades at the Memphis Mall. The boys took her skiing at Cedar Cliff and sky diving at Landis Airport.

Honey's years at college were just as successful socially. At dinner one evening, her father said, "You'll be graduating soon. It's time to think about your future. Do you know what you want to do with your life?"

She answered immediately. "I want to be a nurse."

Her father's face reddened. "You mean a doctor."

"No, Father. I . . ."

"You're a Taft. If you want to go into medicine, you'll be a doctor. Is that understood?"

"Yes, Father."

Honey had meant it when she told her father she wanted to be a nurse. She loved taking care of people, helping them and nurturing them. She was terrified by the idea of becoming a doctor, and being responsible for people's lives. But she knew that she must not disappoint her father. *You're a Taft.*

Honey's college grades were not good enough to get her into medical school, but her father's influence was. He was a heavy contributor to a medical school in Knoxville, Tennessee. He met with Dr. Jim Pearson, the dean.

"You're asking for a big favor," Pearson said, "but I'll tell you what I'll do. I'll admit Honey on a probationary basis. If at the end of six months we feel she's not qualified to continue, we'll have to let her go."

"Fair enough. She's going to surprise you."

He was right.

*　*　*

Honey's father had made arrangements for her to stay in Knoxville with a cousin of his, the Reverend Douglas Lipton.

Douglas Lipton was the minister of the Baptist Church. He was in his sixties, married to a woman ten years older.

The minister was delighted to have Honey in the house.

"She's like a breath of fresh air," he told his wife.

He had never seen anyone so eager to please.

Honey did fairly well in medical school, but she lacked dedication. She was there only to please her father.

Honey's teachers liked her. There was a genuine niceness about her that made her professors want her to succeed.

Ironically, she was particularly weak in anatomy. During the eighth week, her anatomy teacher sent for her. "I'm afraid I'm going to have to fail you," he said unhappily.

I can't fail, Honey thought. *I can't let my father down. What would Boccaccio have advised?*

Honey moved closer to the professor. "I came to this school because of you. I had heard so much about you." She moved closer to him. "I want to be like you." And closer. "Being a doctor means everything to me." And closer. "Please help me . . ."

One hour later, when Honey left his office, she had the answers to the next examination.

Before Honey was finished with medical school, she had seduced several of her professors. There was a helplessness about her that they were unable to resist. They were all under the impression that it was *they* who were seducing *her,* and they felt guilty about taking advantage of her innocence.

Dr. Jim Pearson was the last to succumb to Honey. He was intrigued by all the reports he had heard about her. There were rumors of her extraordinary sexual skills. He sent for Honey one day to discuss her grades. She brought a small box of powdered sugar with her, and before the afternoon was over, Dr. Pearson was as hooked as all the others. Honey made him feel young and insatiable. She made him feel that he was a king who had subjugated her and made her his slave.

He tried not to think of his wife and children.

* * *

Honey was genuinely fond of the Reverend Douglas Lipton, and it upset her that his wife was a cold, frigid woman who was always criticizing him. Honey felt sorry for the minister. *He doesn't deserve that,* Honey thought. *He needs comforting.*

In the middle of the night, when Mrs. Lipton was out of town visiting a sister, Honey walked into the minister's bedroom. She was naked. "Douglas . . ."

His eyes flew open. "Honey? Are you all right?"

"No," she said. "Can I talk to you?"

"Of course." He reached for the lamp.

"Don't turn on the light." She crept into bed beside him.

"What's the matter? Aren't you feeling well?"

"I'm worried."

"About what?"

"You. You deserve to be loved. I want to make love to you."

He was wide awake. "My God!" he said. "You're just a child. You can't be serious."

"I am. Your wife's not giving you any love. . . ."

"Honey, this is impossible! You'd better get back to your room now, and . . ."

He could feel her naked body pressing against his. "Honey, we can't do this. I'm . . ."

Her lips were on his, and her body was on top of him, and he was completely swept away. She spent the night in his bed.

At six o'clock in the morning, the door to the bedroom opened and Mrs. Lipton walked in. She stood there, staring at the two of them, then walked out without a word.

Two hours later, the Reverend Douglas Lipton committed suicide in his garage.

When Honey heard the news, she was devastated, unable to believe what had happened.

The sheriff arrived at the house and had a talk with Mrs. Lipton.

When he was through, he went to find Honey. "Out of respect for his family, we're going to list the death of the Reverend Douglas Lipton as a 'suicide for reasons unknown,' but I would suggest that you get the fuck out of this town fast, and stay out."

Honey had gone to Embarcadero County Hospital in San Francisco.

With a glowing recommendation from Dr. Jim Pearson.

Chapter Nine

Time had lost all meaning for Paige. There was no beginning and no end, and the days and nights flowed into one another in a seamless rhythm. The hospital had become her whole life. The outside world was a foreign, faraway planet.

Christmas came and went, and a new year began. In the world outside, U.S. troops liberated Kuwait from Iraq.

There was no word from Alfred. *He'll find out he made a mistake*, Paige thought. *He'll come back to me.*

The early morning crank telephone calls had stopped as suddenly as they had started. Paige was relieved that no new mysterious or threatening incidents had befallen her. It was almost as if they had all been a bad dream . . . except, of course, they hadn't been.

The routine continued to be frantic. There was no time to know patients. They were simply gallbladders and ruptured livers, fractured femurs and broken backs.

The hospital was a jungle filled with mechanical demons—respirators, heart rate monitors, CAT scan equipment, X-ray machines. And each had its own peculiar sound. There were whistles, and buzzers, and the constant chatter on the PA system, and they all blended into a loud, insane cacophony.

The second year of residency was a rite of passage. The residents moved up to more demanding duties and watched the new group come in, feeling a mixture of scorn and arrogance toward them.

"Those poor devils," Kat said to Paige. "They have no idea what they're in for."

"They'll find out soon enough."

Paige and Honey were becoming worried about Kat. She was losing weight, and seemed depressed. In the middle of conversations, they would find Kat looking off into space, her mind preoccupied. From time to time, she would receive a mysterious phone call, and after each one her depression seemed to worsen.

Paige and Honey sat down to have a talk with her.

"Is everything all right?" Paige asked. "You know we love you, and if there's a problem, we'd like to help."

"Thanks. I appreciate it, but there's nothing you can do. It's a money problem."

Honey looked at her in surprise. "What do you need money for? We never go anyplace. We haven't any time to buy anything. We—"

"It's not for me. It's for my brother." Kat had not mentioned her brother before.

"I didn't know you had a brother," Paige said.

"Does he live in San Francisco?" Honey asked.

Kat was hesitant. "No. He lives back East. In Detroit. You'll have to meet him one day."

"We'd like to. What does he do?"

"He's kind of an entrepreneur," Kat said vaguely. "He's a little down on his luck right now, but Mike will bounce back. He always does." *I hope to God I'm right*, Kat thought.

Harry Bowman had transferred from a residency program in Iowa. He was a good-humored, happy-go-lucky fellow who went out of his way to be pleasant to everyone.

One day, he said to Paige, "I'm giving a little party tomorrow night. If you and Dr. Hunter and Dr. Taft are free, why don't you come? I think you'll have a good time."

"Fine," Paige said. "What shall we bring?"

Bowman laughed. "Don't bring anything."

"Are you sure?" Paige asked. "A bottle of wine, or . . ."

"Forget it! It's going to be at my little apartment."

Bowman's little apartment turned out to be a ten-room penthouse, filled with antique furniture.

The three women walked in and stared in amazement.

"My God!" Kat said. "Where did all this come from?"

"I was smart enough to have a clever father," Bowman said. "He left all his money to me."

"And you're working?" Kat marveled.

Bowman smiled. "I like being a doctor."

The buffet consisted of Beluga Malossol caviar, *pâté de campagne*, smoked Scottish salmon, oysters on the half shell, backfin lump crabmeat, *crudités* with a shallot vinaigrette dressing, and Cristal champagne.

Bowman had been right. The three of

them did have a wonderful time.

"I can't thank you enough," Paige told Bowman at the end of the evening when they were leaving.

"Are you free Saturday?" he asked.

"Yes."

"I have a little motorboat. I'll take you out for a spin."

"Sounds great."

At four o'clock in the morning, Kat was awakened out of a deep sleep in the on-call room. "Dr. Hunter, Emergency Room Three. . . . Dr. Hunter, Emergency Three."

Kat got out of bed, fighting exhaustion. Rubbing sleep from her eyes, she took the elevator down to the ER.

An orderly greeted her at the door. "He's over on the gurney in the corner. He's in a lot of pain."

Kat walked over to him. "I'm Dr. Hunter," she said sleepily.

He groaned. "Jesus, doc. You've got to do somethin'. My back is killin' me."

Kat stifled a yawn. "How long have you been in pain?"

"About two weeks."

Kat was looking at him, puzzled. "Two

weeks? Why didn't you come in sooner?"

He tried to move, and winced. "To tell you the truth, I hate hospitals."

"Then why are you coming in now?"

He brightened. "There's a big golf tournament coming up, and if you don't fix my back, I won't be able to enjoy it."

Kat took a deep breath. "A golf tournament."

"Yeah."

She was fighting to control herself. "I'll tell you what. Go home. Take two aspirins, and if you aren't feeling better in the morning give me a call." She turned and stormed out of the room, leaving him gaping after her.

Harry Bowman's little motorboat was a sleek fifty-foot motor cruiser.

"Welcome aboard!" he said as he greeted Paige, Kat, and Honey at the dock.

Honey looked at the boat admiringly.

"It's beautiful," Paige said.

They cruised around the bay for three hours, enjoying the warm, sunny day. It was the first time any of them had relaxed in weeks.

While they were anchored off Angel Island, eating a delicious lunch, Kat said, "This is the life. Let's not go back to shore."

"Good thinking," Honey said.

All in all, it was a heavenly day.

When they returned to the dock, Paige said, "I can't tell you how much I've enjoyed this."

"It's been my pleasure." Bowman patted her arm. "We'll do it again. Anytime. You three are always welcome."

What a lovely man, Paige thought.

Honey liked working in obstetrics. It was a ward filled with new life and new hope, in a timeless, joyful ritual.

The first-time mothers were eager and apprehensive. The veterans could not wait to get it over with.

One of the women who was about to deliver said to Honey, "Thank God! I'll be able to see my toes again."

If Paige had kept a diary, she would have marked the fifteenth of August as a red-letter day. That was the day Jimmy Ford came into her life.

Jimmy was a hospital orderly, with the brightest smile and the sunniest disposition Paige had ever seen. He was small and thin, and looked seventeen. He was twenty-five, and moved around the hospital corridors like a cheerful tornado. Nothing was too much trouble for him.

He was constantly running errands for everyone. He had absolutely no sense of status and treated doctors, nurses, and janitors alike.

Jimmy Ford loved to tell jokes.

"Did you hear about the patient in a body cast? The fellow in the bed next to him asked him what he did for a living.

"He said, 'I was a window washer at the Empire State Building.'

"The other fellow said, 'When did you quit?'

" 'Halfway down.' "

And Jimmy would grin and hurry off to help somebody.

He adored Paige. "I'm going to be a doctor one day. I want to be like you."

He would bring her little presents— candy bars, and stuffed toys. A joke went with each gift.

"In Houston, a man stopped a pedestrian and asked, 'What's the quickest way to the hospital?'

" 'Say something bad about Texas.' "

The jokes were terrible, but Jimmy made them sound funny.

He would arrive at the hospital the same

time as Paige, and he would race up to her on his motorcycle.

"The patient asked, 'Will my operation be dangerous?'

"And the surgeon said, 'No. You can't get a dangerous operation for two hundred dollars.'"

And he would be gone.

Whenever Paige, Kat, and Honey were free on the same day, they went out exploring San Francisco. They visited the Dutch Mill and the Japanese Tea Garden. They went to Fisherman's Wharf and rode the cable car. They went to see plays at the Curran Theater, and had dinner at the Maharani on Post Street. All the waiters were Indian, and to the astonishment of Kat and Honey, Paige addressed them in Hindi.

"*Hum Hindustani baht bahut ocho bolta hi.*" And from that moment, the restaurant was theirs.

"Where in the world did you learn to talk Indian?" Honey asked.

"Hindi," Paige said. She hesitated. "We . . . I lived in India for a while." It was still so vivid. She and Alfred were at Agra, staring at the Taj Mahal. *Shah Jahan built that for his wife. It took twenty years, Alfred.*

I'm going to build you a Taj Mahal. I don't care how long it takes!

This is Karen Turner. My wife.

She heard her name called, and turned.

"Paige . . ." There was a look of concern on Kat's face. "Are you all right?"

"Fine. I'm fine."

The impossible hours continued. Another New Year's Eve came and went, and the second year slid into the third, and nothing had changed. The hospital was untouched by the outside world. The wars and famines and disasters of far-off countries paled by comparison with the life-and-death crises they coped with twenty-four hours a day.

Whenever Kat and Paige met in the hospital corridors, Kat would grin and say, "Having a good time?"

"When did you sleep last?" Paige asked.

Kat sighed. "Who can remember?"

They stumbled through the long days and nights, trying to keep up with the incessant, demanding pressure, grabbing sandwiches when they had time, and drinking cold coffee out of paper cups.

*   *   *

The sexual harassment seemed to have become a part of Kat's life. There were the constant innuendos not only from the doctors, but also from patients who tried to get her into bed. They got the same response as the doctors. *There's not a man in the world I'll let touch me.*

And she really believed it.

In the middle of a busy morning, there was another telephone call from Mike.

"Hi, sis."

And Kat knew what was coming. She had sent him all the money she could spare, but deep down inside, she knew that whatever she sent would never be enough.

"I hate like hell to bother you, Kat. I really do. But I got into a small jam." His voice sounded strained.

"Mike . . . are you all right?"

"Oh, yeah. It's nothing serious. It's just that I owe somebody who needs his money back right away, and I was wondering . . ."

"I'll see what I can do," Kat said wearily.

"Thanks. I can always count on you, can't I, sis? I love you."

"I love you, too, Mike."

* * *

One day, Kat said to Paige and Honey, "Do you know what we all need?"

"A month's sleep?"

"A vacation. That's where we should be, strolling down the Champs Elysées, looking in all those expensive shop windows."

"Right. First-class all the way!" Paige giggled. "We'll sleep all day and play all night."

Honey laughed. "Sounds good."

"We have some vacation time coming up in a few months," Paige observed. "Why don't we make some plans for the three of us to go away somewhere?"

"That's a great idea," Kat said enthusiastically. "Saturday, let's stop in at a travel agency."

They spent the next three days excitedly making plans.

"I'm dying to see London. Maybe we'll run into the queen."

"Paris is where I want to go. It's supposed to be the most romantic city in the world."

"I want to ride a gondola in the moonlight in Venice."

Maybe we'll go to Venice on our honeymoon, Paige, Alfred had said. *Would you like that?*

Oh, yes!

She wondered if Alfred had taken Karen to Venice on their honeymoon.

Saturday morning the three of them stopped in at the Corniche Travel Agency on Powell Street.

The woman behind the counter was polite. "What kind of trip are you interested in?"

"We'd like to go to Europe—London, Paris, Venice . . ."

"Lovely. We have some economical package tours that—"

"No, no, no." Paige looked at Honey and grinned. "First-class."

"Right. First-class air travel," Kat chimed in.

"First-class hotels," Honey added.

"Well, I can recommend the Ritz in London, the Crillon in Paris, the Cipriani in Venice, and—"

Paige said, "Why don't we just take some brochures with us? We can study them and make up our minds."

"That will be fine," the travel agent said.

Paige was looking at a brochure. "You arrange yacht charters, too?"

"Yes."

"Good. We may be chartering one."

"Excellent." The travel agent collected a handful of brochures and handed them to Paige. "Whenever you're ready, just let me know and I'll be happy to make your reservations."

"You'll hear from us," Honey promised.

When they got outside, Kat laughed and said, "Nothing like dreaming big, is there?"

"Don't worry," Paige assured her. "One day we'll be able to go to all those places."

Chapter Ten

Seymour Wilson, the chief of medicine at Embarcadero County Hospital, was a frustrated man with an impossible job. There were too many patients, too few doctors and nurses, and too few hours in a day. He felt like the captain of a sinking ship, running around vainly trying to plug up the holes.

At the moment, Dr. Wilson's immediate concern was Honey Taft. While some doctors seemed to like her a great deal, reliable residents and nurses kept reporting that Dr. Taft was incapable of doing her job.

Wilson finally went to see Ben Wallace. "I want to get rid of one of our doctors," he said. "The residents she makes rounds with tell me she's incompetent."

Wallace remembered Honey. She was the one who had the extraordinarily high grades and glowing recommendation. "I don't understand it," he said. "There must be some mistake." He was thoughtful for a moment. "I'll tell you what we'll do, Seymour. Who's the meanest son of a bitch on your staff?"

"Ted Allison."

"All right. Tomorrow morning, send Honey Taft out on rounds with Dr. Allison. Have him give you a report on her. If he says she's incompetent, I'll get rid of her."

"Fair enough," Dr. Wilson said. "Thanks, Ben."

At lunch, Honey told Paige that she had been assigned to make the rounds with Dr. Allison the following morning.

"I know him," Paige said. "He has a miserable reputation."

"That's what I hear," Honey said thoughtfully.

At that moment, in another part of the hospital, Seymour Wilson was talking to Ted Allison. Allison was a hard-bitten veteran of twenty-five years. He had served as a medical officer in the navy, and he still took pride in "kicking ass."

Seymour Wilson was saying, "I want you

182

to keep a close eye on Dr. Taft. If she can't cut it, she's out. Understood?"

"Understood."

He was looking forward to this. Like Seymour Wilson, Ted Allison despised incompetent doctors. In addition, he had a strong conviction that if women wanted to be in the medical profession, they should be nurses. If it was good enough for Florence Nightingale, it was good enough for the rest of them.

At six o'clock the following morning, the residents gathered in the corridor to begin their rounds. The group consisted of Dr. Allison, Tom Benson, who was his chief assistant, and five residents, including Honey Taft.

Now, as Allison looked at Honey, he thought, *Okay, sister, let's see what you've got.* He turned to the group. "Let's go."

The first patient in Ward One was a teenage girl lying in bed, covered with heavy blankets. She was asleep when the group approached her.

"All right," Dr. Allison said. "I want you all to take a look at her chart."

The residents began to study the patient's chart. Dr. Allison turned to Honey. "This patient has fever, chills, general malaise, and anorexia. She has a temperature, a cough, and pneumonia. What's your diagnosis, Dr. Taft?"

Honey stood there, frowning, silent.

"Well?"

"Well," Honey said thoughtfully, "I would say she probably has psittacosis—parrot fever."

Dr. Allison was looking at her in surprise. "What . . . what makes you say that?"

"Her symptoms are typical of psittacosis, and I noticed that she works part-time as a clerk in a pet shop. Psittacosis is transmitted by infected parrots."

Allison nodded slowly. "That's . . . that's very good. Do you know what the treatment is?"

"Yes. Tetracycline for ten days, strict bed rest, and plenty of fluids."

Dr. Allison turned to the group, "Did you all hear that? Dr. Taft is absolutely right."

They moved on to the next patient.

Dr. Allison said, "If you'll examine his chart, you'll find that he has mesothelial tumors, bloody effusion, and fatigue. What's the diagnosis?"

One of the residents said, hopefully, "It sounds like some form of pneumonia."

A second resident spoke up. "It could be cancer."

Dr. Allison turned to Honey. "What is your diagnosis, doctor?"

Honey looked thoughtful. "Offhand, I'd say it was fibrous pneumoconiosis, a form of asbestos poisoning. His chart shows that he works in a carpet mill."

Ted Allison could not conceal his admiration. "Excellent! Excellent! Do you happen to know what the therapy is?"

"Unfortunately, no specific therapy is available yet."

It became even more impressive. In the next two hours, Honey diagnosed a rare case of Reiter's syndrome, osteitis deformans polycythemia, and malaria.

When the rounds were over, Dr. Allison shook Honey's hand. "I'm not easily impressed, doctor, but I want to tell you that you have a tremendous future!"

Honey blushed. "Thank you, Dr. Allison."

"And I intend to tell Ben Wallace so," he said as he walked away.

Tom Benson, Allison's senior assistant, looked at Honey and smiled. "I'll meet you in half an hour, baby."

Paige tried to stay out of the way of Dr. Arthur Kane—007. But at every opportunity, Kane asked for Paige to assist him with operations. And each time, he would become more offensive.

"What do you mean, you won't go out with me? You must be getting it from someone else."

And, "I may be short, honey, but not everywhere. You know what I mean?"

She came to dread the occasions she had to work with him. Time after time, Paige watched Kane perform unnecessary surgery and take out organs that were healthy.

One day, as Paige and Kane were walking toward the operating room, Paige asked, "What are we going to operate on, doctor?"

"His wallet!" He saw the look on Paige's face. "Just kidding, honey."

"He should be working in a butcher shop," Paige later said angrily to Kat. "He has no right to be operating on people."

After a particularly inept liver operation, Dr. Kane turned to Paige and shook his head. "Too bad. I don't know if he's going to make it."

It was all Paige could do to contain her anger. She decided to have a talk with Tom Chang.

"Someone should report Dr. Kane," Paige said. "He's murdering his patients!"

"Take it easy."

"I can't! It's not right that they let a man like that operate. It's criminal. He should be brought up before the credentials committee."

"What good would it do? You'd have to get other doctors to testify against him, and no one would be willing to do that. This is a close community, and we all have to live in it, Paige. It's almost impossible to get one doctor to testify against another. We're all vulnerable and we need each other too much. Calm down. I'll take you out and buy you lunch."

Paige sighed. "All right, but it's a lousy system."

At lunch, Paige asked, "How are you and Sye doing?"

He took a moment to answer. "I . . . we're having problems. My work is destroying our marriage. I don't know what to do."

"I'm sure it will work out," Paige said.

Chang said fiercely, "It had better."

Paige looked up at him.

"I would kill myself if she left me."

The following morning, Arthur Kane was scheduled to perform a kidney operation. The chief of surgery said to Paige, "Dr. Kane asked for you to assist him in OR Four."

Paige's mouth was suddenly dry. She hated the thought of being near him.

Paige said, "Couldn't you get someone else to . . . ?"

"He's waiting for you, doctor."

Paige sighed. "Right."

By the time Paige had scrubbed up, the operation was already in progress.

"Give me a hand here, darling," Kane said to Paige.

The patient's abdomen had been painted with an iodine solution and an incision had been made in the right upper quadrant of the abdomen, just below the rib cage. *So far, so good*, Paige thought.

"Scalpel!"

The scrub nurse handed Dr. Kane a scalpel.

He looked up. "Put some music on."

A moment later a CD began to play.

Dr. Kane kept cutting. "Let's have something a little peppier." He looked over at Paige. "Start the bovie, sweetheart."

Sweetheart. Paige gritted her teeth and picked up a bovie—an electric cautery tool. She began to cauterize the arteries to reduce the amount of blood in the abdomen. The operation was going well.

Thank God, Paige thought.

"Sponge."

The scrub nurse handed Kane a sponge.

"Good. Let's have some suction." He cut around the kidney until it was exposed. "There's the little devil," Dr. Kane said. "More suction." He lifted up the kidney with forceps.

"Right. Let's sew him back up."

For once, everything had gone well, yet something was bothering Paige. She took a closer look at the kidney. It looked healthy. She frowned, wondering if . . .

As Dr. Kane began sewing up the patient, Paige hurried over to the X-ray in the lighted wall frame. She studied it for a moment and said softly, "Oh, my God!"

The X-ray had been put up backward. Dr. Kane had removed the wrong kidney.

Thirty minutes later, Paige was in Ben Wallace's office.

"He took out a healthy kidney and left in a diseased one!" Paige's voice was trembling. "The man should be put in jail!"

Benjamin Wallace said soothingly, "Paige, I agree with you that it's regrettable. But it certainly wasn't intentional. It was a mistake, and—"

"A *mistake?* That patient is going to have to live on dialysis for the rest of his life. Someone should pay for that!"

"Believe me, we're going to have a peer review evaluation."

Paige knew what that meant: a group of physicians would review what had happened, but it would be done in confidence. The information would be withheld from the public and the patient.

"Dr. Wallace . . ."

"You're part of our team, Paige. You've got to be a team player."

"He has no business working in this hospital. Or any other hospital."

"You've got to look at the whole picture. If he were removed, there would be bad publicity and the reputation of the hospital would be hurt. We'd probably face a lot of malpractice suits."

"What about the patients?"

"We'll keep a closer eye on Dr. Kane." He leaned forward in his chair. "I'm going to give you some advice. When you get into private practice, you're going to need the goodwill of other doctors for referrals. Without that, you'll go nowhere, and if you get the reputation of being a maverick and blowing the whistle on your fellow doctors, you won't get any referrals. I can promise you that."

Paige rose. "So you aren't going to do anything?"

"I told you, we're going to do a peer review evaluation."

"And that's it?"

"That's it."

* * *

"It's not fair," Paige said. She was in the cafeteria having lunch with Kat and Honey.

Kat shook her head. "Nobody said life has to be fair."

Paige looked around the antiseptic white-tiled room. "This whole place depresses me. Everybody is sick."

"Or they wouldn't be here," Kat pointed out.

"Why don't we give a party?" Honey suggested.

"A party? What are you talking about?"

Honey's voice was suddenly filled with enthusiasm. "We could order up some decent food and liquor, and have a celebration! I think we could all use a little cheering up."

Paige thought for a second. "You know," she said, "that's not a bad idea. Let's do it!"

"It's a deal. I'll organize things," Honey told them. "We'll do it tomorrow after rounds."

Arthur Kane approached Paige in the corridor. There was ice in his voice. "You've been a naughty girl. Someone should teach you to keep your mouth shut!" And he walked away.

Paige looked after him in disbelief. *Wallace told him what I said. He shouldn't have done that. 'If you get the reputation of being a maverick and blowing the whistle on your fel-*

low doctors...' Would I do it again? Paige pondered. *Darned right I would!*

News of the forthcoming party spread rapidly. All the residents chipped in. A lavish menu was ordered from Ernie's, and liquor was delivered from a nearby store. The party was set for five o'clock in the doctors' lounge. The food and drinks arrived at four-thirty. There was a feast: seafood platters with lobster and shrimp, a variety of pâtés, Swedish meatballs, hot pasta, fruit, and desserts. When Paige, Kat, and Honey walked into the lounge at five-fifteen, it was already crowded with eager residents, interns, and nurses, eating and having a wonderful time.

Paige turned to Honey. "This was a great idea!"

Honey smiled. "Thank you."

An announcement came over the loudspeaker. "Dr. Finley and Dr. Ketler to the ER. Stat." And the two doctors, in the middle of downing shrimp, looked at each other, sighed, and hurriedly left the room.

Tom Chang came up to Paige. "We ought to do this every week," he said.

"Right. It's—"

The loudspeaker came on again. "Dr.

Chang . . . Room 7. . . . Dr. Chang . . . Room 7."

And a minute later, "Dr. Smythe . . . ER Two. . . . Dr. Smythe to ER Two."

The loudspeaker never stopped. Within thirty minutes, almost every doctor and nurse had been called away on some emergency. Honey heard her name called, and then Paige's, and Kat's.

"I can't believe what's happening," Kat said. "You know how people talk about having a guardian angel? Well, I think the three of us are under the spell of a guardian devil."

Her words proved to be prophetic.

The next Monday morning, when Paige got off duty and went to get into her car, two of the tires had been slashed. She stared at them in disbelief. *Someone should teach you to keep your mouth shut!*

When she got back to the apartment she said to Kat and Honey, "Watch out for Arthur Kane. He's crazy."

Chapter Eleven

Kat was awakened by the ring of the telephone. Without opening her eyes, she reached out for it and put the receiver to her ear.

"H'lo?"

"Kat? It's Mike."

She sat up, her heart suddenly pounding. "Mike, are you all right?" She heard him laugh.

"Never better, sis. Thanks to you and your friend."

"My friend?"

"Mr. Dinetto."

"Who?" Kat tried to concentrate, groggy with sleep.

"Mr. Dinetto. He really saved my life."

Kat had no idea what he was talking about. "Mike . . ."

"You know the fellows I owed money to? Mr. Dinetto got them off my back. He's a real gentleman. And he thinks the world of you, Kat."

Kat had forgotten the incident with Dinetto, but now it suddenly flashed into her mind: *Lady, you don't know who you're talking to. You better do what the man says. This is Mr. Lou Dinetto.*

Mike was going on. "I'm sending you some cash, Kat. Your friend arranged for me to get a job. It pays real good money."

Your friend. Kat was nervous. "Mike, listen to me. I want you to be careful."

She heard him laugh again.

"Don't worry about me. Didn't I tell you everything would be coming up roses? Well, I was right."

"Take care of yourself, Mike. Don't—"

The connection was broken.

Kat was unable to go back to sleep. *Dinetto! How did he find out about Mike, and why is he helping him?*

The following night, when Kat left the hospital, a black limousine was waiting for her at the curb. The Shadow and Rhino were standing beside it.

As Kat started to pass, Rhino said, "Get in, doctor. Mr. Dinetto wants to see you."

She studied the man for a moment. Rhino was ominous-looking, but it was the Shadow who frightened Kat. There was something deadly about his stillness. Under other circumstances, Kat would never have gotten into the car, but Mike's telephone call had puzzled her. And worried her.

She was driven to a small apartment on the outskirts of the city, and when she arrived, Dinetto was waiting for her.

"Thanks for coming, Dr. Hunter," he said. "I appreciate it. A friend of mine had a little accident. I want you to take a look at him."

"What are you doing with Mike?" Kat demanded.

"Nothing," he said innocently. "I heard he was in a little trouble, and I got it taken care of."

"How did . . . how did you find out about him? I mean, that he was my brother and . . ."

Dinetto smiled. "In my business, we're all friends. We help each other. Mike got mixed up with some bad boys, so I helped him out. You should be grateful."

"I am," Kat said. "I really am."

"Good! You know the saying 'One hand washes the other'?"

Kat shook her head. "I won't do anything illegal."

"Illegal?" Dinetto said. He seemed hurt. "I wouldn't ask you to do anything like that. This friend of mine was in a little accident and he hates hospitals. Would you take a look at him?"

What am I letting myself in for? Kat wondered. "Very well."

"He's in the bedroom."

Dinetto's friend had been badly beaten up. He was lying in bed, unconscious.

"What happened to him?" Kat asked.

Dinetto looked at her and said, "He fell down a flight of stairs."

"He should be in a hospital."

"I told you, he doesn't like hospitals. I can get you whatever hospital equipment you need. I had another doctor who took care of my friends, but he had an accident."

The words sent a chill through Kat. She wanted nothing more than to run out of the place and go home, and never hear Dinetto's name again, but nothing in life was free. *Quid pro quo.* Kat took off her coat and went to work.

Chapter Twelve

By the beginning of her fourth year of residency, Paige had assisted in hundreds of operations. They had become second nature to her. She knew the surgery procedures for the gallbladder, spleen, liver, appendix, and, most exciting, the heart. But Paige was frustrated because she was not doing the operations herself. *Whatever happened to "Watch one, do one, teach one"?* she wondered.

The answer came when George Englund, chief of surgery, sent for her.

"Paige, there's a hernia operation scheduled for tomorrow in OR Three, seven-thirty A.M."

She made a note. "Right. Who's doing the operation?"

"You are."

"Right. I . . ." The words suddenly sank in. "*I am?*"

"Yes. Any problem with that?"

Paige's grin lit up the room. "No, sir! I . . . thanks!"

"You're ready for it. I think the patient's lucky to have you. His name is Walter Herzog. He's in 314."

"Herzog. Room 314. Right."

And Paige was out the door.

Paige had never been so excited. *I'm going to do my first operation! I'm going to hold a human being's life in my hands. What if I'm not ready? What if I make a mistake? Things can go wrong. It's Murphy's Law.* By the time Paige was through arguing with herself, she was in a state of panic.

She went into the cafeteria and sat down to have a cup of black coffee. *It's going to be all right,* she told herself. *I've assisted in dozens of hernia operations. There's nothing to it. He's lucky to have me.* By the time she finished her coffee, she was calm enough to face her first patient.

*   *   *

Walter Herzog was in his sixties, thin, bald, and very nervous. He was in bed, clutching his groin, when Paige walked in, carrying a bouquet of flowers. Herzog looked up.

"Nurse . . . I want to see a doctor."

Paige walked over to the bed and handed him the flowers. "I'm the doctor. I'm going to operate on you."

He looked at the flowers, and looked at her. "You're *what?*"

"Don't worry," Paige said reassuringly. "You're in good hands." She picked up his chart at the foot of the bed and studied it.

"What does it say?" the man asked anxiously. *Why did she bring me flowers?*

"It says you're going to be just fine."

He swallowed. "Are you really going to do the operation?"

"Yes."

"You seem awfully . . . awfully young."

Paige patted his arm. "I haven't lost a patient yet." She looked around the room. "Are you comfortable? Can I get you anything to read? A book or magazine? Candy?"

He was listening, nervously. "No, I'm okay." *Why was she being so nice to him? Was there something she wasn't telling him?*

"Well, then, I'll see you in the morning," Paige said cheerfully. She wrote something on a piece of paper and handed it to him. "Here's my home number. You call me if you need me tonight. I'll stay right by the phone."

By the time Paige left, Walter Herzog was a nervous wreck.

A few minutes later, Jimmy found Paige in the lounge. He walked up to her with his wide grin. "Congratulations! I hear you're going to do a procedure."

Word gets around fast, Paige thought. "Yes."

"Whoever he is, he's lucky," Jimmy said. "If anything ever happened to me, you're the only one I'd let operate on me."

"Thanks, Jimmy."

And, of course, with Jimmy, there was always a joke.

"Did you hear the one about the man who had a strange pain in his ankles? He was too cheap to go to a doctor, so when his friend told him he had exactly the same pain, he said, 'You'd better get to a doctor right away. And tell me exactly what he says.'

"The next day, he learns his friend is dead. He rushes to a hospital and has five thousand dollars' worth of tests. They can't find anything wrong. He calls his friend's widow, and says, 'Was Chester in a lot of pain before he died?'

" 'No,' she says. 'He didn't even see the truck that hit him!' "

And Jimmy was gone.

Paige was too excited to eat dinner. She spent the evening practicing tying surgical knots on table legs and lamps. *I'm going to get a good night's sleep,* Paige decided, *so I'll be nice and fresh in the morning.*

She was awake all night, going over the operation again and again in her mind.

There are three types of hernias: reducible hernia, where it's possible to push the testicles back into the abdomen; irreducible hernia, where adhesions prevent returning the contents to the abdomen; and the most dangerous, strangulated hernia, where the blood flow through the hernia is shut off, damaging the intestines. Walter Herzog's was a reducible hernia.

At six o'clock in the morning, Paige drove to the hospital parking lot. A new red Ferrari was next to her parking space. Idly, Paige wondered who owned it. Whoever it was had to be rich.

At seven o'clock, Paige was helping Walter Herzog change from pajamas to a blue hospital gown. The nurse had already given him a sedative to relax him while they waited for the gurney that would take him to the operating room.

"This is my first operation," Walter Herzog said.

Mine, too, Paige thought.

The gurney arrived and Walter Herzog was on his way to OR Three. Paige walked down the corridor beside him, and her heart was pounding so loudly that she was afraid he could hear it.

OR Three was one of the larger operating rooms, able to accommodate a heart monitor, a heart-lung machine, and an array of other technical paraphernalia. When Paige walked into the room, the staff were already there, preparing the equipment. There was an attending physician, the anesthesiologist, two residents, a scrub nurse, and two circulating nurses.

The staff were watching her expectantly, eager to see how she would handle her first operation.

Paige walked up to the operating table. Walter Herzog had had his groin shaved and scrubbed with an antiseptic solution. Sterile drapes had been placed around the operating area.

Herzog looked up at Paige and said drowsily, "You're not going to let me die, are you?"

Paige smiled. "What? And spoil my perfect record?"

She looked over at the anesthesiologist, who would give the patient an epidural anesthesia, a saddle block. Paige took a deep breath and nodded.

The operation began.

"Scalpel."

As Paige was about to make the first cut through the skin, the circulating nurse said something.

"What?"

"Would you like some music, doctor?"

It was the first time she had been asked that question. Paige smiled. "Right. Let's have some Jimmy Buffet."

The moment Paige made the first incision, her nervousness vanished. It was as though she had done this all her life. Skillfully, she cut through the first layers of fat and muscle, to the site of the hernia. All the while, she was aware of the familiar litany that was echoing through the room.

"Sponge. . . ."

"Give me a bovie. . . ."

"There it is. . . ."

"Looks like we got there just in time. . . ."

"Clamp. . . ."

"Suction, please. . . ."

Paige's mind was totally focused on what she was doing. Locate the hernial sac . . . free it . . . place the contents back into the abdominal cavity . . . tie off the base of the sac . . . cut off the remainder . . . inguinal ring . . . suture it . . .

One hour and twenty minutes after the first incision, the operation was finished.

Paige should have felt drained, but instead she felt wildly exhilarated.

When Walter Herzog had been sewn up, the scrub nurse turned to Paige. "Dr. Taylor . . ."

Paige looked up. "Yes?"

The nurse grinned. "That was beautiful, doctor."

It was Sunday and the three women had the day off.

"What should we do today?" Kat asked.

Paige had an idea. "It's such a lovely day, why don't we drive out to Tree Park? We can pack a picnic lunch and eat outdoors."

"That sounds lovely," Honey said.

"Let's do it!" Kat agreed.

The telephone rang. The three of them stared at it.

"Jesus!" Kat said. "I thought Lincoln freed us. Don't answer it. It's our day off."

"We *have* no days off," Paige reminded her.

Kat walked over to the telephone and picked it up. "Dr. Hunter." She listened for a moment and handed the telephone to Paige. "It's for you, Dr. Taylor."

Paige said resignedly, "Right." She picked up the receiver. "Dr. Taylor. . . . Hello, Tom. . . . What? . . . No, I was just going out. . . . I see. . . . All right. I'll be there in fifteen minutes." She replaced the receiver. *So much for the picnic,* she thought.

"Is it bad?" Honey asked.

"Yes, we're about to lose a patient. I'll try to be back for dinner tonight."

When Paige arrived at the hospital, she drove into the doctors' parking lot and parked next to the new bright red Ferrari. *I wonder how many operations it took to pay for that?*

Twenty minutes later, Paige was walking into the visitors' waiting room. A man in a dark suit was seated in a chair, staring out the window.

"Mr. Newton?"

He rose to his feet. "Yes."

"I'm Dr. Taylor. I was just in to see your little boy. He was brought in with abdominal pains."

"Yes. I'm going to take him home."

"I'm afraid not. Peter has a ruptured spleen. He needs an immediate transfusion and an operation, or he'll die."

Mr. Newton shook his head. "We are Jehovah's Witnesses. The Lord will not let him die, and I will not let him be tainted with someone else's blood. It was my wife who brought him here. She will be punished for that."

"Mr. Newton, I don't think you understand how serious the situation is. If we don't operate right away, your son is going to die."

The man looked at her and smiled. "You don't know God's ways, do you?"

Paige was angry. "I may not know a lot about God's ways, but I do know a lot about a ruptured spleen." She took out a piece of paper. "He's a minor, so you'll have to sign this consent form for him." She held it out.

"And if I don't sign it?"

"Why . . . then we can't operate."

He nodded. "Do you think your powers are stronger than the Lord's?"

Paige was staring at him. "You're not going to sign, are you?"

"No. A higher power than yours will help my son. You will see."

When Paige returned to the ward, six-year-old Peter Newton had lapsed into unconsciousness.

"He's not going to make it," Chang said. "He's lost too much blood. What do you want to do?"

Paige made her decision. "Get him into OR One. Stat."

Chang looked at her in surprise. "His father changed his mind?"

Paige nodded. "Yes. He changed his mind. Let's move it."

"Good for you! I talked to him for an hour and I couldn't budge him. He said God would take care of it."

"God is taking care of it," Paige assured him.

Two hours and four pints of blood later, the operation was successfully completed. All the boy's vital signs were strong.

Paige gently stroked his forehead. "He's going to be fine."

An orderly hurried into the operating room. "Dr. Taylor? Dr. Wallace wants to see you right away."

Benjamin Wallace was so angry his voice was cracking. "How could you do such an outrageous thing? You gave him a blood transfusion and operated without permission? You broke the law!"

"I saved a boy's life!"

Wallace took a deep breath. "You should have gotten a court order."

"There was no time," Paige said. "Ten minutes more and he would have been dead. God was busy elsewhere."

Wallace was pacing back and forth. "What are we going to do now?"

"Get a court order."

"What for? You've already *done* the operation."

"I'll backdate the court order one day. No one will ever know the difference."

Wallace looked at her and began to hyperventilate. "Jesus!" He mopped his brow. "This could cost me my job."

Paige looked at him for a long moment. Then she turned and started toward the door.

"Paige . . . ?"

She stopped. "Yes?"

"You'll never do anything like this again, will you?"

"Only if I have to," Paige assured him.

Chapter Thirteen

All hospitals have problems with drug theft. By law, each narcotic that is taken from the dispensary must be signed for, but no matter how controlled the security is, drug addicts almost invariably find a way to circumvent it.

Embarcadero County Hospital was having a major problem. Margaret Spencer went to see Ben Wallace.

"I don't know what to do, doctor. Our fentanyl keeps disappearing."

Fentanyl is a highly addictive narcotic and anesthetic drug.

"How much is missing?"

"A great deal. If it were just a few bottles, there could be an innocent explanation for it, but it's happening now on a regular basis. More than a dozen bottles a week are disappearing."

"Do you have any idea who might be taking it?"

"No, sir. I've talked to security. They're at a loss."

"Who has access to the dispensary?"

"That's the problem. Most of the anesthetists have pretty free access to it, and most of the nurses and surgeons."

Wallace was thoughtful. "Thank you for coming to me. I'll take care of it."

"Thank you, doctor." Nurse Spencer left.

I don't need this right now, Wallace thought angrily. A hospital board meeting was coming up, and there were already enough problems to be dealt with. Ben Wallace was well aware of the statistics. More than 10 percent of the doctors in the United States became addicted, at one time or another, to either drugs or alcohol. The easy accessibility of the drugs made them a temptation. It was simple for a doctor to open a cabinet, take out the drug he wanted, and use a tourniquet and syringe to inject it. An addict could need a fix as often as every two hours.

Now it was happening at his hospital. Something had to be done about it before the board meeting. *It would look bad on my record.*

Ben Wallace was not sure whom he could trust to help him find the culprit. He had to be careful. He was certain that neither Dr. Taylor nor Dr. Hunter was involved, and after a great deal of thought, he decided to use them.

He sent for the two of them. "I have a favor to ask of you," he told them. He explained about the missing fentanyl. "I want you to keep your eyes open. If any of the doctors you work with have to step out of the OR for a moment, in the middle of an operation, or show any other signs of addiction, I want you to let me know. Look for any changes in personality—depression or mood swings—or tardiness, or missed appointments. I would appreciate it if you would keep this strictly confidential."

When they left the office, Kat said, "This is a big hospital. We're going to need Sherlock Holmes."

"No, we won't," Paige said unhappily. "I know who it is."

Mitch Campbell was one of Paige's favorite doctors. Dr. Campbell was a likable gray-haired man in his fifties, always good-humored, and one of the hospital's best surgeons. Paige had noticed lately that he was always a few minutes late for an operation, and that he had developed a noticeable tremor. He used Paige to assist him as often as possible, and he usually let her do a major part of the surgery. In the middle of an operation, his hands would begin to shake and he would hand the scalpel to Paige.

"I'm not feeling well," he would mumble. "Would you take over?"

And he would leave the operating room.

Paige had been concerned about what could be wrong with him. Now she knew. She debated what to do. She was aware that if she brought her information to Wallace, Dr. Campbell would be fired, or worse, his career would be destroyed. On the other hand, if she did nothing, she would be putting patients' lives in danger. *Perhaps I could talk to him,* Paige thought. *Tell him what I know, and insist that he get treatment.* She discussed it with Kat.

"It's a problem," Kat agreed. "He's a nice guy, and a good doctor. If you blow the whistle, he's finished, but if you don't, you have to think about the harm he might do. What do you think will happen if you confront him?"

"He'll probably deny it, Kat. That's the usual pattern."

"Yeah. It's a tough call."

The following day, Paige had an operation scheduled with Dr. Campbell. *I hope I'm wrong,* Paige prayed. *Don't let him be late, and don't let him leave during the operation.*

Campbell was fifteen minutes late, and in the middle of the operation, he said, "Take over, will you, Paige? I'll be right back."

I must talk to him, Paige decided. *I can't destroy his career.*

The following morning, as Paige and Honey drove into the doctors' parking lot, Harry Bowman pulled up next to them in the red Ferrari.

"That's a beautiful car," Honey said. "How much does one of those cost?"

Bowman laughed. "If you have to ask, you can't afford it."

But Paige wasn't listening. She was staring at the car, and thinking about the penthouse, the lavish parties, and the boat. *I was smart enough to have a clever father. He left all his money to me.* And yet Bowman worked at a county hospital. Why?

Ten minutes later, Paige was in the personnel office, talking to Karen, the secretary in charge of records.

"Do me a favor, will you, Karen? Just between us, Harry Bowman has asked me to go out with him and I have a feeling he's married. Would you let me have a peek at his personnel file?"

"Sure. Those horny bastards. They never get enough, do they? You're darn right I'll let you look at his file." She went over to a cabinet and found what she was looking for. She brought some papers back to Paige.

Paige glanced through them quickly. Dr. Harry Bowman's application showed that he had come from a small university in the Midwest and, according to the records, had worked his way through medical school. He was an anesthesiologist.

His father was a barber.

Honey Taft was an enigma to most of the doctors at Embarcadero County Hospital. During the morning rounds, she appeared to be unsure of herself. But on the afternoon rounds, she seemed like a different person. She was surprisingly knowledgeable about each patient, and crisp and efficient in her diagnoses.

One of the senior residents was discussing her with a colleague.

"I'll be damned if I understand it," he said. "In the morning, the complaints about Dr. Taft keep piling up. She keeps making mistakes. You know the joke about the nurse who gets everything wrong? A doctor is complaining that he told her to give the patient in Room 4 three pills, and she gave the patient in Room 3 four pills, and just as he's talking about her, he sees her chasing a naked patient down the hall, holding a pan of boiling water. The doctor says, 'Look at that! I told her to prick his boil!' "

His colleague laughed.

"Well, that's Dr. Taft. But in the afternoon she's absolutely brilliant. Her diagnoses are correct, her notes are wonderful, and she's as sharp as hell. She must be taking some kind of miracle pill that only works afternoons." He scratched his head. "It beats the hell out of me."

Dr. Nathan Ritter was a pedant, a man who lived and worked by the book. While he lacked the spark of brilliance, he was capable and dedicated, and he expected the same qualities from those who worked with him.

Honey had the misfortune to be assigned to his team.

Their first stop was a ward containing a dozen patients. One of them was just finishing breakfast. Ritter looked at the chart at the foot of the bed. "Dr. Taft, the chart says this is your patient."

Honey nodded. "Yes."

"He's having a bronchoscopy this morning."

Honey nodded. "That's right."

"And you're allowing him to *eat*?" Dr. Ritter snapped. "*Before* a bronchoscopy?"

Honey said, "The poor man hasn't had anything to eat since—"

Nathan Ritter turned to his assistant. "Postpone the procedure." He started to say something to Honey, then controlled himself. "Let's move on."

The next patient was a Puerto Rican who was coughing badly. Dr. Ritter examined him. "Whose patient is this?"

"Mine," Honey said.

He frowned. "His infection should have cleared up before now." He took a look at the chart. "You're giving him fifty milligrams of ampicillin four times a day?"

"That's right."

"That's *not* right. It's *wrong*! That's supposed to be *five hundred* milligrams four times a day. You left off a zero."

"I'm sorry, I . . ."

"No wonder the patient's not getting any better! I want it changed immediately."

"Yes, doctor."

When they came to another patient of Honey's, Dr. Ritter said impatiently, "He's scheduled for a colonoscopy. Where is the radiology report?"

"The radiology report? Oh. I'm afraid I forgot to order one."

Ritter gave Honey a long, speculative look.

The morning went downhill from there.

The next patient they saw was moaning tearfully. "I'm in such pain. What's wrong with me?"

"We don't know," Honey said.

Dr. Ritter glared at her. "Dr. Taft, may I see you outside for a moment?"

In the corridor, he said, "Never, *never* tell a patient that you don't know. You're the one they're looking to for help! And if you don't know the answer, make one up. Do you understand?"

"It doesn't seem right to . . ."

"I didn't ask you whether it seemed right. Just do as you're told."

They examined a hiatal hernia, a hepatitis patient, a patient with Alzheimer's disease, and two dozen others. The minute the rounds were over, Dr. Ritter went to Benjamin Wallace's office.

"We have a problem," Ritter said.

"What is it, Nathan?"

"It's one of the residents here. Honey Taft."

Again! "What about her?"

"She's a disaster."

"But she had such a wonderful recommendation."

"Ben, you'd better get rid of her before the hospital gets in real trouble, before she kills a patient or two."

Wallace thought about it for a moment, then made his decision. "Right. She'll be out of here."

Paige was busy in surgery most of the morning. As soon as she was free, she went to see Dr. Wallace, to tell him of her suspicions about Harry Bowman.

"Bowman? Are you sure? I mean . . . I've seen no signs of any addiction."

"He doesn't use it," Paige explained. "He sells it. He's living like a millionaire on a resident's salary."

Ben Wallace nodded. "Very well. I'll check it out. Thank you, Paige."

Wallace sent for Bruce Anderson, head of security. "We may have identified the drug thief," Wallace told him. "I want you to keep a close watch on Dr. Harry Bowman."

"Bowman?" Anderson tried to conceal his surprise. Dr. Bowman was constantly giving the guards Cuban cigars and other little gifts. They all loved him.

"If he goes into the dispensary, search him when he comes out."

"Yes, sir."

Harry Bowman was headed for the dispensary. He had orders to fill. A *lot* of orders. It had started as a lucky accident. He had been working in a small hospital in Ames, Iowa, struggling to get by on a resident's salary. He had champagne taste and a beer pocketbook, and then Fate had smiled on him.

One of his patients who had been discharged from the hospital telephoned him one morning.

"Doctor, I'm in terrible pain. You have to give me something for it."

"Do you want to check back in?"

"I don't want to leave the house. Couldn't you bring something here for me?"

Bowman thought about it. "All right. I'll drop by on my way home."

When he visited the patient, he brought with him a bottle of fentanyl.

The patient grabbed it. "That's wonderful!" he said. He pulled out a handful of bills. "Here."

Bowman looked at him, surprised. "You don't have to pay me for that."

"Are you kidding? This stuff is like gold. I have a lot of friends who will pay you a fortune if you bring them this stuff."

That was how it had begun. Within two months, Harry Bowman was making more money than he had ever dreamed possible. Unfortunately, the head of the hospital got wind of what was going on. Fearing a public scandal, he told Bowman that if he left quietly, nothing would appear on his record.

I'm glad I left, Bowman thought. *San Francisco has a much bigger market.*

He reached the dispensary. Bruce Anderson was standing outside. Bowman nodded to him. "Hi, Bruce."

"Good afternoon, Dr. Bowman."

Five minutes later when Bowman came out of the dispensary, Anderson said, "Excuse me. I'm going to have to search you."

Harry Bowman stared at him. "Search me? What are you talking about, Bruce?"

"I'm sorry, doctor. We have orders to search everyone who uses the dispensary," Anderson lied.

Bowman was indignant. "I've never heard of such a thing. I absolutely refuse!"

"Then I'll have to ask you to come along with me to Dr. Wallace's office."

"Fine! He's going to be furious when he hears about this."

Bowman stormed into Wallace's office. "What's going on, Ben? This man wanted to search me, for God's sake!"

"And did you refuse to be searched?"

"Absolutely."

"All right." Wallace reached for the telephone. "I'll let the San Francisco police do it, if you prefer." He began to dial.

Bowman panicked. "Wait a minute! That's not necessary." His face suddenly cleared. "Oh! I know what this is all about!" He reached in his pocket and took out a bottle of fentanyl. "I was taking these to use for an operation, and . . ."

Wallace said quietly, "Empty your pockets."

A look of desperation came over Bowman's face. "There's no reason to . . ."

"Empty your pockets."

Two hours later, the San Francisco office of the Drug Enforcement Agency had a signed confession and the names of the people to whom Bowman had been selling drugs.

When Paige heard the news, she went to see Mitch Campbell. He was sitting in an office, resting. His hands were on the desk when Paige walked in, and she could see the tremor in them.

Campbell quickly moved his hands to his lap. "Hello, Paige. How're you doing?"

"Fine, Mitch. I wanted to talk to you."

"Sit down."

She took a seat opposite him. "How long have you had Parkinson's?"

He turned a shade whiter. "What?"

"That's it, isn't it? You've been trying to cover it up."

There was a heavy silence. "I . . . I . . . yes. But I . . . I can't give up being a doctor. I . . . I just can't give it up. It's my whole life."

Paige leaned forward and said earnestly, "You don't have to give up being a doctor, but you shouldn't be operating."

He looked suddenly old. "I know. I was going to quit last year." He smiled wanly. "I guess I'll have to quit now, won't I? You're going to tell Dr. Wallace."

"No," Paige said gently. "*You're* going to tell Dr. Wallace."

* * *

Paige was having lunch in the cafeteria when Tom Chang joined her.

"I heard what happened," he said. "Bowman! Unbelievable. Nice work."

She shook her head. "I almost had the wrong man."

Chang sat there, silent.

"Are you all right, Tom?"

"Do you want the 'I'm fine,' or do you want the truth?"

"We're friends. I want the truth."

"My marriage has gone to hell." His eyes suddenly filled with tears. "Sye has left. She's gone back home."

"I'm so sorry."

"It's not her fault. We didn't have a marriage anymore. She said I'm married to the hospital, and she's right. I'm spending my whole life here, taking care of strangers, instead of being with the people I love."

"She'll come back. It will work out," Paige said soothingly.

"No. Not this time."

"Have you thought about counseling, or . . .?"

"She refuses."

"I'm sorry, Tom. If there's anything I . . ."
She heard her name on the loudspeaker.

"Dr. Taylor, Room 410 . . ."

Paige felt a sudden pang of alarm. "I have to go," she said. Room 410. That was Sam Bernstein's room. He was one of her favorite patients, a gentle man in his seventies who had been brought in with inoperable stomach cancer. Many of the patients at the hospital were constantly complaining, but Sam Bernstein was an exception. Paige admired his courage and his dignity. He had a wife and two grown sons who visited him regularly, and Paige had grown fond of them, too.

He had been put on life-support systems with a note, DNR—Do Not Resuscitate—if his heart stopped.

When Paige walked into his room, a nurse was at the bedside. She looked up as Paige entered. "He's gone, doctor. I didn't start emergency procedures, because . . ." Her voice trailed off.

"You were right not to," Paige said slowly. "Thank you."

"Is there anything I . . . ?"

"No. I'll make the arrangements." Paige stood by the bedside and looked down at the body of what had been a living, laughing human being, a man who had a family and friends, someone who had spent his life working hard, taking care of the ones he loved. And now . . .

She walked over to the drawer where he kept his possessions. There was an inexpensive watch, a set of keys, fifteen dollars in cash, dentures, and a letter to his wife. All that remained of a man's life.

Paige was unable to shake the feeling of depression that hung over her. "He was such a dear man. Why . . . ?"

Kat said, "Paige, you can't let yourself get emotionally involved with your patients. It will tear you apart."

"I know. You're right, Kat. It's just that . . . it's over so quickly, isn't it? This morning he and I were talking. Tomorrow is his funeral."

"You're not thinking of going to it?"

"No."

The funeral took place at the Hills of Eternity Cemetery.

In the Jewish religion, burial must take place as soon as possible following the death, and the service usually takes place the next day.

The body of Sam Bernstein was dressed in a *takhrikhim,* a white robe, and wrapped in a *talit.* The family was gathered around the graveside. The rabbi was intoning, *"Hamakom y'nathaim etkhem b'tokh sh'ar availai tziyon veeyerushalayim."*

A man standing next to Paige saw the puzzled expression on her face, and he translated for her. " 'May the Lord comfort you with all the mourners of Zion and Jerusalem.' "

To Paige's astonishment, the members of the family began tearing at the clothes they were wearing as they chanted, *"Baruch ata adonai elohainu melech haolam dayan haemet."*

"What . . . ?"

"That's to show respect," the man whispered. "From dust you are and to dust you have returned, but the spirit returns to God who gave it."

The ceremony was over.

The following morning, Kat ran into Honey in the corridor. Honey looked nervous.

"Anything wrong?" Kat asked.

"Dr. Wallace sent for me. He asked me to be in his office at two o'clock."

"Do you know why?"

"I think I messed up at rounds the other day. Dr. Ritter is a monster."

"He can be," Kat said. "But I'm sure everything will be all right."

"I hope so. I just have a bad feeling."

Promptly at two o'clock, she arrived at Benjamin Wallace's office, carrying a small jar of honey in her purse. The receptionist was at lunch. Dr. Wallace's door was open. "Come in, Dr. Taft," he called.

Honey walked into his office.

"Close the door behind you, please."

Honey closed the door.

"Take a seat."

Honey sat down across from him. She was almost trembling.

Benjamin Wallace looked across at her and thought, *It's like kicking a puppy. But what has to be done has to be done.* "I'm afraid I have some unfortunate news for you," he said.

One hour later, Honey met Kat in the solarium. Honey sank into a chair next to her, smiling.

"Did you see Dr. Wallace?" Kat asked.

"Oh, yes. We had a long talk. Did you know that his wife left him last September? They were married for fifteen years. He has two grown children from an earlier marriage, but he hardly ever sees them. The poor darling is so lonely."

BOOK II

Chapter Fourteen

It was New Year's Eve again, and Paige, Kat, and Honey ushered in 1994 at Embarcadero County Hospital. It seemed to them that nothing in their lives had changed except the names of their patients.

As Paige walked through the parking lot, she was reminded of Harry Bowman and his red Ferrari. *How many lives were destroyed by the poison Harry Bowman was selling?* she wondered. Drugs were so seductive. And, in the end, so deadly.

* * *

Jimmy Ford showed up with a small bouquet of flowers for Paige.

"What's this for, Jimmy?"

He blushed. "I just wanted you to have it. Did you know I'm getting married?"

"No! That's wonderful. Who's the lucky girl?"

"Her name is Betsy. She works at a dress shop. We're going to have half a dozen kids. The first girl is going to be named Paige. I hope you don't mind."

"Mind? I'm flattered."

He was embarrassed. "Did you hear the one about the doctor who gave a patient two weeks to live? 'I can't pay you right now,' the man said. 'All right, I'll give you another two weeks.' "

And Jimmy was gone.

Paige was worried about Tom Chang. He was having violent mood swings from euphoria to deep depression.

One morning during a talk with Paige, he said, "Do you realize that most of the people in here would die without us? We have the power to heal their bodies and make them whole again."

And the next morning: "We're all kidding ourselves, Paige. Our patients would get better faster without us. We're hypocrites, pretending that we have all the answers. Well, we don't."

Paige studied him a moment. "What do you hear from Sye?"

"I talked to her yesterday. She won't come back here. She's going ahead with the divorce."

Paige put her hand on his arm. "I'm so sorry, Tom."

He shrugged. "Why? It doesn't bother me. Not anymore. I'll find another woman." He grinned. "And have another child. You'll see."

There was something unreal about the conversation.

That night Paige said to Kat, "I'm worried about Tom Chang. Have you talked to him lately?"

"Yes."

"Did he seem normal to you?"

"No man seems normal to me," Kat said.

Paige was still concerned. "Let's invite him for dinner tomorrow night."

"All right."

The next morning when Paige reported to the hospital, she was greeted with the news that a janitor had found Tom Chang's body in a basement equipment room. He had died of an overdose of sleeping pills.

Paige was near hysteria. "I could have

saved him," she cried. "All this time he was calling out for help, and I didn't hear him."

Kat said firmly, "There's no way you could have helped him, Paige. You were not the problem, and you were not the solution. He didn't want to live without his wife and child. It's as simple as that."

Paige wiped the tears from her eyes. "Damn this place!" she said. "If it weren't for the pressure and the hours, his wife never would have left him."

"But she did," Kat said gently. "It's over."

Paige had never been to a Chinese funeral before. It was an incredible spectacle. It began at the Green Street Mortuary in Chinatown early in the morning, where a crowd started gathering outside. A parade was assembled, with a large brass marching band, and at the head of the parade, mourners carried a huge blowup of a photograph of Tom Chang.

The march began with the band loudly playing, winding through the streets of San Francisco, with a hearse at the end of the procession. Most of the mourners were on foot, but the more elderly rode in cars.

To Paige, the parade seemed to be moving around the city at random. She was puzzled.

"Where are they going?" she asked one of the mourners.

He bowed slightly and said, "It is our custom to take the departed past some of the places that have meaning in his life—restaurants where he ate, shops that he used, places he visited . . ."

"I see."

The parade ended in front of Embarcadero County Hospital.

The mourner turned to Paige and said, "This is where Tom Chang worked. This is where he found his happiness."

Wrong, Paige thought. *This is where he lost his happiness.*

Walking down Market Street one morning, Paige saw Alfred Turner. Her heart started pounding. She had not been able to get him out of her mind. He was starting to cross the street as the light was changing. When Paige got to the corner, the light had turned to red. She ignored it and ran out into the street, oblivious to the honking horns and the outraged cries of motorists.

Paige reached the other side and hurried to catch up with him. She grabbed his sleeve. "Alfred . . ."

The man turned. "I beg your pardon?"
It was a total stranger.

Now that Paige and Kat were fourth-year residents, they were performing operations on a regular basis.

Kat was working with doctors in neurosurgery, and she never ceased to be amazed at the miracle of the hundred billion complex digital computers called neurons that lived in the skull. The work was exciting.

Kat had enormous respect for most of the doctors she worked with. They were brilliant, skilled surgeons. There were a few doctors who gave her a hard time. They tried to date her, and the more Kat refused to go out with them, the more of a challenge she became.

She heard one doctor mutter, "Here comes old ironpants."

She was assisting Dr. Kibler at a brain operation. A tiny incision was made in the cortex, and Dr. Kibler pushed the rubber cannula into the left lateral ventricle, the cavity in the center of the left half of the brain, while Kat held the incision open with a small retractor. Her entire concentration was focused on what was happening in front of her.

Dr. Kibler glanced at her and, as he worked, said, "Did you hear about the wino who staggered into a bar and said, 'Give me a drink, quick!' 'I can't do that,' the bartender said. 'You're already drunk.' "

The burr was cutting in deeper.

" 'If you don't give me a drink, I'll kill myself.' "

Cerebral spinal fluid flowed out of the cannula from the ventricle.

" 'I'll tell you what I'll do,' the bartender said. 'There are three things I want. You do them for me, and I'll give you a bottle.' "

As he went on talking, fifteen milliliters of air were injected into the ventricle, and X-rays were taken of the anterior-posterior view and the lateral view.

" 'See that football player sitting in the corner? I can't get him out of here. I want you to throw him out. Next, I have a pet crocodile in my office with a bad tooth. He's so mean I can't get a vet to go near him. Lastly, there's a lady doctor from the Department of Health who's trying to close up this place. You fuck her, and you get the bottle.' "

A scrub nurse was using suction to reduce the amount of blood in the field.

"The wino throws out the football player, and goes into the office where the crocodile is. He comes out fifteen minutes later, all bloody, and his clothes torn, and he says, 'Where's the lady doctor with the bad tooth?' "

Dr. Kibler roared with laughter. "Do you get it? He fucked the crocodile instead of the doctor. It was probably a better experience!"

Kat stood there, furious, wanting to slap him.

When the operation was over, Kat went to the on-call room to try to get over her anger. *I'm not going to let the bastards beat me down. I'm not.*

From time to time, Paige went out with doctors from the hospital, but she refused to get romantically involved with any of them. Alfred Turner had hurt her too deeply, and she was determined never to go through that again.

Most of her days and nights were spent at the hospital. The schedule was grueling, but Paige was doing general surgery and she enjoyed it.

One morning, George Englund, the chief of surgery, sent for her.

"You're starting your specialty this year. Cardiovascular surgery."

She nodded. "That's right."

"Well, I have a treat for you. Have you heard of Dr. Barker?"

Paige looked at him in surprise. "Dr. *Lawrence* Barker?"

"Yes."

"Of course."

Everyone had heard of Lawrence Barker. He was one of the most famous cardiovascular surgeons in the world.

"Well, he returned last week from Saudi Arabia, where he operated on the king. Dr. Barker's an old friend of mine, and he's agreed to give us three days a week here. *Pro bono.*"

"That's fantastic!" Paige exclaimed.

"I'm putting you on his team."

For a moment, Paige was speechless. "I . . . I don't know what to say. I'm very grateful."

"It's a wonderful opportunity for you. You can learn a lot from him."

"I'm sure I can. Thank you, George. I really appreciate this."

"You'll start your rounds with him tomorrow morning at six o'clock."

"I'm looking forward to it."

"Looking forward to it" was an understatement. It had been Paige's dream to work with someone like Dr. Lawrence Barker. *What do I mean, "someone like Dr. Lawrence Barker"? There's only one Dr. Lawrence Barker.*

She had never seen a photograph of him, but she could visualize what he looked like. He would be tall and handsome, with silver-gray hair, and slender, sensitive hands. A warm and gentle man. *We'll be working closely together,* Paige thought, *and I'm going to make myself absolutely indispensable. I wonder if he's married?*

That night, Paige had an erotic dream about Dr. Barker. They were performing an operation in the nude. In the middle of it, Dr. Barker said, "I want you." A nurse moved the patient off the operating table and Dr. Barker picked Paige up and put her on the table, and made love to her.

When Paige woke up, she was falling off the bed.

At six o'clock the following morning, Paige was nervously waiting in the second-floor corridor with Joel Philips, the senior resident, and five other residents, when a short, sour-faced man stormed toward them. He leaned forward as he walked, as though battling a stiff wind.

He approached the group. "What the hell are you all standing around for? Let's go!"

It took Paige a moment to regain her composure. She hurried along to catch up with the rest of the group. As they moved along the corridor, Dr. Barker snapped, "You'll have between thirty and thirty-five patients to care for every day. I'll expect you to make detailed notes on each one of them. Clear?"

There were murmurs of "Yes, sir."

They had reached the first ward. Dr. Barker walked over to the bed of a patient, a man in his forties. Barker's gruff and forbidding manner went through an instant change. He touched the patient gently on the shoulder and smiled. "Good morning. I'm Dr. Barker."

"Good morning, doctor."

"How are you feeling this morning?"

"My chest hurts."

Dr. Barker studied the chart at the foot of the bed, then turned to Dr. Philips. "What do his X-rays show?"

"No change. He's healing nicely."

"Let's do another CBC."

Dr. Philips made a note.

Dr. Barker patted the young man on the arm and smiled. "It's looking good. We'll have you out of here in a week." He turned to the residents and snapped, "Move it! We have a lot of patients to see."

My God! Paige thought. *Talk about Dr. Jekyll and Mr. Hyde!*

The next patient was an obese woman who had had a pacemaker put in. Dr. Barker studied her chart. "Good morning, Mrs. Shelby." His voice was soothing. "I'm Dr. Barker."

"How long are you going to keep me in this place?"

"Well, you're so charming, I'd like to keep you here forever, but I have a wife."

Mrs. Shelby giggled. "She's a lucky woman."

Barker was examining her chart again. "I'd say you're just about ready to go home."

"Wonderful."

"I'll stop by to see you this afternoon."

Lawrence Barker turned to the residents. "Move on."

They obediently trailed behind the doctor to a semiprivate room where a young Guatemalan boy lay in bed, surrounded by his anxious family.

"Good morning," Dr. Barker said warmly. He scanned the patient's chart. "How are you feeling this morning?"

"I am feeling good, doctor."

Dr. Barker turned to Philips. "Any change in the electrolytes?"

"No, doctor."

"That's good news." He patted the boy's arm. "You hang in there, Juan."

The mother asked anxiously, "Is my son going to be all right?"

Dr. Barker smiled. "We're going to do everything we can for him."

"Thank you, doctor."

Dr. Barker stepped out into the corridor, the others trailing behind him. He stopped. "The patient has myocardiopathy, irregular fever tremors, headaches, and localized edema. Can any of you geniuses tell me what the most common cause of it is?"

There was a silence. Paige said hesitantly, "I believe it's congenital . . . hereditary."

Dr. Barker looked at her and nodded encouragingly.

Pleased, Paige went on. "It skips . . . wait . . ." She was struggling to remember. "It skips a generation and is passed along by the genes of the mother." She stopped, flushed, proud of herself.

Dr. Barker stared at her a moment. "Horseshit! It's Chagas' disease. It affects people from Latin American countries." He looked at Paige with disgust. "Jesus! Who told you you were a doctor?"

Paige's face was flaming red.

The rest of the rounds was a blur to her. They saw twenty-four patients and it seemed to Paige that Dr. Barker spent the morning trying to humiliate her. She was always the one Barker addressed his questions to, testing, probing. When she was right, he never complimented her. When she was wrong, he yelled at her. At one point, when Paige made a mistake, Barker roared, "I wouldn't let you operate on my dog!"

When the rounds were finally over, Dr. Philips, the senior resident, said, "We'll start rounds again at two o'clock. Get your scut books, make notes on each patient, and don't leave anything out."

He looked at Paige pityingly, started to say something, then turned away to join Dr. Barker.

Paige thought, *I never want to see that bastard again.*

The following night, Paige was on call. She ran from one crisis to the next, frantically trying to stem the tide of disasters that flooded the emergency rooms.

At 1:00 A.M., she finally fell asleep. She did not hear the sound of a siren screaming out its warning as an ambulance roared to a stop in front of the emergency entrance of the hospital. Two paramedics swung open the ambulance door, transferred the unconscious patient from his stretcher to a gurney, and ran it through the entrance doors of ER One.

The staff had been alerted by radiophone.

A nurse ran alongside the patient, while a second nurse waited at the top of the ramp. Sixty seconds later, the patient was transferred from the gurney to the examination table.

He was a young man, and he was covered with so much blood that it was difficult to tell what he looked like.

A nurse went to work, cutting his torn clothes off with large shears.

"It looks like everything's broken."

"He's bleeding like a stuck pig."

"I'm not getting a pulse."

"Who's on call?"

"Dr. Taylor."

"Get her. If she hurries, he may still be alive."

Paige was awakened by the ringing of the telephone.

"H'lo . . ."

"We have an emergency in ER One, doctor. I don't think he's going to make it."

Paige sat up on the cot. "Right. I'm coming."

She looked at her wristwatch. 1:30 A.M. She stumbled out of bed and made her way to the elevator.

A minute later, she was walking into ER One. In the middle of the room, on the examining table, was the blood-covered patient.

"What do we have here?" Paige asked.

"Motorcycle accident. He was hit by a bus. He wasn't wearing a helmet."

Paige moved toward the unconscious figure, and even before she saw his face, she somehow knew.

She was suddenly wide awake. "Get three IV lines in him!" Paige ordered. "Get him on oxygen. I want some blood sent down, stat. Call Records to get his blood type."

The nurse looked at her in surprise. "You know him?"

"Yes." She had to force herself to say the words. "His name is Jimmy Ford."

Paige ran her fingers over his scalp. "There's heavy edema. I want a head scan and X-rays. We're going to push the envelope on this one. I want him alive!"

"Yes, doctor."

Paige spent the next two hours making sure that everything possible was being done for Jimmy Ford. The X-rays showed a fractured skull, a brain contusion, broken humerus, and multiple lacerations. But everything would have to wait until he was stabilized.

At 3:30 A.M., Paige decided there was nothing more she could do for the present. He was breathing better, and his pulse was stronger. She looked down at the unconscious figure. *We're going to have half a dozen kids.*

The first girl is going to be named Paige. I hope you don't mind.

"Call me if there's any change at all," Paige said.

"Don't worry, doctor," one of the nurses said. "We'll take good care of him."

Paige made her way back to the on-call room. She was exhausted, but she was too concerned about Jimmy to go back to sleep.

The telephone rang again. She barely had the energy to pick it up. "H'lo."

"Doctor, you'd better come up to the third floor. Stat. I think one of Dr. Barker's patients is having a heart attack."

"Coming," Paige said. *One of Dr. Barker's patients.* Paige took a deep breath, staggered out of bed, threw cold water on her face, and hurried to the third floor.

A nurse was waiting outside a private room. "It's Mrs. Hearns. It looks like she's having another heart seizure."

Paige went into the room.

Mrs. Hearns was a woman in her fifties. Her face still held the remnants of a onetime beauty, but her body was fat and bloated. She was holding her chest and moaning. "I'm dying," she said. "I'm dying. I can't breathe."

"You're going to be all right," Paige said

reassuringly. She turned to the nurse. "Did you do an EKG?"

"She won't let me touch her. She said she's too nervous."

"We must do an EKG," Paige told the patient.

"No! I don't want to die. Please don't let me die . . ."

Paige said to the nurse, "Call Dr. Barker. Ask him to get down here right away."

The nurse hurried off.

Paige put a stethoscope to Mrs. Hearns's chest. She listened. The heartbeat seemed normal, but Paige could not afford to take any chances.

"Dr. Barker will be here in a few minutes," she told Mrs. Hearns. "Try to relax."

"I've never felt this bad. My chest feels so heavy. Please don't leave me."

"I'm not going to leave you," Paige promised her.

While she was waiting for Dr. Barker to arrive, Paige telephoned the intensive care unit. There was no change in Jimmy Ford's condition. He was still in a coma.

Thirty minutes later, Dr. Barker appeared. He had obviously dressed in haste. "What's going on?" he demanded.

Paige said, "I think Mrs. Hearns is having another heart attack."

Dr. Barker moved over to the bedside. "Did you do an EKG?"

"She wouldn't let us."

"Pulse?"

"Normal. No fever."

Dr. Barker put a stethoscope against Mrs. Hearns's back. "Take a deep breath."

She obliged.

"Again."

Mrs. Hearns let out a loud belch. "Excuse me." She smiled. "Oh. That's better."

He studied her a moment. "What did you have for dinner, Mrs. Hearns?"

"I had a hamburger."

"Just a hamburger? That's all? One?"

"Two."

"Anything else?"

"Well, you know . . . onions and french fries."

"And to drink?"

"A chocolate milk shake."

Dr. Barker looked down at the patient. "Your heart is fine. It's your appetite we have to worry about." He turned to Paige. "What you're seeing here is a case of heartburn. I'd like to see you outside, doctor."

When they were in the corridor, he roared, "What the hell did they teach you in medical school? Don't you even know the difference between heartburn and a heart attack?"

"I thought . . ."

"The problem is, you *didn't*! If you ever wake me up again in the middle of the night for a heartburn case, I'll have your ass. You understand that?"

Paige stood there stiffly, her face grim.

"Give her some antacid, *doctor*," Lawrence Barker said sarcastically, "and you'll find that she's cured. I'll see you at six o'clock for rounds."

Paige watched him storm out.

When Paige stumbled back to her cot in the on-call room, she thought, *I'm going to kill Lawrence Barker. I'll do it slowly. He'll be very ill. He'll have a dozen tubes in his body. He'll beg me to put him out of his misery, but I won't. I'll let him suffer, and then when he feels better . . . that's when I'll kill him!*

Chapter Fifteen

Paige was on morning rounds with the Beast, as she secretly referred to Dr. Barker. She had assisted him in three cardiothoracic surgeries, and in spite of her bitter feelings toward him, she could not help but admire his incredible skill. She watched in awe as he opened up a patient, deftly replaced the old heart with a donor heart, and sewed him up. The operation took less than five hours.

Within a few weeks, Paige thought, *that patient will be able to return to a normal life. No wonder surgeons think they're gods. They bring the dead back to life.*

Time after time, Paige watched a heart stop and turn to an inert piece of flesh. And then the miracle would occur, and a lifeless organ would begin to pulsate again and send blood through a body that had been dying.

One morning, a patient was scheduled for a procedure to insert an intra-aortic balloon. Paige was in the operating room assisting Dr. Barker. As they were about to begin, Dr. Barker snapped, "Do it!"

Paige looked at him. "I beg your pardon?"

"It's a simple procedure. Do you think you can handle it?" There was contempt in his voice.

"Yes," Paige said tightly.

"Well, then, get on with it!"

He was infuriating.

Barker watched as Paige expertly inserted a hollow tube into the patient's artery and threaded it up into the heart. It was done flawlessly. Barker stood there, without saying a word.

To hell with him, Paige thought. *Nothing I could ever do would please him.*

Paige injected a radiopaque dye through the tube. They watched the monitor as the dye flowed into the coronary arteries. Images appeared on a fluoroscopy screen and showed the degree of blockage and its location in the artery, while an automatic motion-picture camera recorded the X-rays for a permanent record.

The senior resident looked at Paige and smiled. "Nice job."

"Thank you." Paige turned to Dr. Barker.

"Too damned slow," he growled.

And he walked out.

Paige was grateful for the days that Dr. Barker was away from the hospital, working at his private practice. She said to Kat, "Being away from him for a day is like a week in the country."

"You really hate him, don't you?"

"He's a brilliant doctor, but he's a miserable human being. Have you ever noticed how some people fit their names? If Dr. Barker doesn't stop barking at people, he's going to have a stroke."

"You should see some of the beauties I have to put up with." Kat laughed. "They all think they're God's gift to pussies. Wouldn't it be great if there were no men in the world!"

Paige looked at her, but said nothing.

Paige and Kat went to check on Jimmy Ford. He was still in a coma. There was nothing they could do.

Kat sighed. "Dammit. Why does it happen to the good guys?"

"I wish I knew."

"Do you think he'll make it?"

Paige hesitated. "We've done everything we can. Now it's up to God."

"Funny. I thought *we* were God."

The following day when Paige was in charge of afternoon rounds, Kaplan, a senior resident, stopped her in the corridor. "This is your lucky day." He grinned. "You're getting a new medical school student to take around."

"Really?"

"Yeah, the IN."

"IN?"

"Idiot nephew. Dr. Wallace's wife has a nephew who wants to be a doctor. They threw him out of his last two schools. We've all had to put up with him. Today it's your turn."

Paige groaned. "I don't have time for this. I'm up to my . . ."

"It's not an option. Be a good girl and Dr. Wallace will give you brownie points." Kaplan moved off.

Paige sighed and walked over to where the new residents were waiting to start the rounds. *Where's the IN?* She looked at her watch. He was already three minutes late. *I'll give him one more minute,* Paige decided, *and then to hell with him.* She saw him then, a tall, lean-looking man, hurrying toward her, down the hall.

He walked up to Paige, out of breath, and said, "Excuse me. Dr. Wallace asked me to—"

"You're late," Paige said curtly.

"I know. I'm sorry. I was held up at—"

"Never mind. What's your name?"

"Jason. Jason Curtis." He was wearing a sport jacket.

"Where's your white coat?"

"My white coat?"

"Didn't anyone tell you to wear a white coat on rounds?"

He looked flustered. "No. I'm afraid I . . ."

Paige said irritably, "Go back to the head nurse's office and tell her to give you a white coat. And you don't have a scut book."

"No."

Idiot nephew doesn't begin to describe *him.* "Meet us in Ward One."

"Are you sure? I . . ."

"Just do it!" Paige and the others started off, leaving Jason Curtis staring after them.

They were examining their third patient when Jason Curtis came hurrying up. He was wearing a white coat. Paige was saying, ". . . tumors of the heart can be primary, which is rare, or secondary, which is much more common."

She turned to Curtis. "Can you name the three types of tumors?"

He stared at her. "I'm afraid I . . . I can't."

Of course not. "Epicardial. Myocardial. Endocardial."

He looked at Paige and smiled. "That's really interesting."

My God! Paige thought. *Dr. Wallace or no Dr. Wallace, I'm going to get rid of him fast.*

They moved on to the next patient, and when Paige was through examining him, she took the group into the corridor, out of earshot. "We're dealing here with a thyroid storm, with fever and extreme tachycardia. It came on after surgery." She turned to Jason Curtis. "How would you treat him for that?"

He stood there, thoughtful for a moment. Then he said, "Gently?"

Paige fought for self-control. "You're not his mother, you're his doctor! He needs continuous IV fluids to combat dehydration, along with IV iodine and antithyroid drugs and sedatives for convulsions."

Jason nodded. "That sounds about right."

The rounds got no better. When they were over, Paige called Jason Curtis aside. "Do you mind my being frank with you?"

"No. Not at all," he said agreeably. "I'd appreciate it."

"Look for another profession."

He stood there, frowning. "You don't think I'm cut out for this?"

"Quite honestly, no. You don't enjoy this, do you?"

"Not really."

"Then why did you choose to go into this?"

"To tell you the truth, I was pushed into it."

"Well, you tell Dr. Wallace that he's making a mistake. I think you should find something else to do with your life."

"I really appreciate your telling me this," Jason Curtis said earnestly. "I wonder if we could discuss this further. If you aren't doing anything for dinner tonight . . . ?"

"We have nothing further to discuss," Paige said curtly. "You can tell your uncle . . ."

At that moment Dr. Wallace came into view. "Jason!" he called. "I've been looking all over for you." He turned to Paige. "I see you two have met."

"Yes, we've met," Paige said grimly.

"Good. Jason is the architect in charge of designing the new wing we're building."

Paige stood there, motionless. "He's . . . *what*?"

"Yes. Didn't he tell you?"

She felt her face getting red. *Didn't any-*

*one tell you to wear a white coat on rounds?
Why did you go into this? To tell you the truth,
I was pushed into it.*

By me!

Paige wanted to crawl into a hole. He had
made a complete fool of her. She turned to Jason. "Why didn't you tell me who you were?"

He was watching her, amused. "Well, you
really didn't give me a chance."

"She didn't give you a chance to what?"
Dr. Wallace asked.

"If you'll excuse me . . ." Paige said
tightly.

"What about dinner tonight?"

"I don't eat. And I'm busy." And Paige was
gone.

Jason looked after her, admiringly.
"That's quite a woman."

"She is, isn't she? Shall we go to my office
and talk about the new designs?"

"Fine." But his thoughts were on Paige.

It was July, time for the ritual that took
place every twelve months at hospitals all
over the United States, as new residents came
in to begin their journey toward becoming real
doctors.

The nurses had been looking forward to
the new crop of residents, staking out claims

on the ones they thought would make good lovers or husbands. On this particular day, as the new residents appeared, nearly every female eye was fixed on Dr. Ken Mallory.

No one knew why Ken Mallory had transferred from an exclusive private hospital in Washington, D.C., to Embarcadero County Hospital in San Francisco. He was a fifth-year resident and a general surgeon. There were rumors that he had had to leave Washington in a hurry because of an affair with a congressman's wife. There was another rumor that a nurse had committed suicide because of him and he had been asked to leave. The only thing the nurses were sure of was that Ken Mallory was, without doubt, the best-looking man they had ever seen. He had a tall, athletic body, wavy blond hair, and a face that would have looked great on a movie screen.

Mallory blended into the hospital routine as though he had been there forever. He was a charmer, and almost from the beginning, the nurses were fighting for his attention. Night after night, the other doctors would watch Mallory disappear into an empty on-call room with a different nurse. His reputation as a stud was becoming legendary around the hospital.

Paige, Kat, and Honey were discussing him.

"Can you believe all those nurses throwing themselves at him?" Kat laughed. "They're actually fighting to be the flavor of the week!"

"You have to admit, he *is* attractive," Honey pointed out.

Kat shook her head. "No. I don't."

One morning, half a dozen residents were in the doctors' dressing room when Mallory walked in.

"We were just talking about you," one of them said. "You must be exhausted."

Mallory grinned. "It was not a bad night." He had spent the night with two nurses.

Grundy, one of the residents, said, "You're making the rest of us look like eunuchs, Ken. Isn't there anyone in this hospital you can't lay?"

Mallory laughed. "I doubt it."

Grundy was thoughtful for a moment. "I'll bet I can name someone."

"Really? Who's that?"

"One of the senior residents here. Her name is Kat Hunter."

Mallory nodded. "The black doll. I've seen her. She's very attractive. What makes you think I can't take her to bed?"

"Because we've all struck out. I don't think she likes men."

"Or maybe she just hasn't met the right one," Mallory suggested.

Grundy shook his head. "No. You wouldn't have a chance."

It was a challenge. "I'll bet you're wrong."

One of the other residents spoke up. "You mean you're willing to bet on it?"

Mallory smiled. "Sure. Why not?"

"All right." The group began to crowd around Mallory. "I'll bet you five hundred dollars you can't lay her."

"You're on."

"I'll bet you three hundred."

Another one spoke up. "Let me in on it. I'll bet you six hundred."

In the end, five thousand dollars was bet.

"What's the time limit?" Mallory asked.

Grundy thought for a moment. "Let's say thirty days. Is that fair?"

"More than fair. I won't need that much time."

Grundy said, "But you have to prove it. She has to admit that she went to bed with you."

"No problem." Mallory looked around the group and grinned. "Suckers!"

Fifteen minutes later, Grundy was in the cafeteria where Kat, Paige, and Honey were having breakfast. He walked over to their table. "Can I join you ladies—you doctors—for a moment?"

Paige looked up. "Sure."

Grundy sat down. He looked at Kat and said apologetically, "I hate to tell you this, but I'm really mad, and I think it's only fair that you should know . . ."

Kat was looking at him, puzzled. "Know what?"

Grundy sighed. "That new senior resident who came in—Ken Mallory?"

"Yes. What about him?"

Grundy said, "Well, I . . . God, this is embarrassing. He bet some of the doctors five thousand dollars that he could get you into bed in the next thirty days."

Kat's face was grim. "He did, did he?"

Grundy said piously, "I don't blame you for being angry. It made me sick when I heard about it. Well, I just wanted to warn you. He'll be asking you out, and I thought it was only right that you should know why he was doing it."

"Thanks," Kat said. "I appreciate your telling me."

"It was the least I could do."

They watched Grundy leave.

In the corridor outside the cafeteria, the

other residents were waiting for him.

"How did it go?" they asked.

Grundy laughed. "Perfect. She's as mad as hell. The son of a bitch is dead meat!"

At the table, Honey was saying, "I think that's just terrible."

Kat nodded. "Someone should give him a dick-otomy. They'll be ice skating in hell before I go out with that bastard."

Paige sat there thinking. After a moment, she said, "You know something, Kat? It might be interesting if you *did* go out with him."

Kat looked at her in surprise. *"What?"*

There was a glint in Paige's eye. "Why not? If he wants to play games, let's help him—only he'll play *our* game."

Kat leaned forward. "Go on."

"He has thirty days, right? When he asks you out, you'll be warm and loving and affectionate. I mean, you'll be absolutely *crazy* about the man. You'll drive him out of his mind. The only thing you *won't* do, bless your heart, is to go to bed with him. We'll teach him a five-thousand-dollar lesson."

Kat thought of her stepfather. It was a way of getting revenge. "I like it," Kat said.

"You mean you're going to do it?" Honey said.

"I am."

And Kat had no idea that with those words, she had signed her death warrant.

Chapter Sixteen

Jason Curtis had been unable to get Paige Taylor out of his mind. He telephoned Ben Wallace's secretary. "Hi. This is Jason Curtis. I need a home telephone number for Dr. Paige Taylor."

"Certainly, Mr. Curtis. Just a moment." She gave him the number.

Honey answered the telephone. "Dr. Taft."

"This is Jason Curtis. Is Dr. Taylor there?"

"No, she's not. She's on call at the hospital."

"Oh. That's too bad."

Honey could hear the disappointment in

his voice. "If it's some kind of emergency, I can . . ."

"No, no."

"I could take a message for her and have her call you."

"That will be fine." Jason gave her his telephone number.

"I'll give her the message."

"Thank you."

"Jason Curtis called," Honey said when Paige returned to the apartment. "He sounded cute. Here's his number."

"Burn it."

"Aren't you going to call him back?"

"No. Never."

"You're still hung up on Alfred, aren't you?"

"Of course not."

And that was all Honey could get out of her.

Jason waited two days before he called again.

This time Paige answered the telephone. "Dr. Taylor."

"Hello there!" Jason said. "This is Dr. Curtis."

"Doctor . . . ?"

"You may not remember me," Jason said lightly. "I was on rounds with you the other day, and I asked you to have dinner with me. You said—"

"I said I was busy. I still am. Goodbye, Mr. Curtis." She slammed the receiver down.

"What was that all about?" Honey asked.

"About nothing."

At six o'clock the following morning, when the residents gathered with Paige for morning rounds, Jason Curtis appeared. He was wearing a white coat.

"I hope I'm not late," he said cheerfully. "I had to get a white coat. I know how upset you get when I don't wear one."

Paige took a deep, angry breath. "Come in here," she said. She led Jason into the deserted doctors' dressing room. "What are you doing here?"

"To tell you the truth, I've been worried about some of the patients we saw the other day," he said earnestly. "I came to see if everyone is all right."

The man was infuriating.

"Why aren't you out building something?"

Jason looked at her and said quietly, "I'm trying to." He pulled out a handful of tickets.

271

"Look, I don't know what your tastes are, so I got tickets for tonight's Giants game, the theater, the opera, and a concert. Take your choice. They're nonrefundable."

The man was exasperating. "Do you always throw your money away like this?"

"Only when I'm in love," Jason said.

"Wait a min—"

He held the tickets out to her. "Take your choice."

Paige reached out and took them all. "Thank you," she said sweetly. "I'll give them to my outpatients. Most of them don't have a chance to go to the theater or opera."

He smiled. "Great! I hope they enjoy it. Will you have dinner with me?"

"No."

"You have to eat, anyway. Won't you change your mind?"

Paige felt a small frisson of guilt about the tickets. "I'm afraid I wouldn't be very good company. I was on call last night, and . . ."

"We'll make it an early evening. Scout's honor."

She sighed. "All right, but . . ."

"Wonderful! Where shall I pick you up?"

"I'll be through here at seven."

"I'll pick you up here then." He yawned. "Now I'm going home and going back to bed.

What an ungodly hour to be up. What makes you do it?"

Paige watched him walk away, and she could not help smiling.

At seven o'clock that evening when Jason arrived at the hospital to pick up Paige, the supervising nurse said, "I think you'll find Dr. Taylor in the on-call room."

"Thanks." Jason walked down the corridor to the on-call room. The door was closed. He knocked. There was no answer. He knocked again, then opened the door and looked inside. Paige was on the cot, in a deep sleep. Jason walked over to where she lay and stood there for a long time, looking down at her. *I'm going to marry you, lady,* he thought. He tiptoed out of the room and quietly closed the door behind him.

The following morning, Jason was in a meeting when his secretary came in with a small bouquet of flowers. The card read: *I'm sorry. RIP.* Jason laughed. He telephoned Paige at the hospital. "This is your date calling."

"I really am sorry about last night," Paige said. "I'm embarrassed."

"Don't be. But I have a question."

"Yes?"

"Does RIP stand for Rest in Peace or Rip as in Van Winkle?"

Paige laughed. "Take your choice."

"My choice is dinner tonight. Can we try again?"

She hesitated. *I don't want to become involved. You're not still hung up on Alfred, are you?*

"Hello. Are you there?"

"Yes." *One evening won't do any harm,* Paige decided. "Yes. We can have dinner."

"Wonderful."

As Paige was getting dressed that evening, Kat said, "It looks like you have a heavy date. Who is it?"

"He's a doctor-architect," Paige said.

"A *what?*"

Paige told her the story.

"He sounds like fun. Are you interested in him?"

"Not really."

The evening went by pleasantly. Paige found Jason easy to be with. They talked about everything and nothing, and the time seemed to fly.

"Tell me about you," Jason said. "Where did you grow up?"

"You won't believe me."

"I promise I will."

"All right. The Congo, India, Burma, Nigeria, Kenya . . ."

"I don't believe you."

"It's true. My father worked for WHO."

"Who? I give up. Is this going to be an Abbott and Costello rerun?"

"The World Health Organization. He was a doctor. I spent my childhood traveling to most of the Third World countries with him."

"That must have been difficult for you."

"It was exciting. The hardest part was that I was never able to stay long enough to make friends." *We don't need anyone else, Paige. We'll always have each other. . . . This is my wife, Karen.* She shook off the memory. "I learned a lot of strange languages, and exotic customs."

"For instance?"

"Well, for instance, I . . ." She thought for a moment. "In India they believe in life after death, and that the next life depends on how you behaved in this one. If you were bad, you would come back as an animal. I remember that in one village, we had a dog, and I used to wonder who he used to be and what he did that was bad."

Jason said, "He probably barked up the wrong tree."

Paige smiled. "And then there was the *gherao*."

"The *gherao*?"

"It's a very powerful form of punishment. A crowd surrounds a man." She stopped.

"And?"

"That's it."

"That's it?"

"They don't say anything or do anything. But he can't move, and he can't get away. He's trapped until he gives in to what they want. It can last for many, many hours. He stays inside the circle, but the crowd keeps changing shifts. I saw a man try to escape the *gherao* once. They beat him to death."

The memory of it made Paige shudder. The normally friendly people had turned into a screaming, frenzied mob. "Let's get away from here," Alfred had yelled. He had taken her arm and led her to a quiet side street.

"That's terrible," Jason said.

"My father moved us away the next day."

"I wish I could have known your father."

"He was a wonderful doctor. He would have been a big success on Park Avenue, but he wasn't interested in money. His only interest was in helping people." *Like Alfred,* she thought.

"What happened to him?"

"He was killed in a tribal war."

"I'm sorry."

"He loved doing what he did. In the beginning, the natives fought him. They were very superstitious. In the remote Indian villages, everyone has a *jatak,* a horoscope done by the village astrologer, and they live by it." She smiled. "I loved having mine done."

"And did they tell you that you were going to marry a handsome young architect?"

Paige looked at him and said firmly, "No." The conversation was getting too personal. "You're an architect, so you'll appreciate this. I grew up in huts made of wattle, with earthen floors and thatched roofs where mice and bats liked to nest. I lived in *tukuls* with grass roofs and no windows. My dream was to live one day in a comfortable two-story house with a veranda and a green lawn and a white picket fence, and . . ." Paige stopped. "Sorry. I didn't mean to go on like this, but you *did* ask."

"I'm glad I asked," Jason said.

Paige looked at her watch. "I had no idea it was so late."

"Can we do this again?"

I don't want to lead him on, Paige

thought. *Nothing is going to come of this.* She thought of something Kat had said to her. *You're clinging to a ghost. Let go.* She looked at Jason and said, "Yes."

Early the following morning, a messenger arrived with a package. Paige opened the door for him.

"I have something for Dr. Taylor."

"I'm Dr. Taylor."

The messenger looked at her in surprise. "You're a doctor?"

"Yes," Paige said patiently. "I'm a doctor. Do you mind?"

He shrugged. "No, lady. Not at all. Would you sign here, please?"

The package was surprisingly heavy. Curious, Paige carried it to the living-room table and unwrapped it. It was a miniature model of a beautiful white two-story house with a veranda. In front of the house was a little lawn and garden, surrounded by a white picket fence. *He must have stayed up all night, making it.* There was a card that read:

Mine [ ]
Ours [ ]
Please check one.

She sat there looking at it for a long time. It was the right house, but it was the wrong man.

What's the matter with me? Paige asked herself. *He's bright and attractive and charming.* But she knew what the matter was. He was not Alfred.

The telephone rang. It was Jason. "Did you get your house?" he asked.

"It's beautiful!" Paige said. "Thank you so much."

"I'd like to build you the real thing. Did you fill in the box?"

"No."

"I'm a patient man. Are you free for dinner tonight?"

"Yes, but I have to warn you, I'm going to be operating all day, and by this evening I'll be exhausted."

"We'll make it an early evening. By the way, it's going to be at my parents' home."

Paige hesitated a moment. "Oh?"

"I've told them all about you."

"That's fine," Paige said. Things were moving too quickly. It made her nervous.

When Paige hung up, she thought: *I really shouldn't be doing this. By tonight I'm going to be too tired to do anything but go to sleep.* She was tempted to telephone Jason back and cancel their date. *It's too late to do that now. We'll make it an early evening.*

As Paige was getting dressed that night, Kat said, "You look exhausted."

"I am."

"Why are you going out? You should be going to bed. Or is that redundant?"

"No. Not tonight."

"Jason again?"

"Yes. I'm going to meet his parents."

"Ah." Kat shook her head.

"It's not like that at all," Paige said. *It's really not.*

Jason's mother and father lived in a charming old house in the Pacific Heights district. Jason's father was an aristocratic-looking man in his seventies. Jason's mother was a warm, down-to-earth woman. They made Paige feel instantly at home.

"Jason has told us so much about you," Mrs. Curtis said. "He didn't tell us how beautiful you are."

"Thank you."

They went into the library, filled with miniature models of buildings that Jason and his father had designed.

"I guess that between us, Jason, his great-grandfather, and I have done a lot of the landscape of San Francisco," Jason's father said. "My son is a genius."

"That's what I keep telling Paige," Jason said.

Paige laughed. "I believe it." Her eyes were getting heavy and she was fighting to stay awake.

Jason was watching her, concerned. "Let's go in to dinner," he suggested.

They went into the large dining room. It was oak-paneled, furnished with attractive antiques and portraits on the wall. A maid began serving.

Jason's father said, "That painting over there is Jason's great-grandfather. All the buildings he designed were destroyed in the earthquake of 1906. It's too bad. They were priceless. I'll show you some photographs of them after dinner if you . . ."

Paige's head had dropped to the table. She was sound asleep.

"I'm glad I didn't serve soup," Jason's mother said.

Ken Mallory had a problem. As word of the wager about Kat had spread around the hospital, the bets had quickly increased to ten thousand dollars. Mallory had been so confident of his success that he had bet much more than he could afford to pay off.

If I fail, I'm in a hell of a lot of trouble. But I'm not going to fail. Time for the master to go to work.

Kat was having lunch in the cafeteria with Paige and Honey when Mallory approached the table.

"Mind if I join you doctors?"

Not ladies, not girls. Doctors. The sensitive type, Kat thought cynically. "Not at all. Sit down," Kat said.

Paige and Honey exchanged a look.

"Well, I have to get going," Paige said.

"Me, too. See you later."

Mallory watched Paige and Honey leave.

"Busy morning?" Mallory asked. He made it sound as though he really cared.

"Aren't they all?" Kat gave him a warm, promising smile.

Mallory had planned his strategy carefully. *I'm going to let her know I'm interested in her as a person, not just as a woman. They hate the sex-object thing. Discuss medicine with her. I'll take it slow and easy. I have a whole month to get her in the sack.*

"Did you hear about the postmortem on Mrs. Turnball?" Mallory began. "The woman had a Coca-Cola bottle in her stomach! Can you imagine how . . . ?"

Kat leaned forward. "Are you doing anything Saturday night, Ken?"

Mallory was caught completely off guard. "What?"

"I thought you might like to take me out to dinner."

He found himself almost blushing. *My God!* he thought. *Talk about shooting fish in a barrel! This is no lesbian. The guys said that because they couldn't get into her pants. Well, I'm going to. She's actually asking for it!* He tried to remember with whom he had a date on Saturday. *Sally, the little nurse in OR. She can wait.*

"Nothing important," Mallory said. "I'd love to take you to dinner."

Kat put her hand over his. "Wonderful," she said softly. "I'll really be looking forward to it."

He grinned. "So will I." *You have no idea how much, baby. Ten thousand dollars' worth!*

That afternoon, Kat reported back to Paige and Honey.

"His mouth dropped open!" Kat laughed. "You should have seen the look on his face! He looked like the cat that swallowed the canary."

Paige said, "Remember, you're the Kat. He's the canary."

"What are you going to do Saturday night?" Honey asked.

"Any suggestions?"

"I have," Paige answered. "Here's the plan . . ."

Saturday evening, Kat and Ken Mallory had dinner at Emilio's, a restaurant on the bay. She had dressed carefully for him, in a white cotton dress, off the shoulder.

"You look sensational," Mallory said. He was careful to strike just the right note. *Appreciative, but not pressing. Admiring, but not suggestive.* Mallory had determined to be at his most charming, but it was not necessary. It quickly became obvious to him that Kat was intent on charming *him.*

Over a drink, Kat said, "Everyone talks about what a wonderful doctor you are, Ken."

"Well," Mallory said modestly, "I've had fine training, and I care a lot about my patients. They're very important to me." His voice was filled with sincerity.

Kat put her hand over his. "I'm sure they are. Where are you from? I want to know all about you. The *real* you."

Jesus! Mallory thought. *That's the line I use.* He could not get over how easy this was going to be. He was an expert on the subject of women. His radar knew all the signals they put out. They could say yes with a look, a smile, a tone of voice. Kat's signals were jamming his radar.

She was leaning close to him, and her voice was husky. "I want to know everything."

He talked about himself during dinner, and every time he tried to change the subject and bring it around to Kat, she said, "No, no. I want to hear more. You've had such a fascinating life!"

She's crazy about me, Mallory decided. He wished now that he had taken more bets. *I might even win tonight*, he thought. And he was sure of it when Kat said, as they were having coffee, "Would you like to come up to my apartment for a nightcap?"

Bingo! Mallory stroked her arm and said softly, "I'd love to." *The guys were all crazy,* Mallory decided. *She's the horniest broad I've ever met.* He had a feeling that he was about to be raped.

Thirty minutes later, they were walking into Kat's apartment.

"Nice," Mallory said, looking around. "Very nice. Do you live here alone?"

"No. Dr. Taylor and Dr. Taft live with me."

"Oh." She could hear the note of regret in his voice.

Kat gave him a beguiling smile. "But they won't be home until much later."

Mallory grinned. "Good."

"Would you like a drink?"

"Love one." He watched as Kat walked over to the little bar and mixed two drinks. *She's got great buns*, Mallory thought. *And she's damned good-looking, and I'm getting ten thousand dollars to lay her.* He laughed aloud.

Kat turned. "What's so funny?"

"Nothing. I was just thinking how lucky I am to be here alone with you."

"I'm the lucky one," Kat said warmly. She handed him his drink.

Mallory raised his glass and started to say, "Here's to . . ."

Kat beat him to it. "Here's to us!" she said.

He nodded. "I'll drink to that."

He started to say, "How about a little music?" and as he opened his mouth, Kat said, "Would you like some music?"

"You're a mind reader."

Kat put on an old Cole Porter standard. She surreptitiously glanced at her watch, then turned to Mallory. "Do you like to dance?"

Mallory moved closer to her. "It depends on whom I'm dancing with. I'd love to dance with you."

Kat moved into his arms, and they began to dance to the slow and dreamy music. He felt Kat's body pressing hard against his, and he could feel himself getting aroused. He held her tighter, and Kat smiled up at him.

Now is the time to go in for the kill.

"You're lovely, you know," Mallory said huskily. "I've wanted you since the first moment I saw you."

Kat looked into his eyes. "I've felt the same way about you, Ken." His lips moved toward hers, and he gave her a warm, passionate kiss.

"Let's go into the bedroom," Mallory said. There was a sudden urgency in him.

"Oh, yes!"

He took her by the arm and she started leading him toward her bedroom. And at that moment, the front door opened and Paige and Honey walked in.

"Hi there!" Paige called. She looked at Ken Mallory in surprise. "Oh, Dr. Mallory! I didn't expect to see you here."

"Well, I . . . I . . ."

"We went out to dinner," Kat said.

Mallory was filled with a dark rage. He fought to control it. He turned to Kat. "I should go. It's late and I have a big day to-morrow."

"Oh. I'm sorry you're leaving," Kat said. There was a world of promise in her eyes.

Mallory said, "What about tomorrow night?"

"I'd love to . . ."

"Great!"

". . . but I can't."

"Oh. Well, what about Friday?"

Kat frowned. "Oh, dear. I'm afraid Friday isn't good, either."

Mallory was getting desperate. "Satur-day?"

Kat smiled. "Saturday would be lovely."

He nodded, relieved. "Good. Saturday it is, then."

He turned to Paige and Honey. "Good night."

"Good night."

Kat walked Mallory to the door. "Sweet dreams," she said softly. "I'm going to dream about you."

Mallory squeezed her hand. "I believe in making dreams come true. We'll make up for this Saturday night."

"I can't wait."

* * *

That night, Kat lay in her bed thinking about Mallory. She hated him. But to her surprise, she had enjoyed the evening. She was sure that Mallory had enjoyed it too, in spite of the fact that he was playing a game. *If only this were real,* Kat thought, *and not a game.* She had no idea how dangerous a game it was.

Chapter Seventeen

Maybe it's the weather, Paige thought wearily. It was cold and dreary outside, with a gray driving rain that depressed the spirits. Her day had begun at six o'clock in the morning, and it was filled with constant problems. The hospital seemed to be full of gomers, all complaining at once. The nurses were surly and careless. They drew blood from the wrong patients, lost X-rays that were urgently needed, and snapped at the patients. In addition, there was a staff shortage because of a flu epidemic. It was that kind of day.

The only bright spot was the telephone call from Jason Curtis.

"Hello," he said cheerily. "Just thought I'd check in and see how all our patients are doing."

"They're surviving."

"Any chance of our having lunch?"

Paige laughed. "What's lunch? If I'm lucky, I'll be able to grab a stale sandwich about four o'clock this afternoon. It's pretty hectic around here."

"All right. I won't keep you. May I call you again?"

"All right." *No harm in that.*

"Bye."

Paige worked until midnight without a moment to rest, and when she was finally relieved, she was almost too tired to move. She briefly debated staying at the hospital and sleeping on the cot in the on-call room, but the thought of her warm, cozy bed at home was too tempting. She changed clothes and lurched her way to the elevator.

Dr. Peterson came up to her. "My God!" he said. "Where's the cat that dragged you in?"

Paige smiled wearily. "Do I look that bad?"

"Worse." Peterson grinned. "You're going home now?"

Paige nodded.

"You're lucky. I'm just starting."

The elevator arrived. Paige stood there half asleep.

Peterson said gently, "Paige?"

She shook herself awake. "Yes?"

"Are you going to be able to drive home?"

"Sure," Paige mumbled. "And when I get there, I'm going to sleep for twenty-four hours straight."

She walked to the parking lot and got into her car. She sat there drained, too tired to turn on the ignition. *I mustn't go to sleep here. I'll sleep at home.*

Paige drove out of the parking lot and headed toward the apartment. She was unaware of how erratically she was driving until a driver yelled at her, "Hey, get off the road, you drunken broad!"

She forced herself to concentrate. *I must not fall asleep . . . I must not fall asleep.* She snapped the radio on and turned the volume up loud. When she reached her apartment building, she sat in the car for a long time before she was able to summon enough strength to go upstairs.

Kat and Honey were in their beds, asleep. Paige looked at the clock at her bedside. *One o'clock in the morning.* She stumbled into her bedroom and started to get undressed, but the effort was too much for her. She fell into bed with her clothes on, and in an instant was sound asleep.

She was awakened by the shrill ringing of a telephone that seemed to be coming from some far-off planet. Paige fought to stay asleep, but the ringing was like needles penetrating her brain. She sat up groggily and reached for the phone. "H'lo?"

"Dr. Taylor?"

"Yes." Her voice was a hoarse mumble.

"Dr. Barker wants you in OR Four to assist him, stat."

Paige cleared her throat. "There must be some mistake," she mumbled. "I just got off duty."

"OR Four. He's waiting." The line went dead.

Paige sat on the edge of the bed, numb, her mind clouded by sleep. She looked at the clock on the bedside table. Four-fifteen. Why was Dr. Barker asking for her in the middle of the night? There was only one answer. Something had happened to one of her patients.

Paige staggered into the bathroom and threw cold water on her face. She looked in the mirror and thought, *My God! I look like my mother. No. My mother never looked this bad.*

Ten minutes later, Paige was making her way back to the hospital. She was still half asleep when she took the elevator to the fourth floor to OR Four. She went into the dressing room and changed, then scrubbed up and stepped into the operating room.

There were three nurses and a resident assisting Dr. Barker.

He looked up as Paige entered and yelled, "For Christ's sake, you're wearing a hospital gown! Didn't anyone ever inform you that you're supposed to wear *scrubs* in an operating room?"

Paige stood there, stunned, jolted wide awake, her eyes blazing. "You listen to me," she said, furiously. "I'm supposed to be off duty. I came in as a favor to you. I don't—"

"Don't argue with me," Dr. Barker said curtly. "Get over here and hold this retractor."

Paige walked over to the operating table and looked down. It was not her patient on the table. It was a stranger. *Barker had no reason to call me. He's trying to force me to quit the hospital. Well, I'll be damned if I will!* She gave him a baleful look, picked up the retractor, and went to work.

The operation was an emergency coronary artery bypass graft. The skin incision had already been made down the center of the chest to the breastbone, which had been split with an electric saw. The heart and major blood vessels were exposed.

Paige inserted the metal retractor between the cut sides of the breastbone, forcing the edges apart. She watched as Dr. Barker skillfully opened the pericardial sac, exposing the heart.

He indicated the coronary arteries. "Here's the problem," Barker said. "We're going to do some grafting."

He had already removed a long strip of vein from one leg. He sewed a piece of it into the main artery coming out of the heart. The other end he attached to one of the coronary arteries, beyond the obstructed area, sending the blood through the vein graft, bypassing the obstruction.

Paige was watching a master at work. *If only he weren't such a bastard!*

The operation took three hours. By the time it was over, Paige was only half conscious. When the incision had been closed, Dr. Barker turned to the staff and said, "I want to thank all of you." He was not looking at Paige.

Paige stumbled out of the room without a word and went upstairs to the office of Dr. Benjamin Wallace.

Wallace was just arriving. "You look exhausted," he said. "You should get some rest."

Paige took a deep breath to control her anger. "I want to be transferred to another surgical team."

Wallace studied her a moment. "You're assigned to Dr. Barker, right?"

"Right."

"What's the problem?"

"Ask *him*. He hates me. He'll be glad to get rid of me. I'll go with anyone else. Anyone."

"I'll talk to him," Wallace said.

"Thank you."

Paige turned and walked out of the office. *They'd better take me away from him. If I see him again, I'll kill him.*

Paige went home and slept for twelve hours. She woke up with a feeling that something wonderful had happened, and then she remembered. *I don't have to see the Beast anymore!* She drove to the hospital, whistling.

As Paige was walking down the corridor, an orderly came up to her. "Dr. Taylor . . ."

"Yes?"

"Dr. Wallace would like to see you in his office."

"Thank you," Paige said. She wondered who the new senior surgeon would be. *Anybody will be an improvement,* Paige thought. She walked into Benjamin Wallace's office.

"Well, you look much better today, Paige."

"Thanks. I feel much better." And she did.

She felt great, filled with an enormous sense of relief.

"I talked to Dr. Barker."

Paige smiled. "Thank you. I really appreciate it."

"He won't let you go."

Paige's smile faded. *What?*

"He said you're assigned to his team and you'll stay there."

She could not believe what she was hearing. "But *why?*" She knew why. The sadistic bastard needed a whipping girl, someone to humiliate. "I'm not going to stand for it."

Dr. Wallace said ruefully, "I'm afraid you have no choice. Unless you want to leave the hospital. Would you like to think about it?"

Paige did not have to think about it. "No." She was not going to let Barker force her to quit. That was his plan. "No," she repeated slowly. "I'll stay."

"Good. Then that's settled."

Not by a long shot, Paige thought. *I'm going to find some way to pay him back.*

In the doctors' dressing room, Ken Mallory was getting ready to make his rounds. Dr. Grundy and three other doctors walked in.

"There's our man!" Grundy said. "How are you doing, Ken?"

"Fine," Mallory said.

Grundy turned to the others. "He doesn't look like he just got laid, does he?" He turned back to Mallory. "I hope you have our money ready. I plan to make a down payment on a little car."

Another doctor joined in. "I'm buying a whole new wardrobe."

Mallory shook his head pityingly. "I wouldn't count on it, suckers. Get ready to pay me off!"

Grundy was studying him. "What do you mean?"

"If she's a lesbian, I'm a eunuch. She's the horniest broad I ever met. I practically had to hold her off the other night!"

The men were looking at one another, worried.

"But you didn't get her into the sack?"

"The only reason I didn't, my friends, is because we were interrupted on the way to the bedroom. I have a date with her Saturday night, and it will all be over but the shouting." Mallory finished dressing. "Now, if you gentlemen will excuse me . . ."

An hour later, Grundy stopped Kat in the corridor.

"I've been looking for you," he said. He looked angry.

"Is something wrong?"

"It's that bastard Mallory. He's so sure of himself that he's telling everyone he's going to get you into bed by Saturday night."

"Don't worry," Kat said grimly. "He's going to lose."

When Ken Mallory picked Kat up Saturday night, she had on a low-cut dress that accentuated her voluptuous figure.

"You look gorgeous," he said admiringly.

She put her arms around him. "I want to look good for you." She was clinging to him.

God, she really wants it! When Mallory spoke, his voice was husky. "Look, I have an idea, Kat. Before we go out to dinner, why don't we slip into the bedroom and . . ."

She was stroking his face. "Oh, darling, I wish we could. Paige is home." Paige was actually at the hospital, working.

"Oh."

"But after dinner . . ." She let the suggestion hang in the air.

"Yes?"

"We could go to your place."

Mallory put his arms around her and kissed her. "That's a wonderful idea!"

He took her to the Iron Horse, and they had a delicious dinner. In spite of herself, Kat was having a wonderful time. He was charming and amusing, and incredibly attractive. He seemed genuinely interested in knowing everything about her. She knew he was flattering her, but he really seemed to mean the compliments he paid her.

If I didn't know better . . .

Mallory had hardly tasted his food. All he could think was, *In two hours I will be making ten thousand dollars. . . . In one hour, I will be making ten thousand dollars. . . . In thirty minutes . . .*

They finished their coffee.

"Are you ready?" Mallory asked.

Kat put her hand over his. "You have no idea how ready, darling. Let's go."

They took a taxi to Mallory's apartment. "I'm absolutely crazy about you," Mallory murmured. "I've never known anyone like you."

And she could hear Grundy's voice: *He's so sure of himself that he says he's going to get you into bed by Saturday night.*

When they arrived at the apartment, Mallory paid the taxi driver and led Kat into the elevator. It seemed to Mallory to take forever to get up to his apartment. He opened the door and said eagerly, "Here it is."

Kat stepped inside.

It was an ordinary little bachelor's apartment that desperately needed a woman's touch.

"Oh, it's lovely," Kat breathed. She turned to Mallory. "It's *you*."

He grinned. "Let me show you *our* room. I'll put some music on."

As he went over to the tape deck, Kat glanced at her watch. The voice of Barbra Streisand filled the room.

Mallory took her hand. "Let's go, honey."

"Wait a minute," Kat said softly.

He was looking at her, puzzled. "What for?"

"I just want to enjoy this moment with you. You know, before we . . ."

"Why don't we enjoy it in the bedroom?"

"I'd love a drink."

"A drink?" He tried to hide his impatience. "Fine. What would you like?"

"A vodka and tonic, please."

He smiled. "I think we can handle that." He went over to the little bar and hurriedly mixed two drinks.

Kat looked at her watch again.

Mallory returned with the drinks and handed one to Kat. "Here you are, baby." He raised his glass. "To togetherness."

"To togetherness," Kat said. She took a

sip of the drink. "Oh, my God!"

He looked at her, startled. "What's the matter?"

"This is vodka!"

"That's what you asked for."

"Did I? I'm sorry. I hate vodka!" She stroked his face. "May I have a scotch and soda?"

"Sure." He swallowed his impatience and went back to the bar to mix another drink.

Kat glanced at her watch again.

Ken Mallory returned. "Here you are."

"Thank you, darling."

She took two sips of her drink. Mallory took the glass from her and set it on a table. He put his arms around Kat and held her close, and she could feel that he was aroused.

"Now," Ken said softly, "let's make history."

"Oh, yes!" Kat said. "Yes!"

She let him lead her into the bedroom.

I've done it! Mallory exulted. *I've done it! Here go the walls of Jericho!* He turned to Kat. "Get undressed, baby."

"You first, darling. I want to watch you get undressed. It excites me."

"Oh? Well, sure."

As Kat stood there watching, Mallory slowly took his clothes off. First his jacket, then his shirt and tie, then his shoes and stockings, and then his trousers. He had the firm figure of an athlete.

"Does this excite you, baby?"

"Oh, yes. Now take off your shorts."

Slowly Mallory let his shorts fall to the floor. He had a turgid erection.

"That's beautiful," Kat said.

"Now it's your turn."

"Right."

And at that moment, Kat's beeper went off.

Mallory was startled. "What the hell . . . ?"

"They're calling me," Kat said. "May I use your telephone?"

"Now?"

"Yes. It must be an emergency."

"Now? Can't it wait?"

"Darling, you know the rules."

"But . . ."

As Mallory watched, Kat walked over to the telephone and dialed a number. "Dr. Hunter." She listened. "Really? Of course. I'll be right there."

Mallory was staring at her, stupefied. "What's going on?"

"I have to get back to the hospital, angel."

"Now?"

"Yes. One of my patients is dying."

"Can't he wait until . . . ?"

"I'm sorry. We'll do this another night."

Ken Mallory stood there, buck naked, watching Kat walk out of his apartment, and as the door closed behind her, he picked up her drink and slammed it into the wall. *Bitch . . . bitch . . . bitch . . .*

When Kat got back to the apartment, Paige and Honey were eagerly waiting for her.

"How did it go?" Paige asked. "Was I on time?"

Kat laughed. "Your timing was perfect."

She began to describe the evening. When she came to the part about Mallory standing in the bedroom naked, with an erection, they laughed until tears came to their eyes.

Kat was tempted to tell them how enjoyable she really found Ken Mallory, but she felt foolish. After all, he was seeing her only so he could win a bet.

Somehow, Paige seemed to sense how Kat felt. "Be careful of him, Kat."

Kat smiled. "Don't worry. But I will admit that if I didn't know about that bet . . . He's a snake, but he gives good snake oil."

"When are you going to see him again?" Honey asked.

"I'm going to give him a week to cool off."

Paige was studying her. "Him or you?"

*   *   *

Dinetto's black limousine was waiting outside the hospital for Kat. This time, the Shadow was alone. Kat wished that Rhino were there. There was something about the Shadow that petrified her. He never smiled and seldom spoke, but he exuded menace.

"Get in," he said as Kat approached the car.

"Look," Kat said indignantly, "you tell Mr. Dinetto that he can't order me around. I don't work for him. Just because I did him a favor once . . . "

"Get in. You can tell him yourself."

Kat hesitated. It would be easy to walk away and not get involved any further, but how would it affect Mike? Kat got into the car.

The victim this time had been badly beaten, whipped with a chain. Lou Dinetto was there with him.

Kat took one look at the patient and said, "You've got to get him to a hospital right away."

"Kat," Dinetto said, "you have to treat him here."

"Why?" Kat demanded. But she knew the answer, and it terrified her.

Chapter Eighteen

It was one of those clear days in San Francisco when there was a magic in the air. The night wind had swept away the rainclouds, producing a crisp, sunny Sunday morning.

Jason had arranged to pick up Paige at the apartment. When he arrived, Paige was surprised at how pleased she was to see him.

"Good morning," Jason said. "You look beautiful."

"Thank you."

"What would you like to do today?"

Paige said, "It's your town. You lead, I'll follow."

"Fair enough."

"If you don't mind," Paige said, "I'd like to

make a quick stop at the hospital."

"I thought this was your day off."

"It is, but there's a patient I'm concerned about."

"No problem." Jason drove her to the hospital.

"I won't be long," Paige promised as she got out of the car.

"I'll wait for you here."

Paige went up to the third floor and into Jimmy Ford's room. He was still in a coma, attached to an array of tubes feeding him intravenously.

A nurse was in the room. She looked up as Paige entered. "Good morning, Dr. Taylor."

"Good morning." Paige walked over to the boy's bedside. "Has there been any change?"

"I'm afraid not."

Paige felt Jimmy's pulse and listened to his heartbeat.

"It's been several weeks now," the nurse said. "It doesn't look good, does it?"

"He's going to come out of it," Paige said firmly. She turned to the unconscious figure on the bed and raised her voice. "Do you hear me? You're going to get well!" There was no reaction. She closed her eyes a moment and said a silent prayer. "Have them beep me at once if there's any change."

"Yes, doctor."

He's not going to die, Paige thought. *I'm not going to let him die. . . .*

Jason got out of the car as Paige approached. "Is everything all right?"

There was no point in burdening him with her problems. "Everything's fine," Paige said.

"Let's play real tourists today," Jason said. "There's a state law that all tours have to start at Fisherman's Wharf."

Paige smiled. "We mustn't break the law."

Fisherman's Wharf was like an outdoor carnival. The street entertainers were out in full force. There were mimes, clowns, dancers, and musicians. Vendors were selling steaming caldrons of Dungeness crabs and clam chowder with fresh sourdough bread.

"There's no place like this in the world," Jason said warmly.

Paige was touched by his enthusiasm. She had seen Fisherman's Wharf before and most of the other tourist sites of San Francisco, but she did not want to spoil his fun.

"Have you ridden a cable car yet?" Jason asked.

"No." *Not since last week.*

"You haven't lived! Come along."

They walked to Powell Street and boarded a cable car. As they started up the steep grade, Jason said, "This was known as Hallidie's Folly. He built it in 1873."

"And I'll bet they said it wouldn't last!"

Jason laughed. "That's right. When I was going to high school, I used to work weekends as a tour guide."

"I'm sure you were good."

"The best. Would you like to hear some of my spiel?"

"I'd love to."

Jason adopted the nasal tone of a tour guide. "Ladies and gentlemen, for your information, the oldest street in San Francisco is Grant Avenue, the longest is Mission Street—seven and a half miles long—the widest is Van Ness Avenue at one hundred twenty-five feet, and you'll be surprised to know that the narrowest, DeForest Street, is only four and a half feet. That's right, ladies and gentlemen, four and a half feet. The steepest street we can offer you is Filbert Street, with a thirty-one and a half percent grade." He looked at Paige and grinned. "I'm surprised that I still remember all that."

When they alighted from the cable car, Paige looked up at Jason and smiled. "What's next?"

"We're going to take a carriage ride."

Ten minutes later, they were seated in a horse-drawn carriage that took them from Fisherman's Wharf to Ghirardelli Square to North Beach. Jason pointed out the places of interest along the way, and Paige was surprised at how much she was enjoying herself. *Don't let yourself get carried away.*

They went up to Coit Tower for a view of the city. As they ascended, Jason asked, "Are you hungry?"

The fresh air had made Paige very hungry. "Yes."

"Good. I'm going to take you to one of the best Chinese restaurants in the world—Tommy Toy's."

Paige had heard the hospital staff speak of it.

The meal turned out to be a banquet. They started with lobster pot stickers with chili sauce, and hot and sour soup with seafood. That was followed by filet of chicken with snow peas and pecans, veal filet with Szechuan sauce, and four-flavored fried rice. For dessert, they had a peach mousse. The food was wonderful.

"Do you come here often?" Paige asked.

"As often as I can."

There was a boyish quality about Jason

that Paige found very attractive.

"Tell me," Paige said, "did you always want to be an architect?"

"I had no choice." Jason grinned. "My first toys were Erector sets. It's exciting to dream about something and then watch that dream become concrete and bricks and stone, and soar up into the sky and become a part of the city you live in."

I'm going to build you a Taj Mahal. I don't care how long it takes!

"I'm one of the lucky ones, Paige, spending my life doing what I love to do. Who was it who said, 'Most people live lives of quiet desperation'?"

Sounds like a lot of my patients, Paige thought.

"There's nothing else I would want to do, or any other place I would want to live. This is a fabulous city." His voice was filled with excitement. "It has everything anyone could want. I never get tired of it."

Paige studied him for a moment, enjoying his enthusiasm. "You've never been married?"

Jason shrugged. "Once. We were both too young. It didn't work out."

"I'm sorry."

"No need to be. She's married to a very wealthy meat packer. Have you been married?"

I'm going to be a doctor, too, when I grow up. We'll get married, and we'll work together.
"No."

They took a bay cruise under the Golden Gate and Bay Bridge. Jason assumed his tour guide's voice again. "And there, ladies and gentlemen, is the storied Alcatraz, former home of some of the world's most infamous criminals—Machine Gun Kelly, Al Capone, and Robert Stroud, known as the Birdman! 'Alcatraz' means pelican in Spanish. It was originally called Isla de los Alcatraces, after the birds that were its only inhabitants. Do you know why they had hot showers every day for the prisoners here?"
"No."
"So that they wouldn't get used to the cold bay water when they were trying to escape."
"Is that true?" Paige asked.
"Have I ever lied to you?"

It was late afternoon when Jason said, "Have you ever been to Noe Valley?"
Paige shook her head. "No."
"I'd like to show it to you. It used to be farms and streams. Now it's filled with brightly colored Victorian homes and gardens.

The houses are very old, because it was about the only area spared in the 1906 earthquake."

"It sounds lovely."

Jason hesitated. "My home is there. Would you like to see it?" He saw Paige's reaction. "Paige, I'm in love with you."

"We hardly know each other. How could you . . . ?"

"I knew it from the moment you said, 'Don't you know you're supposed to wear a white coat on rounds?' That's when I fell in love with you."

"Jason . . ."

"I'm a firm believer in love at first sight. My grandfather saw my grandmother riding a bicycle in the park and he followed her, and they got married three months later. They were together for fifty years, until he died. My father saw my mother crossing a street, and he knew she was going to be his wife. They've been married for forty-five years. You see, it runs in the family. I want to marry you."

It was the moment of truth.

Paige looked at Jason and thought, *He's the first man I've been attracted to since Alfred. He's adorable and bright and genuine. He's everything a woman could want in a man. What's the matter with me? I'm holding on to a ghost.* Yet deep inside her, she still had the overpowering feeling that one day Alfred was going to come back to her.

She looked at Jason and made her decision. "Jason . . ."

And at that moment, Paige's beeper went off. It sounded urgent, ominous.

"Paige . . ."

"I have to get to a telephone." Two minutes later, she was talking to the hospital.

Jason watched Paige's face turn pale.

She was shouting into the telephone, "No! Absolutely not! Tell them I'll be right there." She slammed the phone down.

"What is it?" Jason asked.

She turned to him, and her eyes were filled with tears. "It's Jimmy Ford, my patient. They're going to take him off the respirator. They're going to let him die."

When Paige reached Jimmy Ford's room, there were three people there beside the comatose figure in bed: George Englund, Benjamin Wallace, and a lawyer, Silvester Damone.

"What's going on here?" Paige demanded.

Benjamin Wallace said, "At the hospital ethics committee meeting this morning, it was decided that Jimmy Ford's condition is hopeless. We've decided to remove—"

"No!" Paige said. "You can't! I'm his doctor. I say he has a chance to come out of it! We're *not* going to let him die."

Silvester Damone spoke up. "It's not your decision to make, doctor."

Paige looked at him defiantly. "Who are you?"

"I'm the family's attorney." He pulled out a document and handed it to Paige. "This is Jimmy Ford's living will. It specifically states that if he has a life-threatening trauma, he's not to be kept alive by mechanical means."

"But I've been monitoring his condition," Paige pleaded. "He's been stabilized for weeks. He could come out of it any moment."

"Can you guarantee that?" Damone asked.

"No, but . . ."

"Then you'll have to do as you're ordered, doctor."

Paige looked down at the figure of Jimmy. "No! You have to wait a little longer."

The lawyer said smoothly, "Doctor, I'm sure it benefits the hospital to keep patients here as long as possible, but the family cannot afford the medical expenses any longer. I'm ordering you now to take him off the respirator."

"Just another day or two," Paige said

desperately, "and I'm sure . . ."

"No," Damone said firmly. "Today."

George Englund turned to Paige. "I'm sorry, but I'm afraid we have no choice."

"Thank you, doctor," the lawyer said. "I'll leave it to you to handle it. I'll notify the family that it will be taken care of immediately, so they can begin to make the funeral arrangements." He turned to Benjamin Wallace. "Thank you for your cooperation. Good day."

They watched him walk out of the room.

"We can't do this to Jimmy!" Paige said.

Dr. Wallace cleared his throat. "Paige . . ."

"What if we got him out of here and hid him in another room? There must be something we haven't thought of. Something . . ."

Benjamin Wallace said, "This isn't a request. It's an order." He turned to George Englund. "Do you want to . . . ?"

"No!" Paige said. "I'll . . . I'll do it."

"Very well."

"If you don't mind, I'd like to be alone with him."

George Englund squeezed her arm. "I'm sorry, Paige."

"I know."

Paige watched the two men leave the room.

She was alone with the unconscious boy.

She looked at the respirator that was keeping him alive and the IVs that were feeding his body. It would be so simple to turn the respirator off, to snuff out a life. But he had had so many wonderful dreams, such high hopes.

I'm going to be a doctor one day. I want to be like you.

Did you know I'm getting married? . . . Her name is Betsy. . . . We're going to have half a dozen kids. The first girl is going to be named Paige.

He had so very much to live for.

Paige stood there looking down at him, tears blurring the room. "Damn you!" she said. "You're a quitter!" She was sobbing now. "What happened to those dreams of yours? I thought you wanted to become a doctor! Answer me! Do you hear me? Open your eyes!" She looked down at the pale figure. There was no reaction. "I'm sorry," Paige said. "I'm so sorry." She leaned down to kiss him on the cheek, and as she slowly straightened up, she was looking into his open eyes.

"Jimmy! *Jimmy!*"

He blinked and closed his eyes again. Paige squeezed his hand. She leaned forward and said through her sobs, "Jimmy, did you hear the one about the patient who was being fed intravenously? He asked the doctor for an extra bottle. He was having a guest for lunch."

Chapter Nineteen

Honey was happier than she had ever been in her life. She had a warm relationship with patients that few of the other doctors had. She genuinely cared about them. She worked in geriatrics, in pediatrics, and in various other wards, and Dr. Wallace saw to it that she was given assignments that kept her out of harm's way. He wanted to make sure that she stayed at the hospital and was available to him.

Honey envied the nurses. They were able to nurture their patients without worrying about major medical decisions. *I never wanted to be a doctor,* Honey thought. *I always wanted to be a nurse.*

There are no nurses in the Taft family.

*　*　*

In the afternoons when Honey left the hospital, she would go shopping at the Bay Company, and Streetlight Records, and buy gifts for the children in pediatric care.

"I love children," she told Kat.

"Are you planning to have a large family?"

"Someday," Honey said wistfully. "I have to find their father first."

One of Honey's favorite patients in the geriatric ward was Daniel McGuire, a cheerful man in his nineties who was suffering from a diseased liver condition. He had been a gambler in his youth, and he liked to make bets with Honey.

"I'll bet you fifty cents the orderly is late with my breakfast."

"I'll bet you a dollar it's going to rain this afternoon."

"I'll bet you the Giants win."

Honey always took his bets.

"I'll bet you ten to one I beat this thing," he said.

"This time I'm not going to bet you," Honey told him. "I'm on your side."

He took her hand. "I know you are." He grinned. "If I were a few months younger . . ."

Honey laughed. "Never mind. I like older men."

One morning a letter came to him addressed to the hospital. Honey took it to him in his room.

"Read it to me, would you?" His eyesight had faded.

"Of course," Honey said. She opened the envelope, looked at it a moment, and let out a cry. "You've won the lottery! Fifty thousand dollars! Congratulations!"

"How about that?" He yelled. "I always knew I'd win the lottery one day! Give me a hug."

Honey leaned down and hugged him.

"You know something, Honey? I'm the luckiest man in the world."

When Honey came back to visit him that afternoon, he had passed away.

Honey was in the doctors' lounge when Dr. Stevens walked in. "Is there a Virgo here?"

One of the doctors laughed. "If you mean a virgin, I doubt it."

"A *Virgo*," Stevens repeated. "I need a Virgo."

"I'm a Virgo," Honey said. "What's the problem?"

He walked up to her. "The problem is that

I have a goddam maniac on my hands. She won't let anyone near her but a Virgo."

Honey got up. "I'll go see her."

"Thanks. Her name is Frances Gordon."

Frances Gordon had just had a hip replacement. The moment Honey walked into the room, the woman looked up and said, "You're a Virgo. Born on the cusp, right?"

Honey smiled. "That's right."

"Those Aquarians and Leos don't know what the hell they're doin'. They treat patients like they're meat."

"The doctors here are very good," Honey protested. "They—"

"Ha! Most of them are in it for the money." She looked at Honey more closely. "You're different."

Honey scanned the chart at the foot of the bed, a surprised look on her face.

"What's the matter? What are you lookin' at?"

Honey blinked. "It says here that your occupation is a . . . a psychic."

Frances Gordon nodded. "That's right. Don't you believe in psychics?"

Honey shook her head. "I'm afraid not."

"That's too bad. Sit down a minute."

Honey took a chair.

"Let me hold your hand."

Honey shook her head. "I really don't . . ."

"C'mon, give me your hand."

Reluctantly, Honey let her take her hand.

Frances Gordon held it for a moment, and closed her eyes. When she opened them, she said, "You've had a difficult life, haven't you?"

Everyone has had a difficult life, Honey thought. *Next she'll be telling me that I'll be taking a trip across the water.*

"You've used a lot of men, haven't you?"

Honey felt herself stiffen.

"There's been some kind of change in you—just recently—hasn't there?"

Honey could not wait to get out of the room. The woman was making her nervous. She started to pull away.

"You're going to fall in love."

Honey said, "I'm afraid I really have to . . ."

"He's an artist."

"I don't know any artists."

"You will." Frances Gordon let go of her hand. "Come back and see me," she commanded.

"Sure."

Honey fled.

* * *

Honey stopped in to visit Mrs. Owens, a new patient, a thin woman who appeared to be in her late forties. Her chart noted that she was twenty-eight. She had a broken nose and two black eyes, and her face was puffy and bruised.

Honey walked up to the bed. "I'm Dr. Taft."

The woman looked at her with dull, expressionless eyes. She remained silent.

"What happened to you?"

"I fell down some stairs." When she opened her mouth, she revealed a gap where two front teeth were missing.

Honey glanced at the chart. "It says here that you have two broken ribs and a fractured pelvis."

"Yeah. It was a bad fall."

"How did you get the black eyes?"

"When I fell."

"Are you married?"

"Yeah."

"Any children?"

"Two."

"What does your husband do?"

"Let's leave my husband out of this, okay?"

"I'm afraid it's not okay," Honey said. "Is he the one who beat you up?"

"No one beat me up."

"I'm going to have to file a police report."

Mrs. Owens was suddenly panicky. "No! Please don't!"

"Why not?"

"He'll kill me! You don't know him!"

"Has he beaten you up before?"

"Yes, but he . . . he doesn't mean anything by it. He gets drunk and loses his temper."

"Why haven't you left him?"

Mrs. Owens shrugged, and the movement caused her pain. "The kids and I have nowhere to go."

Honey was listening, furious. "You don't have to take this, you know. There are shelters and agencies that will take care of you and protect you and the children."

The woman shook her head in despair. "I have no money. I lost my job as a secretary when he started . . ." She could not go on.

Honey squeezed her hand. "You're going to be fine. I'll see that you're taken care of."

Five minutes later Honey marched into Dr. Wallace's office. He was delighted to see her. He wondered what she had brought with her this time. At various times, she had used warm honey, hot water, melted chocolate, and—his favorite—maple syrup. Her ingenuity was boundless.

"Lock the door, baby."

"I can't stay, Ben. I have to get back."

She told him about her patient.

"You'll have to file a police report," Wallace said. "It's the law."

"The law hasn't protected her before. Look, all she wants to do is get away from her husband. She worked as a secretary. Didn't you say you needed a new file clerk?"

"Well, yes, but . . . wait a minute!"

"Thanks," Honey said. "We'll get her on her feet, and find her a place to live, and she'll have a new job!"

Wallace sighed. "I'll see what I can do."

"I knew you would," Honey said.

The next morning, Honey went back to see Mrs. Owens.

"How are you feeling today?" Honey asked.

"Better, thanks. When can I go home? My husband doesn't like it when—"

"Your husband is not going to bother you anymore," Honey said firmly. "You'll stay here until we find a place for you and the children to live, and when you're well enough, you're going to have a job here at the hospital."

Mrs. Owens stared at her unbelievingly. "Do . . . do you mean that?"

"Absolutely. You'll have your own apartment with your children. You won't have to put up with the kind of horror you've been living through, and you'll have a decent, respectable job."

Mrs. Owens clutched Honey's hand. "I don't know how to thank you," she sobbed. "You don't know what it has been like."

"I can imagine," Honey said. "You're going to be fine."

The woman nodded, too choked up to speak.

The following day when Honey returned to see Mrs. Owens, the room was empty.

"Where is she?" Honey asked.

"Oh," the nurse said, "she left this morning with her husband."

Her name was on the PA system again. "Dr. Taft . . . Room 215. . . . Dr. Taft . . . Room 215."

In the corridor Honey ran into Kat. "How's your day going?" Kat asked.

"You wouldn't believe it!" Honey told her.

Dr. Ritter was waiting for her in Room 215. In bed was an Indian man in his late twenties.

Dr. Ritter said, "This is your patient?"

"Yes."

"It says here that he speaks no English. Right?"

"Yes."

He showed her the chart. "And this is your writing? Vomiting, cramps, thirst, dehydration . . ."

"That's right," Honey said.

". . . absence of peripheral pulse . . ."

"Yes."

"And what was your diagnosis?"

"Stomach flu."

"Did you take a stool sample?"

"No. What for?"

"Because your patient has cholera, that's what for!" He was screaming. "We're going to have to close down the fucking hospital!"

Chapter Twenty

"*Cholera?* Are you telling me this hospital has a patient with *cholera?*" Benjamin Wallace yelled.

"I'm afraid so."

"Are you absolutely *sure?*"

"No question," Dr. Ritter said. "His stool is swarming with vibrios. He has low arterial pH, with hypotension, tachycardia, and cyanosis."

By law, all cases of cholera and other infectious diseases must immediately be reported to the state health board and to the Centers for Disease Control in Atlanta.

"We're going to have to report it, Ben."

"They'll close us down!" Wallace stood up and began to pace. "We can't afford that. I'll be goddamned if I'm going to put every patient in this hospital under quarantine." He stopped pacing for a moment. "Does the patient know what he has?"

"No. He doesn't speak English. He's from India."

"Who has had contact with him?"

"Two nurses and Dr. Taft."

"And Dr. Taft diagnosed it as stomach flu?"

"Right. I suppose you're going to dismiss her."

"Well, no," Wallace said. "Anyone can make a mistake. Let's not be hasty. Does the patient's chart read stomach flu?"

"Yes."

Wallace made his decision. "Let's leave it that way. Here's what I want you to do. Start intravenous rehydration—use lactated Ringer's solution. Also give him tetracycline. If we can restore his blood volume and fluid immediately, he could be close to normal in a few hours."

"We aren't going to report this?" Dr. Ritter asked.

Wallace looked him in the eye. "Report a case of stomach flu?"

"What about the nurses and Dr. Taft?"

"Give them tetracycline, too. What's the patient's name?"

"Pandit Jawah."

"Put him in quarantine for forty-eight hours. He'll either be cured by then or dead."

Honey was in a panic. She went to find Paige.

"I need your help."

"What's the problem?"

Honey told her. "I wish you would talk to him. He doesn't speak English, and you speak Indian."

"Hindi."

"Whatever. Will you talk to him?"

"Of course."

Ten minutes later, Paige was talking to Pandit Jawah.

"*Aap ki tabyat kaisi hai?*"

"*Karab hai.*"

"*Aap jald acha ko hum kardenge.*"

"*Bhagwan aap ki soney ga.*"

"*Aap ka ilaj hum jalb shuroo kardenge.*"

"*Shukria.*"

"*Dost kiss liay hain?*"

Paige took Honey outside in the corridor.

"What did he say?"

"He said he feels terrible. I told him he's going to get well. He said to tell it to God. I told him we're going to start treatment immediately. He said he's grateful."

"So am I."

"What are friends for?"

Cholera is a disease that can cause death within twenty-four hours from dehydration, or that can be cured within a few hours.

Five hours after his treatment began, Pandit Jawah was nearly back to normal.

Paige stopped in to see Jimmy Ford.

His face lit up when he saw her. "Hi." His voice was weak, but he had improved miraculously.

"How are you feeling?" Paige asked.

"Great. Did you hear about the doctor who said to his patient, 'The best thing you can do is give up smoking, stop drinking, and cut down on your sex life'? The patient said, 'I don't deserve the best. What's the second best?' "

And Paige knew Jimmy Ford was going to get well.

Ken Mallory was getting off duty and was on his way to meet Kat when he heard his name being paged. He hesitated, debating whether or not simply to slip out. His name was paged once more. Reluctantly, he picked up a telephone. "Dr. Mallory."

"Doctor, could you come to ER Two, please? We have a patient here who—"

"Sorry," Mallory said, "I just checked out. Find someone else."

"There's no one else available who can handle this. It's a bleeding ulcer, and the patient's condition is critical. I'm afraid we're going to lose him if . . ."

Damn! "All right. I'll be right there." *I'll have to call Kat and tell her I'll be late.*

The patient in the emergency room was a man in his sixties. He was semiconscious, ghost-pale, perspiring, and breathing hard, obviously in enormous pain. Mallory took one look at him and said, "Get him into an OR, stat!"

Fifteen minutes later, Mallory had the patient on an operating table. The anesthesiologist was monitoring his blood pressure. "It's dropping fast."

"Pump some more blood into him."

Ken Mallory began the operation, working against time. It took only a moment to cut through the skin, and after that, the layer of fat, the fascia, the muscle, and finally the smooth, transparent peritoneum, the lining of the abdomen. Blood was pouring into the stomach.

"Bovie!" Mallory said. "Get me four units of blood from the blood bank." He began to cauterize the bleeding vessels.

The operation took four hours, and when it was over, Mallory was exhausted. He looked down at the patient and said, "He's going to live."

One of the nurses gave Mallory a warm smile. "It's a good thing you were here, Dr. Mallory."

He looked over at her. She was young and pretty and obviously open to an invitation. *I'll get to you later, baby,* Mallory thought. He turned to a junior resident, "Close him up and get him into the recovery room. I'll check on him in the morning."

Mallory debated whether to telephone Kat, but it was midnight. He sent her two dozen roses.

When Mallory checked in at 6:00 A.M., he stopped by the recovery room to see his new patient.

"He's awake," the nurse said.

Mallory walked over to the bed. "I'm Dr. Mallory. How do you feel?"

"When I think of the alternative, I feel

fine," the patient said weakly. "They tell me you saved my life. This was the damnedest thing. I was in the car on my way to a dinner party, and I got this sudden pain and I guess I blacked out. Fortunately, we were only a block away from the hospital, and they brought me to the emergency room here."

"You were lucky. You lost a lot of blood."

"They told me that in another ten minutes, I would have been gone. I want to thank you, doctor."

Mallory shrugged. "I was just doing my job."

The patient was studying him carefully. "I'm Alex Harrison."

The name meant nothing to Mallory. "Glad to know you, Mr. Harrison." He was checking Harrison's pulse. "Are you in any pain now?"

"A bit, but I guess they have me pretty well doped up."

"The anesthetic will wear off," Mallory assured him. "So will the pain. You're going to be fine."

"How long will I have to be in the hospital?"

"We should have you out of here in a few days."

A clerk from the business office came in, carrying some hospital forms. "Mr. Harrison, for our records, the hospital needs to know whether you have medical coverage."

"You mean you want to know if I can pay my bill."

"Well, I wouldn't put it like that, sir."

"You might check with the San Francisco Fidelity Bank," he said dryly. "I own it."

In the afternoon, when Mallory stopped by to see Alex Harrison, there was an attractive woman with him. She was in her early thirties, blond and trim, and elegant-looking. She was wearing an Adolfo dress that Mallory figured must have cost more than his monthly salary.

"Ah! Here's our hero," Alex Harrison said. "It's Dr. Mallory, isn't it?"

"Yes. Ken Mallory."

"Dr. Mallory, this is my daughter, Lauren."

She held out a slim, manicured hand. "Father tells me you saved his life."

He smiled. "That's what doctors are for."

Lauren was looking over him approvingly. "Not all doctors."

It was obvious to Mallory that these two did not belong in a county hospital. He said to Alex Harrison, "You're coming along fine, but perhaps you'd feel more comfortable if you called your own doctor."

Alex Harrison shook his head. "That won't be necessary. He didn't save my life. You did. Do you like it here?"

It was a strange question. "It's interesting, yes. Why?"

Harrison sat up in bed. "Well, I was just thinking. A good-looking fellow as capable as you are could have a damned bright future. I don't think you have much of a future in a place like this."

"Well, I . . ."

"Maybe it was fate that brought me here."

Lauren spoke up. "I think what my father is trying to say is that he would like to show you his appreciation."

"Lauren is right. You and I should have a serious talk when I get out of here. I'd like you to come up to the house for dinner."

Mallory looked at Lauren and said slowly, "I'd like that."

And it changed his life.

Ken Mallory was having a surprisingly difficult time getting together with Kat.

"How's Monday night, Kat?"

"Wonderful."

"Good. I'll pick you up at—"

"Wait! I just remembered. A cousin from New York is coming to town for the night."

"Well, Tuesday?"

"I'm on call Tuesday."

"What about Wednesday?"

"I promised Paige and Honey that we'd do something together Wednesday."

Mallory was getting desperate. His time was running out too fast.

"Thursday?"

"Thursday is fine."

"Great. Shall I pick you up?"

"No. Why don't we meet at Chez Panisse?"

"Very well. Eight o'clock?"

"Perfect."

Mallory waited at the restaurant until nine o'clock and then telephoned Kat. There was no answer. He waited another half hour. *Maybe she misunderstood,* he thought. *She wouldn't deliberately break a date with me.*

The following morning, he saw Kat at the hospital. She ran up to him.

"Oh, Ken, I'm so sorry! It was the silliest thing. I decided to take a little nap before our date. I fell asleep and when I woke up it was the middle of the night. Poor darling. Did you wait for me long?"

"No, no. It's all right." *The stupid woman!* He moved closer to her. "I want to finish what we started, baby. I go crazy when I think about you."

"Me, too," Kat said. "I can't wait."

"Maybe next weekend we can . . ."

"Oh, dear. I'm busy over the weekend."

And so it went.

The clock was running.

Kat was reporting events to Paige when her beeper went off.

"Excuse me." Kat picked up a telephone. "Dr. Hunter." She listened a moment. "Thanks. I'll be right there." She replaced the receiver. "I have to go. Emergency."

Paige sighed. "What else is new?"

Kat strode down the corridor and took an elevator down to the emergency room. Inside were two dozen cots, all of them occupied. Kat thought of it as the suffering room, filled day and night with victims of automobile accidents, gunshots or knife wounds, and twisted limbs. A kaleidoscope of broken lives. To Kat it was a small corner of hell.

An orderly hurried up to her. "Dr. Hunter . . ."

"What have we got?" Kat asked. They were moving toward a cot at the far end of the room.

"He's unconscious. It looks as though someone beat him up. His face and head are battered, he has a broken nose, a dislocated shoulder blade, at least two different fractures to his right arm, and . . ."

"Why did you call me?"

"The paramedics think there's a head injury. There could be brain damage."

They had reached the cot where the victim lay. His face was caked with blood, swollen and bruised. He was wearing alligator shoes and . . . Kat's heart skipped a beat. She leaned forward and took a closer look. It was Lou Dinetto.

Kat ran skillful fingers over his scalp and examined his eyes. There was a definite concussion.

She hurried over to a telephone and dialed. "This is Dr. Hunter. I want a head CAT scan done. The patient's name is Dinetto. Lou Dinetto. Send down a gurney, stat."

Kat replaced the receiver and turned her attention back to Dinetto. She said to the orderly, "Stay with him. When the gurney arrives, take him to the third floor. I'll be waiting."

Thirty minutes later on the third floor, Kat was studying the CAT scan she had ordered. "He has some brain hemorrhaging, he has a high fever, and he's in shock. I want him stabilized for twenty-four hours. I'll decide then when we'll operate."

Kat wondered whether what had happened to Dinetto might affect Mike.

And how.

Paige stopped by to see Jimmy. He was feeling much better.

"Did you hear about the flasher in the garment district? He walked up to a little old lady and opened up his raincoat. She studied him a moment and said, 'You call *that* a lining?' "

Kat was having dinner with Mallory at an intimate little restaurant near the bay. Seated across from Mallory, studying him, Kat felt guilty. *I should never have started this,* she thought. *I know what he is, and yet I'm having a wonderful time. Damn the man! But I can't stop our plan now.*

They had finished their coffee.

Kat leaned forward. "Can we go to your place, Ken?"

"You bet!" *Finally,* Mallory thought.

Kat shifted in her chair uncomfortably and frowned. "Uh, oh!"

"Are you all right?" Mallory asked.

"I don't know. Would you excuse me for a moment?"

"Certainly." He watched her get up and head for the ladies' room.

When she returned, she said, "It's bad timing, darling. I'm so sorry. You'd better get me home."

He stared at her, trying to conceal his frustration. The damned fates were conspiring against him.

"Right," Mallory said curtly. He was ready to explode.

He was going to lose a precious five days.

Five minutes after Kat returned to the apartment, the front doorbell rang. Kat smiled to herself. Mallory had found an excuse to come back, and she hated herself for being so pleased. She walked over to the door and opened it.

"Ken . . ."

Rhino and the Shadow were standing there. Kat felt a sudden sense of fear. The two men pushed past her into the apartment.

Rhino spoke. "You doin' the operation on Mr. Dinetto?"

Kat's throat was dry. "Yes."

"We don't want anything to happen to him."

"Neither do I," Kat said. "Now, if you'll excuse me. I'm tired and—"

"Is there a chance he'll die?" the Shadow asked.

Kat hesitated. "In brain surgery there's always a risk of—"

"You better not let it happen."

"Believe me, I—"

"Don't let it happen." He looked at Rhino. "Let's go."

Kat watched them start to leave.

At the door, the Shadow turned and said, "Say hello to Mike for us."

Kat was suddenly very still. "Is . . . is this some kind of threat?"

"We don't threaten people, doc. We're telling you. If Mr. Dinetto dies, you and your fucking family are gonna be wiped out."

Chapter Twenty-one

In the doctors' dressing room, half a dozen doctors were waiting for Ken Mallory to appear.

When he walked in, Grundy said, "Hail the conquering hero! We want to hear all the lurid details." He grinned. "But the catch is, buddy, we want to hear them from *her*."

"I ran into a little bad luck." Mallory smiled. "But you can all start getting your money ready."

Kat and Paige were getting into scrubs.

"Have you ever done a procedure on a doctor?" Kat asked.

"No."

"You're lucky. They're the worst patients in the world. They know too much."

"Who are you operating on?"

"Dr. Mervyn 'Don't Hurt Me' Franklin."

"Good luck."

"I'll need it."

Dr. Mervyn Franklin was a man in his sixties, thin, bald, and irascible.

When Kat walked into his room, he snapped, "It's about time you got here. Did the damned electrolyte reports come back?"

"Yes," Kat said. "They're normal."

"Who says so? I don't trust the damn lab. Half the time they don't know what they're doing. And make sure there's no mix-up on the blood transfusion."

"I'll make sure," Kat said patiently.

"Who's doing the operation?"

"Dr. Jurgenson and I. Dr. Franklin, I promise you, there's nothing for you to worry about."

"Whose brain are they operating on, yours or mine? All operations are risky. You know why? Because half of the damned surgeons are in the wrong profession. They should have been butchers."

"Dr. Jurgenson is very capable."

"I know he is, or I wouldn't let him touch me. Who's the anesthesiologist?"

"I believe it's Dr. Miller."

"That quack? I don't want him. Get me someone else."

"Dr. Franklin . . ."

"Get me someone else. See if Haliburton is available."

"All right."

"And get me the names of the nurses in the OR. I want to check them out."

Kat looked him in the eye. "Would you prefer to do the operation yourself?"

"What?" He stared at her a moment, then smiled sheepishly. "I guess not."

Kat said gently, "Then why don't you let us handle it?"

"Okay. You know something? I like you."

"I like you, too. Did the nurse give you a sedative?"

"Yes."

"All right. We'll be ready in a few minutes. Is there anything I can do for you?"

"Yeah. Teach my stupid nurse where my veins are located."

In OR Four, the brain surgery on Dr. Mervyn Franklin was going perfectly. He had complained every step of the way from his room to the operating theater.

"Now mind you," he said, "minimal anesthetic. The brain has no feeling, so once you get in there, you won't need much."

"I'm aware of that," Kat said patiently.

"And see that the temperature is kept down to forty degrees. That's maximum."

"Right."

"Let's have some fast music on during the operation. Keep you all on your toes."

"Right."

"And make sure you have a top scrub nurse in there."

"Right."

And on and on it went.

When the opening in Dr. Franklin's skull was drilled, Kat said, "I see the clot. It doesn't look too bad." She went to work.

Three hours later as they were beginning to close the incision, George Englund, the chief of surgery, came into the operating room and went up to Kat.

"Kat, are you almost through here?"

"We're just wrapping it up."

"Let Dr. Jurgenson take over. We need you fast. There's an emergency."

Kat nodded. "Coming." She turned to Jurgenson. "Will you finish up here?"

"No problem."

Kat walked out with George Englund. "What's happening?"

"You were scheduled to do an operation later, but your patient has started to hemorrhage. They're taking him to OR Three now. It doesn't look as though he's going to make it. You'll have to operate right away."

"Who?"

"A Mr. Dinetto."

Kat looked at him aghast. *"Dinetto?" If Mr. Dinetto dies, you and your fucking family are gonna be wiped out.*

Kat hurried down the corridor that led to OR Three. Approaching her were Rhino and the Shadow.

"What's going on?" Rhino demanded.

Kat's mouth was so dry that it was difficult to speak. "Mr. Dinetto started hemorrhaging. We must operate right away."

The Shadow grabbed her arm. "Then do it! But remember what we told you. Keep him alive."

Kat pulled away and hurried into the operating room.

Because of the change in schedule, Dr. Vance was doing the operation with Kat. He was a good surgeon. Kat began the ritual scrub: a half minute on each arm first, then a half minute on each hand. She repeated it and then scrubbed her nails.

Dr. Vance stepped in beside her and started his scrub. "How are you feeling?"

"Fine," Kat lied.

Lou Dinetto was wheeled into the operating room on a gurney, semiconscious, and carefully transferred to the operating table. His shaven head was scrubbed and painted with Merthiolate solution that gleamed a bright orange under the operating lights. He was as pale as death.

The team was in place: Dr. Vance, another resident, an anesthesiologist, two scrub nurses, and a circulating nurse. Kat checked to make sure that everything they might require was there. She glanced at the wall monitors—oxygen saturation, carbon dioxide, temperature, muscle stimulators, precordial stethoscope, EKG, automatic blood pressure, and disconnect alarms. Everything was in order.

The anesthesiologist strapped a blood pressure cuff on Dinetto's right arm, then placed a rubber mask over the patient's face. "All right, now. Breathe deeply. Take three big breaths."

Dinetto was asleep before the third breath.

The procedure began.

Kat was reporting aloud. "There's an area of damage in the middle of the brain, caused by a clot that's broken off the aorta valve. It's blocking a small blood vessel on the right side of the brain and extending slightly into the left half." She probed deeper. "It's at the lower edge of the aqueduct of Sylvius. Scalpel."

A tiny burr hole about the size of a dime was made by an electric drill to expose the dura mater. Next, Kat cut open the dura to expose a segment of the cerebral cortex that lay underneath. "Forceps!"

The scrub nurse handed her the electric forceps.

The incision was held open by a small retractor which maintained itself in place.

"There's a hell of a lot of bleeding," Vance said.

Kat picked up the bovie and started to cauterize the bleeders. "We're going to control it."

Dr. Vance started suction on soft cotton patties that were placed on the dura. The oozing veins on the surface of the dura were identified and coagulated.

"It looks good," Vance said. "He's going to make it."

Kat breathed a sigh of relief.

And at that instant, Lou Dinetto stiffened and his body went into spasm. The anesthesiologist called out, "Blood pressure's dropping!"

Kat said, "Get some more blood into him!"

They were all looking at the monitor. The curve was rapidly flattening out. There were two quick heartbeats followed by ventricular fibrillation.

"Shock him!" Kat snapped. She quickly attached the electric pads to his body and turned on the machine.

Dinetto's chest heaved up once and then fell.

"Inject him with epinephrine! Quick!"

"No heartbeat!" the anesthesiologist called out a moment later.

Kat tried again, raising the dial.

Once again, there was a quick convulsive movement.

"No heartbeat!" the anesthesiologist cried. "Asystole. No rhythm at all."

Desperately, Kat tried one last time. The body rose higher this time, then fell again. Nothing.

"He's dead," Dr. Vance said.

Chapter Twenty-two

Code Red is an alert that immediately brings all-out medical assistance to try to save the life of a patient. When Lou Dinetto's heart stopped in the middle of his operation, the operating room Code Red team rushed to give aid.

Over the public address system Kat could hear, "Code Red, OR Three. . . . Code Red . . ." *Red rhymes with dead.*

Kat was in a panic. She applied the electroshock again. It was not only his life she was trying to save—it was Mike's and her own. Dinetto's body leaped into the air, then fell back, inert.

"Try once more!" Dr. Vance urged.

We don't threaten people, doc. We're tell-

ing you. If Mr. Dinetto dies, you and your fuck-ing family are gonna be wiped out.

Kat turned on the switch and applied the machine to Dinetto's chest again. Once more his body rose a few inches into the air and then fell back.

"Again!"

It's not going to happen, Kat thought de-spairingly. *I'm going to die with him.*

The operating room was suddenly filled with doctors and nurses.

"What are you waiting for?" someone asked.

Kat took a deep breath and pressed down once again. For an instant, nothing happened. Then a faint blip appeared on the monitor. It faltered a moment, then appeared again and faltered, and then began to grow stronger and stronger, until it became a steady, stabilized rhythm.

Kat stared at it unbelievingly.

There was a cheer from the crowded room. "He's going to make it!" someone yelled.

"Jesus, that was close!"

They have no idea how close, Kat thought.

Two hours later, Lou Dinetto was off the table and on a gurney, on his way back to in-tensive care. Kat was at his side. Rhino and the Shadow were waiting in the corridor.

"The operation was successful," Kat said. "He's going to be fine."

Ken Mallory was in deep trouble. It was the last day to make good on his bet. The problem had been growing so gradually that he had hardly been aware of it. From almost the first night, he had been positive that he would have no trouble getting Kat into bed. *Trouble? She's eager for it!* Now his time was up, and he was facing disaster.

Mallory thought about all the things that had gone wrong—Kat's roommates coming in just as she was about to go to bed with him, the difficulty of getting together for a date, Kat's being called away by her beeper and leaving him standing naked, her cousin coming to town, her oversleeping, her period. He stopped suddenly and thought, *Wait a minute! They couldn't have all been coincidences!* Kat was doing this to him deliberately! She had somehow gotten wind of the bet, and had decided to make a fool of him, to play a joke on him, a joke that was going to cost him ten thousand dollars that he didn't have. *The bitch!* He was no closer to winning than he had been at the beginning. She had deliberately led him on. *How the hell did I let myself get into this?* He knew there was no way he could come up with the money.

When Mallory walked into the doctors' dressing room, they were waiting for him.

"Payoff day!" Grundy sang out.

Mallory forced a smile. "I have until midnight, right? Believe me, she's ready, fellows."

There was a snicker. "Sure. We'll believe you when we hear it from the lady herself. Just have the cash ready in the morning."

Mallory laughed. "You'd better have *yours* ready!"

He *had* to find a way. And suddenly he had the answer.

Ken Mallory found Kat in the lounge. He sat down opposite her. "I hear you saved a patient's life."

"And my own."

"What?"

"Nothing."

"How would you like to save my life?"

Kat looked at him quizzically.

"Have dinner with me tonight."

"I'm too tired, Ken." She was weary of the game she was playing with him. *I've had enough,* Kat thought. *It's time to stop. It's over. I've fallen into my own trap.* She wished he were a different kind of man. If only he had been honest with her. *I really could have cared for him,* Kat thought.

There was no way Mallory was going to let Kat get away. "We'll make it an early night," he coaxed. "You have to have dinner somewhere."

Reluctantly, Kat nodded. She knew it was going to be the last time. She was going to tell him she knew about the bet. She was going to end the game. "All right."

Honey finished her shift at 4:00 P.M. She looked at her watch and decided that she had just enough time to do some quick shopping. She went to the Candelier to buy some candles for the apartment, then to the San Francisco Tea and Coffee Company so there would be some drinkable coffee for breakfast, and on to Chris Kelly for linens.

Loaded down with packages, Honey headed for the apartment. *I'll fix myself some dinner at home,* Honey decided. She knew that Kat had a date with Mallory, and that Paige was on call.

Fumbling with her packages, Honey entered the apartment and closed the door behind her. She switched on the light. A huge black man was coming out of the bathroom, dripping blood on the white carpet. He was pointing a gun at her.

"Make one sound, and I'll blow your fucking head off!"

Honey screamed.

Chapter Twenty-three

Mallory was seated across from Kat at Schroeder's restaurant on Front Street.

It's the bottom of the ninth, he thought, *and so far it's a shutout.* What was going to happen when he couldn't pay the ten thousand dollars? Word would spread quickly around the hospital, and he would become known as a welcher, a sick joke.

Kat was chatting about one of her patients, and Mallory was looking into her eyes, not hearing a word she said. He had more important things on his mind.

Dinner was almost over, and the waiter was serving coffee. Kat looked at her watch. "I have an early call, Ken. I think we'd better go."

He sat there, staring down at the table. "Kat . . ." He looked up. "There's something I have to tell you."

"Yes?"

"I have a confession to make." He took a deep breath. "This isn't easy for me."

She watched him, puzzled. "What is it?"

"I'm embarrassed to tell you." He was fumbling for words. "I . . . I made a stupid bet with some of the doctors that . . . that I could take you to bed."

Kat was staring at him. "You . . ."

"Please don't say anything yet. I'm so ashamed of what I did. It started out as a kind of joke, but the joke is on me. Something happened that I didn't count on. I fell in love with you."

"Ken . . ."

"I've never been in love before, Kat. I've known a lot of women, but never felt anything like this. I haven't been able to stop thinking about you." He took a shaky breath. "I want to marry you."

Kat's mind was spinning. Everything was being turned topsy-turvy. "I . . . I don't know what to . . ."

"You're the only woman I've ever proposed to. Please say yes. Will you marry me, Kat?"

So he had really meant all the lovely things he had said to her! Her heart was pounding. It was like a wonderful dream suddenly come true. All she had wanted from him was honesty. And now he was being honest with her. All this time he had been feeling guilty about what he had done. He was not like other men. He was genuine, and sensitive.

When Kat looked at him, her eyes were glowing. "Yes, Ken. Oh, yes!"

His grin lit up the room. "Kat . . ." He leaned over and kissed her. "I'm so sorry about that stupid bet." He shook his head in self-derision. "Ten thousand dollars. We could have used that money for our honeymoon. But it's worth losing it to have you."

Kat was thinking, *Ten thousand dollars.*

"I was such a fool."

"When is your deadline up?"

"At midnight tonight, but that's not important anymore. The important thing is us. That we're going to be married. We—"

"Ken?"

"Yes, darling?"

"Let's go to your place." There was a mischievous glint in Kat's eyes. "You still have time to win your bet."

*   *   *

Kat was a tigress in bed.

My God! This was worth waiting for, Mallory thought. All the feelings that Kat had kept bottled up over the years suddenly exploded. She was the most passionate woman Ken Mallory had ever known. At the end of two hours, he was exhausted. He held Kat in his arms. "You're incredible," he said.

She lifted herself up on her elbows and looked down at him. "So are you, darling. I'm so happy."

Mallory grinned. "So am I." *Ten thousand dollars' worth!* he thought. *And great sex.*

"Promise me it will always be like this, Ken."

"I promise," Mallory said in his sincerest voice.

Kat looked at her watch. "I'd better get dressed."

"Can't you spend the night here?"

"No, I'm riding to the hospital with Paige in the morning." She gave him a warm kiss. "Don't worry. We'll have all our lives to spend together."

He watched her get dressed.

"I can't wait to collect on that bet. It will buy us a great honeymoon." He frowned. "But what if the boys don't believe me? They aren't going to take my word for it."

Kat was thoughtful for a moment. Finally, she said, "Don't worry. I'll let them know."

Mallory grinned. "Come on back to bed."

Chapter Twenty-four

The black man with the gun pointed at Honey screamed, "I told you to shut up!"

"I . . . I'm sorry," Honey said. She was trembling. "Wh . . . what do you want?"

He was pressing his hand against his side, trying to stop the flow of blood. "I want my sister."

Honey looked at him, puzzled. He was obviously insane. "Your sister?"

"Kat." His voice was becoming faint.

"Oh, my God! You're Mike!"

"Yeah."

The gun dropped, and he slipped to the floor. Honey rushed to him. Blood was pouring out from what looked like a gunshot wound.

"Lie still," Honey said. She hurried into the bathroom and gathered up some peroxide and a large bath towel. She returned to Mike. "This is going to hurt," she warned.

He lay there, too weak to move.

She poured peroxide into the wound and pressed the towel against his side. He bit down on his hand to keep from screaming.

"I'm going to call an ambulance and get you to the hospital," Honey said.

He grabbed her arm. "No! No hospitals. No police." His voice was getting weaker. "Where's Kat?"

"I don't know," Honey said helplessly. She knew Kat was out somewhere with Mallory, but she had no idea where. "Let me call a friend of mine."

"Paige?" he asked.

Honey nodded. "Yes." *So Kat told him about the two of us.*

It took the hospital ten minutes to reach Paige.

"You'd better come home," Honey said.

"I'm on call, Honey. I'm in the middle of—"

"Kat's brother is here."

"Oh, well, tell him—"

"He's been shot."

"He *what?*"

"He's been shot!"

"I'll send the paramedics over and—"

"He says no hospitals and no police. I don't know what to do."

"How bad is it?"

"Pretty bad."

There was a pause. "I'll find someone to cover for me. I'll be there in half an hour."

Honey replaced the receiver and turned to Mike. "Paige is coming."

Two hours later, on her way back to the apartment, Kat was filled with a glorious sense of well-being. She had been nervous about making love, afraid that she would hate it after the terrible experience she had had, but instead, Ken Mallory had turned it into something wonderful. He had unlocked emotions in her that she had never known existed.

Smiling to herself at the thought of how they had outwitted the doctors at the last moment and won the bet, Kat opened the door to the apartment and stood there in shock. Paige and Honey were kneeling beside Mike. He was lying on the floor, a pillow under his head, a towel pressed against his side, his clothes soaked with blood.

Paige and Honey looked up as Kat entered.

"Mike! My God!" She rushed over to Mike and knelt beside him. "What happened?"

"Hi, sis." His voice was barely a whisper.

"He's been shot," Paige said. "He's hemorrhaging."

"Let's get him to the hospital," Kat said.

Mike shook his head. "No," he whispered. "You're a doctor. Fix me up."

Kat looked over at Paige.

"I've stopped as much of the bleeding as I can, but the bullet is still inside him. We don't have the instruments here to—"

"He's still losing blood," Kat said. She cradled Mike's head in her arms. "Listen to me, Mike. If you don't get help, you're going to die."

"You . . . can't . . . report . . . this . . . I don't want any police."

Kat asked quietly, "What are you involved in, Mike?"

"Nothing. I was in a . . . a business deal . . . and it went sour . . . and this guy got mad and shot me."

It was the kind of story Kat had been listening to for years. Lies. All lies. She had known that then, and she knew it now, but she had tried to keep the truth from herself.

Mike held on to her arm. "Will you help me, sis?"

"Yes. I'm going to help you, Mike." Kat leaned down and kissed him on the cheek. Then she rose and went to the telephone. She picked up the receiver and dialed the emergency room at the hospital. "This is Dr. Hunter," she said in an unsteady voice. "I need an ambulance right away . . ."

At the hospital, Kat asked Paige to perform the operation to remove the bullet.

"He's lost a lot of blood," Paige said. She turned to the assisting surgeon. "Give him another unit."

It was dawn when the operation was finished. The surgery was successful.

When it was over, Paige called Kat aside. "How do you want me to report this?" she asked. "I could list it as an accident, or . . ."

"No," Kat said. Her voice was filled with pain. "I should have done this a long time ago. I want you to report it as a gunshot wound."

Mallory was waiting for Kat outside the operating theater.

"Kat! I heard about your brother and . . ."

Kat nodded wearily.

"I'm so sorry. Is he going to be all right?"

Kat looked at Mallory and said, "Yes. For the first time in his life, Mike is going to be all right."

Mallory squeezed Kat's hand. "I just want you to know how wonderful last night was. You were a miracle. Oh. That reminds me. The doctors I bet with are in the lounge waiting, but I suppose with all that has happened, you wouldn't want to go in and . . ."

"Why not?"

She took his arm and the two of them walked into the lounge. The doctors watched them as they approached.

Grundy said, "Hi, Kat. We need to have your word on something. Dr. Mallory claims that you and he spent the night together, and it was great."

"It was better than great," Kat said. "It was *fantastic!*" She kissed Mallory on the cheek. "I'll see you later, lover."

The men sat there, gaping, as Kat walked away.

In their dressing room, Kat said to Paige and Honey, "In all the excitement, I haven't had a chance to tell you the news."

"What news?" Paige asked.

"Ken asked me to marry him."

There were looks of disbelief on their faces.

"You're joking!" Paige said.

"No. He proposed to me last night. I accepted."

"But you can't marry him!" Honey exclaimed. "You know what he's like. I mean, he tried to get you to go to bed on a bet!"

"He succeeded." Kat grinned.

Paige looked at her. "I'm confused."

Kat said, "We were wrong about him. Completely wrong. Ken told me about that bet himself. All this time, it's been bothering his conscience. Don't you see what happened? I went out with him to punish him, and he went out with me to win some money, and we ended up falling in love with each other. Oh, I can't tell you how happy I am!"

Honey and Paige looked at each other. "When are you getting married?" Honey asked.

"We haven't discussed it yet, but I'm sure it will be soon. I want you two to be my bridesmaids."

"You can count on it," Paige said. "We'll be there." But there was a nagging doubt in the back of her mind. She yawned. "It's been a long night. I'm going home and get some sleep."

"I'll stay here with Mike," Kat said. "When he wakes up, the police want to talk to him." She took their hands in hers. "Thank you for being such good friends."

On the way home, Paige thought about what had happened that night. She knew how much Kat loved her brother. It had taken a lot of courage to turn him over to the police. *I should have done this a long time ago.*

The telephone was ringing as Paige walked into the apartment. She hurried to pick it up.

It was Jason. "Hi! I just called to tell you how much I miss you. What's going on in your life?"

Paige was tempted to tell him, to share it with somebody, but it was too personal. It belonged to Kat.

"Nothing," Paige said. "Everything is fine."

"Good. Are you free for dinner tonight?"

Paige was aware that it was more than an invitation to dinner. *If I see him any more, I'm going to get involved,* Paige thought. She knew that it was one of the most important decisions of her life.

She took a deep breath. "Jason . . ." The

doorbell rang. "Hold it a minute, will you, Jason?"

Paige put the telephone down and went to the door and opened it.

Alfred Turner was standing there.

Chapter Twenty-five

Paige stood there, frozen.

Alfred smiled. "May I come in?"

She was flustered. "Of . . . of course. I'm . . . sorry." She watched Alfred walk into the living room, and she was filled with conflicting emotions. She was happy and excited and angry at the same time. *Why am I going on like this?* Paige thought. *He probably dropped by to say hello.*

Alfred turned to her. "I've left Karen."

The words were a shock.

Alfred moved closer to her. "I made a big mistake, Paige. I never should have let you go. Never."

"Alfred . . ." Paige suddenly remembered. "Excuse me."

She hurried to the telephone and picked it up. "Jason?"

"Yes, Paige. About tonight, we could—"

"I . . . I can't see you."

"Oh. If tonight is bad, what about tomorrow night?"

"I . . . I'm not sure."

He sensed the tension in her voice. "Is anything wrong?"

"No. Everything is fine. I'll call you tomorrow and explain."

"All right." He sounded puzzled.

Paige replaced the receiver.

"I've missed you, Paige," Alfred said. "Have you missed me?"

No. I just follow strangers on the street and call them Alfred. "Yes," Paige admitted.

"Good. We belong together, you know. We always have."

Have we? Is that why you married Karen? Do you think you can walk in and out of my life any time you please?

Alfred was standing close to her. "Haven't we?"

Paige looked at him and said, "I don't know." It was all too sudden.

Alfred took her hand in his. "Of course you do."

"Wha. happened with Karen?"

Alfred sh. ugged. "Karen was a mistake. I kept thinking about you and all the great times we had. We were always good for each other."

She was watching him, wary, guarded. "Alfred . . ."

"I'm here to stay, Paige. When I say 'here,' I don't exactly mean that. We're going to New York."

"New York?"

"Yes. I'll tell you all about it. I could use a cup of coffee."

"Of course. I'll make a fresh pot. It will just take a few minutes."

Alfred followed her into the kitchen, where Paige began to prepare the coffee. She was trying to get her thoughts in order. She had wanted Alfred back so desperately, and now that he was here . . .

Alfred was saying, "I've learned a lot in the last few years, Paige. I've grown up."

"Oh?"

"Yes. You know I've been working with WHO all these years."

"I know."

"Those countries haven't changed any since we were kids. In fact, some of them are worse. There's more disease down there, more poverty . . ."

"But you were there, helping," Paige said.

"Yes, and I suddenly woke up."

"Woke up?"

"I realized I was throwing my life away. I was down there, living in misery, working twenty-four hours a day, helping those ignorant savages, when I could have been making a bundle of money over here."

Paige was listening in disbelief.

"I met a doctor who has a practice on Park Avenue in New York. Do you know how much he makes a year? Over five hundred thousand dollars! Did you hear me? Five hundred thousand a year!"

Paige was staring at him.

"I said to myself, 'Where has that kind of money been all of my life?' He offered me a position as an associate," Alfred said proudly, "and I'm going in with him. That's why you and I are going to New York."

Paige stood there, numbed by what she was hearing.

"I'll be able to afford a penthouse apartment for us, and to get you pretty dresses, and all the things I've always promised you." He was grinning. "Well, are you surprised?"

Paige's mouth was dry. "I . . . I don't know what to say, Alfred."

He laughed. "Of course you don't. Five

hundred thousand dollars a year is enough to make anyone speechless."

"I wasn't thinking of the money," Paige said slowly.

"No?"

She was studying him, as though seeing him for the first time. "Alfred, when you were working for WHO, didn't you feel you were helping people?"

He shrugged. "Nothing can help those people. And who the hell really cares? Would you believe that Karen wanted me to stay down there in Bangladesh? I told her no way, so she went back." He took Paige's hand. "So here I am. . . . You're a little quiet. I guess you're overwhelmed by all this, huh?"

Paige thought of her father. *He would have been a big success on Park Avenue, but he wasn't interested in money. His only interest was in helping people.*

"I've already divorced Karen, so we can get married right away." He patted her hand. "What do you think of the idea of living in New York?"

Paige took a deep breath. "Alfred . . ."

There was an expectant smile on his face. "Yes?"

"Get out."

The smile slowly faded. "What?"

Paige rose. "I want you to get out of here."

He was confused. "Where do you want me to go?"

"I won't tell you," Paige said. "It would hurt your feelings."

After Alfred had gone, Paige sat lost in thought. Kat had been right. She had been clinging to a ghost. *Helping those ignorant savages, when I could have been making a bundle over here. . . . Five hundred thousand a year!*

And that's what I've been hanging on to, Paige thought wonderingly. She should have felt depressed, but instead she was filled with a feeling of elation. She suddenly felt free. She knew now what she wanted.

She walked over to the telephone and dialed Jason's number.

"Hello."

"Jason, it's Paige. Remember telling me about your house in Noe Valley?"

"Yes . . ."

"I'd love to see it. Are you free tonight?"

Jason said quietly, "Do you want to tell me what's going on, Paige? I'm very confused."

"*I'm* the one who's confused. I thought I was in love with a man I knew a long time ago, but he's not the same man. I know what I want now."

"Yes?"

"I want to see your house."

Noe Valley belonged to another century. It was a colorful oasis in the heart of one of the most cosmopolitan cities in the world.

Jason's house was a reflection of him—comfortable, neat, and charming. He escorted Paige through the house. "This is the living room, the kitchen, the guest bathroom, the study . . ." He looked at her and said, "The bedroom is upstairs. Would you like to see it?"

Paige said quietly, "Very much."

They went up the stairs into the bedroom. Paige's heart was pounding wildly. But what was happening seemed inevitable. *I should have known from the beginning*, she thought.

Paige never knew who made the first move, but somehow they were in each other's arms and Jason's lips were on hers, and it seemed the most natural thing in the world. They started to undress each other, and there was a fierce urgency in both of them. And then they were in bed, and he was making love to her.

"God," he whispered. "I love you."

"I know," Paige teased. "Ever since I told you to put on the white coat."

After they made love, Paige said, "I'd like to spend the night here."

Jason smiled. "You won't hate me in the morning?"

"I promise."

Paige spent the night with Jason, talking . . . making love . . . talking. In the morning, she cooked breakfast for him.

Jason watched her, and said, "I don't know how I got so lucky, but thank you."

"I'm the lucky one," Paige told him.

"You know something? I never got an answer to my proposal."

"You'll have an answer this afternoon."

That afternoon, a messenger arrived at Jason's office, with an envelope. Inside was the card that Jason had sent with the model house.

Mine [ ]
Ours [x]
Please check one.

Chapter Twenty-six

Lou Dinetto was ready to check out of the hospital. Kat went to his room to say goodbye. Rhino and the Shadow were there.

As Kat walked in, Dinetto turned to them and said, "Get lost."

Kat watched them leave the room.

Dinetto looked at Kat and said, "I owe you one."

"You don't owe me anything."

"Is that what you think my life is worth? I hear you're getting married."

"That's right."

"To a doctor."

"Yes."

"Well, tell him to take good care of you, or he'll have to answer to me."

"I'll tell him."

There was a small pause. "I'm sorry about Mike."

"He'll be all right," Kat said. "I had a long talk with him. He'll be fine."

"Good." Dinetto held out a bulky manila envelope. "A little wedding present for you."

Kat shook her head. "No. Thank you."

"But . . ."

"Take care of yourself."

"You, too. You know something? You're a real stand-up broad. I'm going to tell you something I want you to remember. If you ever need a favor—*anything*—you come to me. You hear me?"

"I hear you."

She knew that he meant it. And she knew that she would never go to him.

During the weeks that followed, Paige and Jason spoke on the phone three and four times a day, and were together every time Paige was not on night call.

The hospital was busier than ever. Paige had been on a thirty-six-hour shift that had been filled with emergencies. She had just gone to sleep in the on-call room when she was awakened by the urgent shrill of the telephone.

She fumbled the phone to her ear. "H'lo?"

"Dr. Taylor, will you come to Room 422, stat?"

Paige tried to clear her mind. *Room 422. One of Dr. Barker's patients. Lance Kelly.* He had just had a mitral valve replaced. *Something must have gone wrong.* Paige stumbled off the cot and walked out into the deserted corridor. She decided not to wait for the elevator. She ran up the stairs. *Maybe it's just a nervous nurse. If it's serious, I'll call Dr. Barker,* she thought.

She walked into Room 422 and stood in the doorway, staring. The patient was fighting for breath and moaning. The nurse turned to Paige in obvious relief. "I didn't know what to do, doctor. I . . ."

Paige hurried to the bedside. "You're going to be fine," she said reassuringly. She took his wrist between two fingers. His pulse was jumping wildly. The mitral valve was malfunctioning.

"Let's sedate him," Paige ordered.

The nurse handed Paige a syringe, and Paige injected it into a vein. Paige turned to the nurse. "Tell the head nurse to get an operating team together, stat. And send for Dr. Barker!"

Fifteen minutes later, Kelly was on the operating table. The team consisted of two scrub nurses, a circulating nurse, and two residents. A television monitor was perched high in a corner of the room to display the heart rate, EKG, and blood pressure.

The anesthesiologist walked in, and Paige felt like cursing. Most of the anesthesiologists at the hospital were skilled doctors, but Herman Koch was an exception. Paige had worked with him before and tried to avoid him as much as possible. She did not trust him. Now she had no choice.

Paige watched him secure a tube to the patient's throat, while she unfolded a paper drape with a clear window and placed it over the patient's chest.

"Put a line into the jugular vein," Paige said.

Koch nodded. "Right."

One of the residents asked, "What's the problem here?"

"Dr. Barker replaced the mitral valve yesterday. I think it's ruptured." Paige looked over at Dr. Koch. "Is he out?"

Koch nodded. "Sleeping like he's in bed at home."

I wish you were, Paige thought. "What are you using?"

"Propofol."

She nodded. "All right."

She watched Kelly being connected to the heart-lung machine so she could perform a cardiopulmonary bypass. Paige studied the monitors on the wall. Pulse 140 . . . blood oxygen saturation 92 percent . . . blood pressure 80 over 60. "Let's go," Paige said.

One of the residents put on music.

Paige stepped up to the operating table under eleven hundred watts of hot white light and turned to the scrub nurse. "Scalpel, please . . ."

The operation began.

Paige removed all the sternal wires from the operation the day before. She then cut from the base of the neck to the lower end of the sternum, while one of the residents blotted away the blood with gauze pads.

She carefully went through the layers of fat and muscle, and in front of her was the erratically beating heart. "There's the problem," Paige said. "The atrium is perforated. Blood is collecting around the heart and compressing it." Paige was looking at the monitor on the wall. The pump pressure had dropped dangerously.

"Increase the flow," Paige ordered.

The door to the operating room opened and Lawrence Barker stepped in. He stood to one side, watching what was happening.

Paige said, "Dr. Barker. Do you want to . . .?"

"It's your operation."

Paige took a quick look at what Koch was doing. "Be careful. You'll overanesthetize him, dammit! Slow it down!"

"But I . . ."

"He's in V-tach! His pressure is dropping!"

"What do you want me to do?" Koch asked helplessly.

He should know, Paige thought angrily. "Give him lidocaine and epinephrine! Now!" She was yelling.

"Right."

Paige watched as Koch picked up a syringe and injected it into the patient's IV.

A resident looked at the monitor and called out, "Blood pressure is falling."

Paige was working frantically to stop the flow of blood. She looked up at Koch. "Too much flow! I told you to . . ."

The noise of the heartbeat on the monitor suddenly became chaotic.

"My God! Something's gone wrong!"

"Give me the defibrillator!" Paige yelled.

The circulating nurse reached for the defibrillator on the crash cart, opened two sterile paddles, and plugged them in. She turned the buttons up to charge them and ten seconds later handed them to Paige.

She took the paddles and positioned them directly over Kelly's heart. Kelly's body jumped, then fell back.

Paige tried again, *willing* him to come back to life, willing him to breathe again. Nothing. The heart lay still, a dead, useless organ.

Paige was in a fury. Her part of the operation had been successful. Koch had over-anesthetized the patient.

As Paige was applying the defibrillator to Lance Kelly's body for the third futile time, Dr. Barker stepped up to the operating table and turned to Paige. "You killed him."

Chapter Twenty-seven

Jason was in the middle of a design meeting when his secretary said, "Dr. Taylor is on the phone for you. Shall I tell her you'll call back?"

"No. I'll take it." Jason picked up the phone. "Paige?"

"Jason . . . I need you!" She was sobbing.

"What happened?"

"Can you come to the apartment?"

"Of course. I'll be right there." He stood up. "The meeting is over. We'll pick it up in the morning."

Half an hour later, Jason was at the apartment. Paige opened the door and threw her arms around him. Her eyes were red from crying.

"What happened?" Jason asked.

"It's awful! Dr. Barker told me I . . . I killed a patient, and honestly, it . . . it wasn't my fault!" Her voice broke. "I can't take any more of his . . ."

"Paige," Jason said gently, "you've told me how mean he always is. That's the man's character."

Paige shook her head. "It's more than that. He's been trying to force me out since the day I started working with him. Jason, if he were a bad doctor and didn't think I was any good, I wouldn't mind so much, but the man is brilliant. I have to respect his opinion. I just don't think I'm good enough."

"Nonsense," Jason said angrily. "Of course you are. Everyone I talk to says you're a wonderful doctor."

"Not Lawrence Barker."

"Forget Barker."

"I'm going to," Paige said. "I'm quitting the hospital."

Jason took her in his arms. "Paige, I know you love the profession too much to give it up."

"I won't give it up. I just never want to see that hospital again."

Jason took out a handkerchief and dried Paige's tears.

"I'm sorry to bother you with all of this," Paige said.

"That's what husbands-to-be are for, isn't it?"

She managed a smile. "I like the sound of that. All right." Paige took a deep breath. "I feel better now. Thanks for talking to me. I telephoned Dr. Wallace and told him I was quitting. I'm going over to the hospital and see him now."

"I'll see you at dinner tonight."

Paige walked through the corridors of the hospital, knowing that she was seeing them for the last time. There were the familiar noises and the people hurrying up and down the corridors. It had become more of a home to her than she'd realized. She thought of Jimmy and Chang, and all the wonderful doctors she had worked with. Darling Jason going on rounds with her in his white coat. She passed the cafeteria where she and Honey and Kat had had a hundred breakfasts, and the lounge, where they had tried to have a party. The corridors and rooms were full of so many memories. *I'm going to miss it,* Paige thought, *but I refuse to work under the same roof as that monster.*

She went up to Dr. Wallace's office. He was waiting for her.

"Well, I must say, your telephone call surprised me, Paige! Have you definitely made up your mind?"

"Yes."

Benjamin Wallace sighed. "Very well. Before you go, Dr. Barker would like to see you."

"I want to see him." All of Paige's pent-up anger boiled to the surface.

"He's in the lab. Well . . . good luck."

"Thanks." Paige headed for the lab.

Dr. Barker was examining some slides under a microscope when Paige entered. He looked up. "I'm told you've decided to quit the hospital."

"That's right. You finally got your wish."

"And what was that?" Barker asked.

"You've wanted me out of here from the first moment you saw me. Well, you've won. I can't fight you anymore. When you told me I killed your patient, I . . ." Paige's voice broke. "I . . . I think you're a sadistic, cold-hearted son of a bitch, and I hate you."

"Sit down," Dr. Barker said.

"No. I have nothing more to say."

"Well, I have. Who the hell do you think you . . . ?"

He suddenly stopped and began to gasp.

As Paige watched in horror, he clutched his heart and toppled over in his chair, his face twisted to one side in a horrible rictus.

Paige was at his side instantly. "Dr. Barker!" She grabbed the telephone and shouted into it, "Code Red! Code Red!"

Dr. Peterson said, "He's suffered a massive stroke. It's too early to tell whether he's going to come out of it."

It's my fault, Paige thought. *I wanted him dead.* She felt miserable.

She went back to see Ben Wallace. "I'm sorry about what happened," Paige said. "He was a good doctor."

"Yes. It's regrettable. Very . . ." Wallace studied her a moment. "Paige, if Dr. Barker can't practice here anymore, would you consider staying on?"

Paige hesitated. "Yes. Of course."

Chapter Twenty-eight

His chart read, "John Cronin, white male, age 70. Diagnosis: Cardiac tumor."

Paige had not yet met John Cronin. He was scheduled to have heart surgery. She walked into his room, a nurse and a staff doctor at her side. She smiled warmly and said, "Good morning, Mr. Cronin."

They had just extubated him, and there were the marks of adhesive tape around his mouth. IV bottles hung overhead, and the tubing had been inserted in his left arm.

Cronin looked over at Paige. "Who the hell are you?"

"I'm Dr. Taylor. I'm going to examine you and—"

"Like hell you are! Keep your fucking hands off me. Why didn't they send in a *real* doctor?"

Paige's smile died. "I'm a cardiovascular surgeon. I'm going to do everything I can to get you well again."

"*You're* going to operate on my heart?"

"That's right. I . . ."

John Cronin looked at the resident and said, "For Christ's sake, is this the best this hospital can do?"

"I assure you, Dr. Taylor is thoroughly qualified," the staff doctor said.

"So is my ass."

Paige said stiffly, "Would you rather bring in your own surgeon?"

"I don't have one. I can't afford those high-priced quacks. You doctors are all alike. All you're interested in is money. You don't give a damn about people. We're just pieces of meat to you, aren't we?"

Paige was fighting to control her temper. "I know you're upset right now, but—"

"Upset? Just because you're going to cut my heart out?" He was screaming. "I know I'll die on the operating table. You're going to kill me, and I hope they get you for murder!"

"That's enough!" Paige said.

He was grinning at her maliciously. "It wouldn't look good on your record if I died, would it, doctor? Maybe I *will* let you operate on me."

Paige found that she was hyperventilating. She turned to the nurse. "I want an EKG and a chemistry panel." She took one last look at John Cronin, then turned and left the room.

When Paige returned an hour later with the reports on the tests, John Cronin looked up. "Oh, the bitch is back."

Paige operated on John Cronin at six o'clock the following morning.

The moment she opened him up, she knew that there was no hope. The major problem was not the heart. Cronin's organs showed signs of melanoma.

A resident said, "Oh, my God! What are we going to do?"

"We're going to pray that he doesn't have to live with this too long."

When Paige stepped out of the operating room into the corridor, she found a woman and two men waiting for her. The woman was in her late thirties. She had bright red hair and too much makeup, and she wore a heavy, cheap perfume. She had on a tight dress that accentuated a voluptuous figure. The men were in their forties, and both had red hair. To Paige, they looked like a circus troupe.

The woman said to Paige, "You Dr. Taylor?"

"Yes."

"I'm Mrs. Cronin. These are my brothers. How's my husband?"

Paige hesitated. She said carefully, "The operation went as well as could be expected."

"Oh, thank God!" Mrs. Cronin said melodramatically, dabbing at her eyes with a lace handkerchief. "I'd die if anything happened to John!"

Paige felt as if she were watching an actress in a bad play.

"Can I see my darling now?"

"Not yet, Mrs. Cronin. He's in the recovery room. I suggest that you come back tomorrow."

"We'll be back." She turned to the men. "Come along, fellas."

Paige watched as they walked away. *Poor John Cronin,* she thought.

Paige was given the report the next morning. The cancer had metastasized throughout Cronin's body. It was too late for radiation treatment.

The oncologist said to Paige, "There's

nothing to do but try to keep him comfortable. He's going to be in a hell of a lot of pain."

"How much time does he have?"

"A week or two at the most."

Paige went to visit John Cronin in intensive care. He was asleep. John Cronin was no longer a bitter, vitriolic man, but a human being fighting desperately for his life. He was on a respirator, and being fed intravenously. Paige sat down at his bedside, watching him. He looked tired and defeated. *He's one of the unlucky ones,* Paige thought. *Even with all the modern medical miracles, there's nothing we can do to save him.* Paige touched his arm gently. After a while, she left.

Later that afternoon, Paige stopped by to see John Cronin again. He was off the respirator now. When he opened his eyes and saw Paige, he said drowsily, "The operation's over, huh?"

Paige smiled reassuringly. "Yes. I just came by to make sure that you're comfortable."

"Comfortable?" he snorted. "What the hell do you care?"

Paige said, "Please. Let's not fight."

Cronin lay there, silently studying her. "The other doctor told me you did a good job."

Paige said nothing.

"I have cancer, don't I?"

"Yes."

"How bad is it?"

The question posed a dilemma that all surgeons were faced with sooner or later. Paige said. "It's pretty bad."

There was a long silence. "What about radiation or chemotherapy?"

"I'm sorry. It would make you feel worse, and it wouldn't help."

"I see. Well . . . I've had a good life."

"I'm sure you have."

"You may not think so, looking at me now, but I've had a lot of women."

"I believe it."

"Yeah. Women . . . thick steaks . . . good cigars . . . You married?"

"No."

"You ought to be. Everyone should be married. I've been married. Twice. First, for thirty-five years. She was a wonderful lady. She died of a heart attack."

"I'm sorry."

"It's okay." He sighed. "Then I got sucked into marrying a bimbo. Her and her two hungry brothers. It's my fault for being so horny,

I guess. Her red hair turned me on. She's some piece of work."

"I'm sure she . . ."

"No offense, but do you know why I'm in this cockamamie hospital? My wife put me here. She didn't want to waste money on me for a private hospital. This way there'll be more to leave to her and her brothers." He looked up at Paige. "How much time *do* I have left?"

"Do you want it straight?"

"No . . . yes."

"A week or two."

"Jesus! The pain is going to get worse, isn't it?"

"I'll try to keep you as comfortable as possible, Mr. Cronin."

"Call me John."

"John."

"Life is a bitch, isn't it?"

"You said you've had a good life."

"I did. It's kinda funny, knowing it's about over. Where do you think we go?"

"I don't know."

He forced a smile. "I'll let you know when I get there."

"Some medication is on the way. Can I do anything to make you more comfortable?"

"Yeah. Come back and talk to me tonight."

It was Paige's night off, and she was exhausted. "I'll come back."

That night when Paige went back to see John Cronin, he was awake.

"How are you feeling?"

He winced. "Terrible. I was never very good about pain. I guess I've got a low threshold."

"I understand."

"You met Hazel, huh?"

"Hazel?"

"My wife. The bimbo. She and her brothers were here to see me. They said they talked to you."

"Yes."

"She's something, ain't she? I sure got myself into a bundle of trouble there. They can't wait for me to kick the bucket."

"Don't say that."

"It's true. The only reason Hazel married me was for my money. To tell you the truth, I didn't mind that so much. I really had a good time with her in bed, but then she and her brothers started to get greedy. They always wanted more."

The two of them sat there in a comfortable silence.

"Did I tell you I used to travel a lot?"

"No."

"Yeah. I've been to Sweden . . . Denmark . . . Germany. Have you been to Europe?"

She thought about the day at the travel agency. *Let's go to Venice! No, let's go to Paris! How about London?* "No. I haven't."

"You ought to go."

"Maybe one day I will."

"I guess you don't make much money working at a hospital like this, huh?"

"I make enough."

He nodded to himself. "Yeah. You have to go to Europe. Do me a favor. Go to Paris . . . stay at the Crillon, have dinner at Maxim's, order a big, thick steak and a bottle of champagne, and when you eat that steak and drink that champagne, I want you to think of me. Will you do that?"

Paige said slowly, "I'll do that one day."

John Cronin was studying her. "Good. I'm tired now. Will you come back tomorrow and talk to me again?"

"I'll come back," Paige said.

John Cronin slept.

Chapter Twenty-nine

Ken Mallory was a great believer in Lady Luck, and after meeting the Harrisons, he believed even more firmly that she was on his side. The odds against a man as wealthy as Alex Harrison being brought to Embarcadero County Hospital were enormous. *And I'm the one who saved his life, and he wants to show his gratitude,* Mallory thought gleefully.

He had asked a friend of his about the Harrisons.

"Rich doesn't even begin to cover it," his friend had said. "He's a millionaire a dozen times over. And he has a great-looking daughter. She's been married three or four times. The last time to a count."

"Have you ever met the Harrisons?"

"No. They don't mingle with the *hoi polloi.*"

On a Saturday morning, as Alex Harrison was being discharged from the hospital, he said, "Ken, do you think I'll be in shape to give a dinner party a week from now?"

Mallory nodded. "If you don't overdo it, I don't see why not."

Alex Harrison smiled. "Fine. You're the guest of honor."

Mallory felt a sudden thrill. *The old man really meant what he said.* "Well . . . thank you."

"Lauren and I will expect you at seven-thirty next Saturday night." He gave Mallory an address on Nob Hill.

"I'll be there," Mallory said. *Will I ever!*

Mallory had promised to take Kat to the theater that evening, but it would be easy to cancel. He had collected his winnings, and he enjoyed having sex with her. Several times a week they had managed to get together in one of the empty on-call rooms, or a deserted hospital room, or at her apartment or his. *Her fires were banked a long time,* Mallory thought happily, *but when the explosion came—wow! Well, one of these days, it will be time to say arrivederci.*

On the day he was to have dinner with

the Harrisons, Mallory telephoned Kat. "Bad news, baby."

"What's the matter, darling?"

"One of the doctors is sick and they've asked me to cover for him. I'm afraid I'm going to have to break our date."

She did not want to let him know how disappointed she was, how much she needed to be with him. Kat said lightly, "Oh well, that's the doctor business, isn't it?"

"Yeah. I'll make it up to you."

"You don't have to make anything up to me," she said warmly. "I love you."

"I love you, too."

"Ken, when are we going to talk about us?"

"What do you mean?" He knew exactly what she meant. A commitment. They were all alike. *They use their pussies for bait, hoping to hook a sucker into spending his life with them.* Well, he was too smart for that. When the time came, he would regretfully bow out, as he had done a dozen times before.

Kat was saying, "Don't you think we should set a date, Ken? I have a lot of plans to make."

"Oh, sure. We'll do that."

"I thought maybe June. What do you think?"

You don't want to know what I think. If I

play my cards right, there's going to be a wedding, but it won't be with you. "We'll talk about it, baby. I really have to go now."

The Harrisons' home was a mansion out of a motion picture, situated on acres of manicured grounds. The house itself seemed to go on forever. There were two dozen guests, and in the huge drawing room a small orchestra was playing. When Mallory walked in, Lauren hurried over to greet him. She was wearing a silky clinging gown. She squeezed Mallory's hand, "Welcome, guest of honor. I'm so glad you're here."

"So am I. How is your father?"

"Very much alive, thanks to you. You're quite a hero in this house."

Mallory smiled modestly. "I only did my job."

"I suppose that's what God says every day." She took his hand and began introducing him to the other guests.

The guest list was blue-ribbon. The governor of California was there, the French ambassador, a justice of the Supreme Court, and a dozen assorted politicians, artists, and business tycoons. Mallory could feel the power in the room, and it thrilled him. *This is where I belong,* he thought. *Right here, with these peo-ple.*

The dinner was delicious and elegantly served. At the end of the evening, when the guests started to leave, Harrison said to Mallory, "Don't rush off, Ken. I'd like to talk to you."

"I'd be delighted."

Harrison, Lauren, and Mallory sat in the library. Harrison was seated in a chair next to his daughter.

"When I told you at the hospital that I thought you had a great future before you, I meant it."

"I really appreciate your confidence, sir."

"You should be in private practice."

Mallory laughed self-deprecatingly. "I'm afraid it's not that easy, Mr. Harrison. It takes a long time to build up a practice, and I'm . . ."

"Ordinarily, yes. But you're not an ordi-nary man."

"I don't understand."

"After you finish your residency, Father wants to set you up in your own practice," Lauren said.

For a moment, Mallory was speechless. It was too easy. He felt as though he were living in some kind of wonderful dream. "I . . . I don't know what to say."

"I have a lot of very wealthy friends. I've already spoken to some of them about you. I can promise you that you'll be swamped the minute you put up your shingle."

"Daddy, lawyers put up shingles," Lauren said.

"Whatever. In any case, I'd like to finance you. Are you interested?"

Mallory was finding it difficult to breathe. "Very much so. But I . . . I don't know when I would be able to repay you."

"You don't understand. I'm repaying *you*. You won't owe me anything."

Lauren was looking at Mallory, her eyes warm. "Please say yes."

"I'd be stupid to say no, wouldn't I?"

"That's right," Lauren said softly. "And I'm sure you're not stupid."

On his way home, Ken Mallory was in a state of euphoria. *This is as good as it gets,* he thought. But he was wrong. It got better.

Lauren telephoned him. "I hope you don't mind mixing business with pleasure."

He smiled to himself. "Not at all. What did you have in mind?"

"There's a charity ball next Saturday night. Would you like to take me?"

Oh, baby, I'm going to take you all right.

"I'd love to." He was on duty Saturday night, but he would call in sick and they would have to find someone to take his place.

Mallory was a man who believed in planning ahead, but what was happening to him now went beyond his wildest dreams.

Over the next few weeks he was swept up in Lauren's social circle, and life took on a dizzying pace. He would be out with Lauren dancing half the night, and stumble through his days at the hospital. There were mounting complaints about his work, but he didn't care. *I'll be out of here soon,* he told himself.

The thought of getting away from the dreary county hospital and having his own practice was exciting enough, but Lauren was the bonus that Lady Luck had given him.

Kat was becoming a nuisance. Mallory had to keep finding pretexts to avoid seeing her. When she would press him, he would say, "Darling, I'm crazy about you . . . of course I want to marry you, but right now, I . . ." and he would go into a litany of excuses.

It was Lauren who suggested that the two of them spend a weekend at the family lodge at Big Sur. Mallory was elated. *Everything is coming up roses,* he thought. *I'm going to own the whole damned world!*

* * *

The lodge was spread across pine-covered hills, an enormous structure built of wood and tile and stone, overlooking the Pacific Ocean. It had a master bedroom, eight guest bedrooms, a spacious living room with a stone fireplace, an indoor swimming pool, and a large hot tub. Everything smelled of old money.

When they walked in, Lauren turned to Mallory and said, "I let the servants go for the weekend."

Mallory grinned. "Good thinking." He put his arms around Lauren and said softly, "I'm wild about you."

"Show me," Lauren said.

They spent the day in bed, and Lauren was almost as insatiable as Kat.

"You're wearing me out!" Mallory laughed.

"Good. I don't want you to be able to make love to anyone else." She sat up in bed. "There *is* no one else, is there, Ken?"

"Absolutely not," Mallory said sincerely. "There's no one in the world for me but you. I'm in love with you, Lauren." Now was the time to take the plunge, to wrap his whole future up in one neat package. It would be one thing to be a successful doctor in private practice. It would be something else to be Alex Harrison's son-in-law. "I want to marry you."

He held his breath, waiting for her answer.

"Oh, yes, darling," Lauren said. "Yes."

At the apartment, Kat was frantically trying to reach Mallory. She telephoned the hospital.

"I'm sorry, Dr. Hunter, Dr. Mallory is not on call, and doesn't answer his page."

"Didn't he leave word where he could be reached?"

"We have no record of it."

Kat replaced the receiver and turned to Paige. "Something's happened to him, I know it. He would have called me by now."

"Kat, there could be a hundred reasons why you haven't heard from him. Perhaps he had to go out of town suddenly, or . . ."

"You're right. I'm sure there's some good excuse."

Kat looked at the phone and *willed* it to ring.

When Mallory returned to San Francisco, he telephoned Kat at the hospital.

"Dr. Hunter is off duty," the receptionist told him.

"Thank you." Mallory called the apartment. Kat was there.

"Hi, baby!"

"Ken! Where have you been? I've been worried about you. I tried everywhere to reach—"

"I had a family emergency," he said smoothly. "I'm sorry I didn't have a chance to call you. I had to go out of town. May I come over?"

"You know you may. I'm so glad you're all right. I—"

"Half an hour." He replaced the receiver and thought happily, *The time has come, the walrus said, to speak of many things. Kat, baby, it was great fun, but it was just one of those things.*

When Mallory arrived at the apartment, Kat threw her arms around him. "I've missed you!" She could not tell him how desperately worried she had been. Men hated that kind of thing. She stood back. "Darling, you look absolutely exhausted."

Mallory sighed. "I've been up for the last twenty-four hours." *That part is true,* he thought.

Kat hugged him. "Poor baby. Can I fix something for you?"

"No, I'm fine. All I really need is a good night's sleep. Let's sit down, Kat. We have to have a talk." He sat on the couch next to her.

"Is anything wrong?" Kat asked.

Mallory took a deep breath. "Kat, I've been thinking a lot about us lately."

She smiled. "So have I. I have news for you. I—"

"No, wait. Let me finish. Kat, I think we're rushing into things too fast. I . . . I think I proposed too hastily."

She paled. "What . . . what are you saying?"

"I'm saying that I think we should postpone everything."

She felt as though the room were closing in on her. She was finding it difficult to breathe. "Ken, we can't postpone anything. I'm having your baby."

Chapter Thirty

Paige got home at midnight, drained. It had been an exhausting day. There had been no time for lunch, and dinner had consisted of a sandwich between operations. She fell into her bed and was asleep instantly. She was awakened by the ringing of the telephone. Groggily, Paige reached for the instrument and automatically glanced at the bedside clock. It was three in the morning. "H'lo?"

"Dr. Taylor? I'm sorry to disturb you, but one of your patients is insisting on seeing you right away."

Paige's throat was so dry she could hardly talk. "I'm off duty," she mumbled. "Can't you get someone . . . ?"

"He won't talk to anyone else. He says he needs *you*."

"Who is it?"

"John Cronin."

Paige sat up straighter. "What's happened?"

"I don't know. He refuses to speak with anyone but you."

"All right," Paige said wearily. "I'm on my way."

Thirty minutes later, Paige arrived at the hospital. She went directly to John Cronin's room. He was lying in bed, awake. Tubes were protruding from his nostrils and his arms.

"Thanks for coming." His voice was weak and hoarse.

Paige sat down in a chair next to the bed. She smiled. "That's all right, John. I had nothing to do, anyway, but sleep. What can I do for you that no one else here at this great big hospital couldn't have done?"

"I want you to talk to me."

Paige groaned. "At this hour? I thought it was some kind of emergency."

"It is. I want to leave."

She shook her head. "That's impossible. You can't go home now. You couldn't get the kind of treatment—"

He interrupted her. "I don't want to go home. I want to leave."

She looked at him and said slowly, "What are you saying?"

"You know what I'm saying. The medication isn't working anymore. I can't stand this pain. I want out."

Paige leaned over and took his hand. "John, I can't do that. Let me give you some—"

"No. I'm tired, Paige. I want to go wherever it is I'm going, but I don't want to hang around here like this. Not anymore."

"John . . ."

"How much time do I have left? A few more days? I told you, I'm not good about pain. I'm lying here like a trapped animal, filled with all these goddam tubes. My body is being eaten away inside. This isn't living—it's dying. For God's sake, help me!"

He was racked by a sudden spasm of pain. When he spoke again, his voice was even weaker. "Help me . . . please . . ."

Paige knew what she had to do. She had to report John Cronin's request to Dr. Benjamin Wallace. He would pass it on to the Administration Committee. They would assemble a panel of doctors to assess Cronin's condition, and then make a decision. After that, it would have to be approved by . . .

"Paige . . . it's *my* life. Let me do with it as I like."

She looked over at the helpless figure locked in his pain.

"I'm begging you . . ."

She took his hand and held it for a long time. When she spoke, she said, "All right, John. I'll do it."

He managed a trace of a smile. "I knew I could count on you."

Paige leaned over and kissed him on the forehead. "Close your eyes and go to sleep."

"Good night, Paige."

"Good night, John."

John Cronin sighed and closed his eyes, a beatific smile on his face.

Paige sat there watching him, thinking about what she was about to do. She remembered how horrified she had been on her first day of rounds with Dr. Radnor. *She's been in a coma for six weeks. Her vital signs are failing. There's nothing more we can do for her. We'll pull the plug this afternoon.* Was it wrong to release a fellow human being from his misery?

Slowly, as though she were moving under water, Paige rose and walked to a cabinet in the corner, where a bottle of insulin was kept for emergency use. She removed the bottle and stood there, staring at it. Then she uncapped the bottle. She filled a syringe with the insulin and walked back to John Cronin's bedside. There was still time to go back. *I'm lying here like a trapped animal. . . . This isn't living—it's dying. For God's sake, help me!*

Paige leaned forward and slowly injected the insulin into the IV attached to Cronin's arm.

"Sleep well," Paige whispered. She was unaware that she was sobbing.

Paige drove home and stayed awake the rest of the night, thinking about what she had done.

At six o'clock in the morning, she received a telephone call from one of the residents at the hospital.

"I'm sorry to give you bad news, Dr. Taylor. Your patient John Cronin died of cardiac arrest early this morning."

The staff doctor in charge that morning was Dr. Arthur Kane.

Chapter Thirty-one

The one other time Ken Mallory had gone to an opera, he had fallen asleep. On this night he was watching *Rigoletto* at the San Francisco Opera House and enjoying every minute of it. He was seated in a box with Lauren Harrison and her father. In the lobby of the opera house during intermission, Alex Harrison had introduced him to a large number of friends.

"This is my future son-in-law and a brilliant doctor, Ken Mallory."

Being Alex Harrison's son-in-law was enough to *make* him a brilliant doctor.

After the performance, the Harrisons and Mallory went to the Fairmont Hotel for supper in the elegant main dining room. Mallory enjoyed the deferential greeting that the maître d' gave to Alex Harrison as he led them to their booth. *From now on, I'll be able to afford places like this,* Mallory thought, *and everyone is going to know who I am.*

After they had ordered, Lauren said, "Darling, I think we should have a party to announce our engagement."

"That's a good idea!" her father said. "We'll make it a big one. What do you say, Ken?"

A warning bell sounded in Mallory's mind. An engagement party would mean publicity. *I'll have to set Kat straight first. A little money should take care of that.* Mallory cursed the stupid bet he had made. For a mere ten thousand dollars, his whole shining future might now be in jeopardy. He could just imagine what would happen if he tried to explain Kat to the Harrisons.

By the way, I forgot to mention that I'm already engaged to a doctor at the hospital. She's black. . . .

Or: *Do you want to hear something funny? I bet the boys at the hospital ten thousand dollars I could fuck this black doctor. . . .*

Or: *I already have one wedding planned. . . .*

No, he thought, *I'll have to find a way to buy Kat off.*

They were looking at Mallory expectantly.

Mallory smiled. "A party sounds like a wonderful idea."

Lauren said enthusiastically, "Good. I'll get things started. You men have no idea what it takes to give a party."

Alex Harrison turned to Mallory. "I've already started the ball rolling for you, Ken."

"Sir?"

"Gary Gitlin, the head of North Shore Hospital, is an old golf buddy of mine. I talked to him about you, and he doesn't think there will be any problem about having you affiliated with his hospital. That's quite prestigious, you know. And at the same time, I'll get you set up in your own practice."

Mallory listened, filled with a sense of euphoria. "That's wonderful."

"Of course, it will take a few years to build up a really lucrative practice, but I think you should be able to make two or three hundred thousand dollars the first year or two."

Two or three hundred thousand! My God! Mallory thought. *He makes it sound like peanuts.* "That . . . That would be very nice, sir."

Alex Harrison smiled. "Ken, since I'm going to be your father-in-law, let's get off this 'sir' business. Call me Alex."

"Right, Alex."

"You know, I've never been a June bride," Lauren said. "Is June all right with you, darling?"

He could hear Kat's voice saying: *Don't you think we should set a date? I thought maybe June.*

Mallory took Lauren's hand in his. "That sounds great." *That will give me plenty of time to handle Kat,* Mallory decided. He smiled to himself. *I'll offer her some of the money I won getting her into bed.*

"We have a yacht in the south of France," Alex Harrison was saying, "Would you two like to honeymoon on the French Riviera? You can fly over in our Gulfstream."

A yacht. The French Riviera. It was like a fantasy come true. Mallory looked at Lauren. "I'd honeymoon anywhere with Lauren."

Alex Harrison nodded. "Well, it looks like everything is settled." He smiled at his daughter. "I'm going to miss you, baby."

"You're not losing me, Father. You're gaining a doctor!"

Alex Harrison nodded. "And a damn good one. I can never thank you enough for saving my life, Ken."

Lauren stroked Mallory's hand. "I'll thank him for you."

"Ken, why don't we have lunch next

week?" Alex Harrison said. "We'll pick out some decent office space for you, maybe in the Post Building, and I'll make a date for you to see Gary Gitlin. A lot of my friends are dying to meet you."

"I think you might rephrase that, Father." Lauren suggested. She turned to Ken. "I've been talking to *my* friends about you and they're eager to meet you, too, only I'm not going to let them."

"I'm not interested in anyone but you," Mallory said warmly.

When they got into their chauffeur-driven Rolls-Royce, Lauren asked, "Where can we drop you, darling?"

"The hospital. I've got to check on a few patients." He had no intention of seeing any patients. Kat was on duty at the hospital.

Lauren stroked his cheek. "My poor baby. You work much too hard."

Mallory sighed. "It doesn't matter. As long as I'm helping people."

He found Kat in the geriatric ward.

"Hi, Kat."

She was in an angry mood. "We had a date last night, Ken."

429

"I know. I'm sorry. I wasn't able to make it, and—"

"That's the third time in the last week. What's going on?"

She was becoming a boring nag. "Kat, I have to talk to you. Is there an empty room around here?"

She thought for a moment. "A patient checked out of 315. Let's go in there."

They started down the corridor. A nurse walked up to them. "Oh, Dr. Mallory! Dr. Peterson has been looking for you. He—"

"Tell him I'm busy." He took Kat by the arm and led her to the elevator.

When they arrived at the third floor, they walked silently down the corridor and went into Room 315. Mallory closed the door behind them. He was hyperventilating. His whole golden future depended on the next few minutes.

He took Kat's hand in his. It was time to be sincere. "Kat, you know I'm crazy about you. I've never felt about anyone the way I feel about you. But, honey, the idea of having a baby right now . . . well . . . can't you see how wrong it would be? I mean . . . we're both working day and night, we aren't making enough money to . . ."

"But we can manage," Kat said. "I love you, Ken, and I—"

"Wait. All I'm asking is that we put everything off for a little while. Let me finish my term at the hospital and get started in private practice somewhere. Maybe we'll go back East. In a few years we'll be able to afford to get married and have a baby."

"*In a few years?* But I told you, I'm pregnant."

"I know, darling, but it's been what, now . . . two months? There's still plenty of time to abort it."

Kat looked at him, shocked. "No! I won't abort it. I want us to get married right away. Now."

We have a yacht in the south of France. Would you two like to honeymoon on the French Riviera? You can fly over in our Gulfstream.

"I've already told Paige and Honey that we're getting married. They're going to be my bridesmaids. And I told them about the baby."

Mallory felt a cold chill go through him. Things were getting out of hand. If the Harrisons got wind of this, he would be finished. "You shouldn't have done that."

"Why not?"

Mallory forced a smile. "I want to keep our private lives private." *I'll get you set up in your own practice. . . . You should be able to make two or three hundred thousand dollars*

431

the first year or two. "Kat, I'm going to ask you this for the last time. Will you have an abortion?" He was *willing* her to say yes, trying to keep the desperation out of his voice.

"No."

"Kat . . ."

"I can't, Ken. I told you how I felt about the abortion I had as a girl. I swore I could never live through such a thing again. Don't ask me again."

And it was at that moment that Ken Mallory realized he could not take a chance. He had no choice. He was going to have to kill her.

Chapter Thirty-two

Honey looked forward every day to seeing the patient in Room 306. His name was Sean Reilly, and he was a good-looking Irishman, with black hair and black sparkling eyes. Honey guessed that he was in his early forties.

When Honey first met him on her rounds, she had looked at his chart and said, "I see you're here for a cholecystectomy."

"I thought they were going to remove my gallbladder."

Honey smiled. "Same thing."

Sean fixed his black eyes on her. "They can cut out anything they want except my heart. That belongs to you."

433

Honey laughed. "Flattery will get you everywhere."

"I hope so, darlin'."

When Honey had a few minutes to spare, she would drop by and chat with Sean. He was charming and amusing.

"It's worth bein' operated on just to have you around, little darlin'."

"You aren't nervous about the operation, are you?" she asked.

"Not if you're going to operate, love."

"I'm not a surgeon. I'm an internist."

"Are internists allowed to have dinner with their patients?"

"No. There's a rule against it."

"Do internists ever break rules?"

"Never." Honey was smiling.

"I think you're beautiful," Sean said.

No one had ever told Honey that before. She found herself blushing. "Thank you."

"You're like the fresh mornin' dew in the fields of Killarney."

"Have you ever been to Ireland?" Honey asked.

He laughed. "No, but I promise you we'll go there together one day. You'll see."

It was ridiculous Irish blarney, and yet . . .

That afternoon when Honey went in to see Sean, she said, "How are you feeling?"

"The better for seeing you. Have you thought about our dinner date?"

"No," Honey said. She was lying.

"I was hoping after my operation, I could take you out. You're not engaged, or married, or anything silly like that, are you?"

Honey smiled. "Nothing silly like that."

"Good! Neither am I. Who would have me?"

A lot of women, Honey thought.

"If you like home cooking, I happen to be a great cook."

"We'll see."

When Honey went to Sean's room the following morning, he said, "I have a little present for you." He handed her a sheet of drawing paper. On it was a softened, idealized sketch of Honey.

"I love it!" Honey said. "You're a wonderful artist!" And she suddenly remembered the psychic's words: *You're going to fall in love. He's an artist.* She was looking at Sean strangely.

"Is anything wrong?"

"No," Honey said slowly. "No."

Five minutes later, Honey walked into Frances Gordon's room.

"Here comes the Virgo!"

Honey said, "Do you remember telling me that I was going to fall in love with someone— an artist?"

"Yes."

"Well, I . . . I think I've met him."

Frances Gordon smiled. "See? The stars never lie."

"Could . . . could you tell me a little about him? About us?"

"There are some tarot cards in that drawer over there. Could you give them to me, please?"

As Honey handed her the cards, she thought, *This is ridiculous! I don't believe in this!*

Frances Gordon was laying out the cards. She kept nodding to herself, and nodding and smiling, and suddenly she stopped. Her face went pale. "Oh, my God!" She looked up at Honey.

"What . . . what's the matter?" Honey asked.

"This artist. You say you've already met him?"

"I think so. Yes."

Frances Gordon's voice was filled with sadness. "The poor man." She looked up at Honey. "I'm sorry . . . I'm so sorry."

* * *

Sean Reilly was scheduled to have his operation the following morning.

8:15 A.M. Dr. William Radnor was in OR Two, preparing for the operation.

8:25 A.M. A truck containing a week's supply of bags of blood pulled up at the emergency entrance to Embarcadero County Hospital. The driver carried the bags to the blood bank in the basement. Eric Foster, the resident on duty, was sharing coffee and a danish with a pretty young nurse, Andrea.

"Where do you want these?" the driver asked.

"Just set them down there." Foster pointed to a corner.

"Right." The driver put the bags down and pulled out a form. "I need your John Hancock."

"Okay." Foster signed the form. "Thanks."

"No sweat." The driver left.

Foster turned to Andrea. "Where were we?"

"You were telling me how adorable I am."

"Right. If you weren't married, I'd really go after you," the resident said. "Do you ever fool around?"

"No. My husband is a boxer."

"Oh. Do you have a sister?"

"As a matter of fact, I do."

"Is she as pretty as you are?"

"Prettier."

"What's her name?"

"Marilyn."

"Why don't we double-date one night?"

As they chatted, the fax machine began to click. Foster ignored it.

8:45 A.M. Dr. Radnor began the operation on Sean Reilly. The beginning went smoothly. The operating room functioned like a well-oiled machine, run by capable people doing their jobs.

9:05 A.M. Dr. Radnor reached the cystic duct. A textbook operation up until then. As he started to excise the gallbladder, his hand slipped and the scalpel nicked an artery. Blood began to pour out.

"Jesus!" He tried to stop the flow.

The anesthesiologist called out, "His blood pressure just dropped to ninety-five. He's going into shock!"

Radnor turned to the circulating nurse.

"Get some more blood up here, stat!"

"Right away, doctor."

9:06 A.M. The telephone rang in the blood bank.

"Don't go away," Foster told Andrea. He walked past the fax machine, which had stopped clicking, and picked up the telephone. "Blood supply."

"We need four units of Type O in OR Two, stat."

"Right." Foster replaced the receiver and went to the corner where the new blood had been deposited. He pulled out four bags and placed them on the top shelf of the metal cart used for such emergencies. He double-checked the bags. "Type O," he said aloud. He rang for an orderly.

"What's going on?" Andrea asked.

Foster looked at the schedule in front of him. "It looks like one of the patients is giving Dr. Radnor a bad time."

9:10 A.M. The orderly came into the blood bank. "What have we got?"

"Take this to OR Two. They're waiting for it."

He watched the orderly wheel out the cart, then turned to Andrea. "Tell me about your sister."

"She's married, too."

"Aw . . ."

Andrea smiled. "But she fools around."

"Does she really?"

"I'm only kidding. I have to go back to work, Eric. Thanks for the coffee and danish."

"Anytime." He watched her leave and thought, *What a great ass!*

9:12 A.M. The orderly was waiting for an elevator to take him to the second floor.

9:13 A.M. Dr. Radnor was doing his best to minimize the catastrophe. "Where's the damned blood?"

9:15 A.M. The orderly pushed at the door to OR Two and the circulating nurse opened it.

"Thanks," she said. She carried the bags into the room. "It's here, doctor."

"Start pumping it into him. Fast!"

* * *

In the blood bank, Eric Foster finished his coffee, thinking about Andrea. *All the good-looking ones are married.*

As he started toward his desk, he passed the fax machine. He pulled out the fax. It read:

Recall Warning Alert #687, June 25: Red Blood Cells, Fresh Frozen Plasma. Units CB83711, CB800007. Community Blood Bank of California, Arizona, Washington, Oregon. Blood products testing repeatedly reactive for Antibody HIV Type I were distributed.

He stared at it a moment, then walked over to his desk and picked up the invoice he had signed for the bags of blood that had just been delivered. He looked at the number on the invoice. The number on the warning was identical.

"Oh, my God!" he said. He grabbed the telephone. "Get me OR Two, fast!"

A nurse answered.

"This is the blood bank. I just sent up four units of Type O. Don't use it! I'm sending up some fresh blood immediately."

The nurse said, "Sorry, it's too late."

* * *

Dr. Radnor broke the news to Sean Reilly.

"It was a mistake," Radnor said. "A terrible mistake. I would give anything if it had not happened."

Sean was staring at him, in shock. "My God! I'm going to die."

"We won't know whether you're HIV-positive for six or eight weeks. And even if you are, that does not necessarily mean you will get AIDS. We're going to do everything we can for you."

"What the hell can you do for me that you haven't already done?" Sean said bitterly. "I'm a dead man."

When Honey heard the news, she was devastated. She remembered Frances Gordon's words. *The poor man.*

Sean Reilly was asleep when Honey walked into his room. She sat at his bedside for a long time, watching him.

He opened his eyes and saw Honey. "I dreamed that I was dreaming, and that I wasn't going to die."

"Sean . . ."

"Did you come to visit the corpse?"

"Please don't talk that way."

"How could this happen?" he cried.

"Someone made a mistake, Sean."

"God, I don't want to die of AIDS!"

"Some people who get HIV may never get AIDS. The Irish are lucky."

"I wish I could believe you."

She took his hand in hers. "You've got to."

"I'm not a praying man," Sean said, "but I sure as hell am going to start now."

"I'll pray with you," Honey said.

He smiled wryly. "I guess we can forget about that dinner, huh?"

"Oh, no. You don't get out of it that easily. I'm looking forward to it."

He studied her a moment. "You really mean that, don't you?"

"You bet I do! No matter what happens. Remember, you promised to take me to Ireland."

Chapter Thirty-three

"Are you all right, Ken?" Lauren asked. "You seem tense, darling."

They were alone in the huge Harrison library. A maid and a butler had served a six-course dinner, and during dinner he and Alex Harrison—*Call me Alex*—had chatted about Mallory's brilliant future.

"Why are you tense?"

Because this pregnant black bitch expects me to marry her. Because any minute word is going to leak out about our engagement and she'll hear about it and blow the whistle. Because my whole future could be destroyed.

He took Lauren's hand in his. "I guess I'm working too hard. My patients aren't just patients to me, Lauren. They're people in trouble, and I can't help worrying about them."

She stroked his face. "That's one of the things I love about you, Ken. You're so caring."

"I guess I was brought up that way."

"Oh, I forgot to tell you. The society editor of the *Chronicle* and a photographer are coming here Monday to do an interview."

It was like a blow to the pit of his stomach.

"Is there any chance you could be here with me, darling? They want a picture of you."

"I . . . I wish I could, but I have a busy day scheduled at the hospital." His mind was racing. "Lauren, do you think it's a good idea to do an interview now? I mean, shouldn't we wait until . . . ?"

Lauren laughed. "You don't know the press, darling. They're like bloodhounds. No, it's much better to get it over with now."

Monday!

The following morning, Mallory tracked down Kat in a utility room. She looked tired and haggard. She had no makeup on and her hair was uncurled. *Lauren would never let herself go like that,* Mallory thought.

"Hi, honey!"

Kat did not answer.

Mallory took her in his arms. "I've been

thinking a lot about us, Kat. I didn't sleep at all last night. There's no one else for me. You were right, and I was wrong. I guess the news came as kind of a shock to me. I want you to have our baby." He watched the sudden glow on Kat's face.

"Do you really mean that, Ken?"

"You bet I do."

She put her arms around him. "Thank God! Oh, darling. I was so worried. I don't know what I would do without you."

"You don't have to worry about that. From now on, everything is going to be wonderful." *You'll never know how wonderful.* "Look, I have Sunday night off. Are you free?"

She grasped his hand. "I'll make myself free."

"Great! We'll have a nice quiet dinner and then we'll go back to your place for a nightcap. Do you think you can get rid of Paige and Honey? I want us to be alone."

Kat smiled. "No problem. You don't know how happy you've made me. Did I ever tell you how much I love you?"

"I love you, too. I'll show you how much Sunday night."

Thinking it over, Mallory decided it was a foolproof plan. He had worked it out to the smallest detail. There was no way Kat's death could ever be blamed on him.

It was too risky to get what he needed from the hospital pharmacy because security had been tightened there after the Bowman affair. Instead, early Sunday morning, Mallory went looking for a pharmacy far away from the neighborhood where he lived. Most of them were closed on Sunday, and he went to half a dozen before he found one that was open.

The pharmacist behind the counter said, "Morning. Can I help you?"

"Yes. I'm going to see a patient in this area, and I want to take a prescription to him." He pulled out his prescription pad and wrote on it.

The pharmacist smiled. "Not many doctors make house calls these days."

"I know. It's a pity, isn't it? People just don't care anymore." He handed the slip of paper to the pharmacist.

The pharmacist looked at it and nodded. "This will only take a few minutes."

"Thank you."

Step one.

That afternoon, Mallory made a stop at the hospital. He was there no more than ten minutes, and when he left, he was carrying a small package.

Step two.

Mallory had arranged to meet Kat at Trader Vic's for dinner, and he was waiting for her when she arrived. He watched her walking toward the table and thought, *It's the Last Supper, bitch.*

He rose and gave her a warm smile. "Hello, doll. You look beautiful." And he had to admit that she did. She looked sensational. *She could have been a model. And she's great in bed. All she lacks,* Ken thought, *is about twenty million dollars, give or take a few million.*

Kat was aware again of how the other women in the restaurant were eyeing Ken, envying her. But he only had eyes for her. He was the old Ken, warm and attentive.

"How was your day?" Ken asked.

She sighed. "Busy. Three operations in the morning and two this afternoon." She leaned forward. "I know it's too early, but I swear I could feel the baby kicking when I was getting dressed."

Mallory smiled. "Maybe it wants to get out."

"We should do an ultrasound test and find

out if it's a boy or a girl. Then I can start buying clothes for it."

"Great idea."

"Ken, can we set a wedding date? I'd like to have our wedding as soon as possible."

"No problem," Mallory said easily. "We can apply for a license next week."

"That's wonderful!" She had a sudden thought. "Maybe we could get a few days off and go somewhere on our honeymoon. Somewhere not too far away—up to Oregon or Washington."

Wrong, baby. I'll be honeymooning in June, on my yacht on the French Riviera.

"That sounds great. I'll talk to Wallace."

Kat squeezed his hand. "Thank you," she said huskily. "I'm going to make you the best wife in the whole world."

"I'm sure of it." Mallory smiled. "Now eat your vegetables. We want the baby to be healthy, don't we?"

They left the restaurant at 9:00 P.M. As they approached Kat's apartment building, Mallory said, "Are you sure Paige and Honey won't be home?"

"I made sure," Kat said. "Paige is at the hospital, on call, and I told Honey you and I wanted to be alone here."

Shit!

She saw the expression on his face. "Is anything wrong?"

"No, baby. I told you, I just like our private times to be private." *I'll have to be careful,* he thought. *Very careful.* "Let's hurry."

His impatience warmed Kat.

Inside the apartment, Mallory said, "Let's go into the bedroom."

Kat grinned. "That sounds like a great idea."

Mallory watched Kat undress, and he thought, *She still has a great figure. A baby would ruin it.*

"Aren't you going to get undressed, Ken?"

"Of course." He remembered the time she had gotten him to undress and then walked out on him. Well, now she was going to pay for that.

He took his clothes off slowly. *Can I perform?* he wondered. He was almost trembling with nervousness. *What I'm going to do is her fault. Not mine. I gave her a chance to back out and she was too stupid to take it.*

He slipped into bed beside her and felt her warm body against his. They began to stroke each other, and he felt himself getting

451

aroused. He entered her and she began to moan.

"Oh, darling . . . it feels so wonderful . . ." She began to move faster and faster. "Yes . . . yes . . . oh, my God! . . . don't stop . . ." And her body began to jerk spasmodically, and she shuddered and then lay still in his arms.

She turned to him anxiously. "Did you . . . ?"

"Of course," Mallory lied. He was much too tense. "How about a drink?"

"No. I shouldn't. The baby . . ."

"But this is a celebration, honey. One little drink isn't going to hurt."

Kat hesitated. "All right. A small one." Kat started to get up.

Mallory stopped her. "No, no. You stay in bed, Mama. You have to get used to being pampered."

Kat watched Mallory as he walked into the living room and she thought, *I'm the luckiest woman in the world!*

Mallory walked over to the little bar and poured scotch into two glasses. He glanced toward the bedroom to make sure he could not be seen, then went over to the couch, where he had placed his jacket. He took a small bottle from his pocket and poured the contents into Kat's drink. He returned to the bar and stirred Kat's drink and smelled it. There was no odor. He took the two glasses back to the bedroom, and handed Kat her drink.

"Let's drink a toast to our baby," Kat said.

"Right. To our baby."

Ken watched as Kat took a swallow of her drink.

"We'll find a nice apartment somewhere," Kat said dreamily. "I'll fix up a nursery. We're going to spoil our child rotten, aren't we?" She took another sip.

Mallory nodded. "Absolutely." He was watching her closely. "How do you feel?"

"Wonderful. I've been so worried about us, darling, but I'm not, not anymore."

"That's good," Mallory said. "You have nothing to worry about."

Kat's eyes were getting heavy. "No," she said. "There's nothing to worry about." Her words were beginning to slur. "Ken, I feel funny." She was beginning to sway.

"You should never have gotten pregnant."

She was staring up at him stupidly. "What?"

"You spoiled everything, Kat."

"Spoiled . . . ?" She was having trouble concentrating.

"You got in my way."

"Wha'?"

"No one gets in my way."

"Ken, I feel dizzy."

He stood there, watching her.

"Ken . . . help me, Ken . . ." Her head fell back onto the pillow.

Mallory looked at his watch again. There was plenty of time.

Chapter Thirty-four

It was Honey who arrived at the apartment first and stumbled across Kat's mutilated body, lying in a pool of blood on the floor of the bathroom, obscenely sprawled against the cold white tiles. A blood-stained curette lay beside her. She had hemorrhaged from her womb.

Honey stood there in shock. "Oh, my God!" Her voice was a strangled whisper. She knelt beside the body and placed a trembling finger against the carotid artery. There was no pulse. Honey hurried back into the living room, picked up the telephone, and dialed 911.

A male voice said, "Nine-one-one Emergency."

Honey stood there paralyzed, unable to speak.

"Nine-one-one Emergency . . . Hello . . .?"

"H . . . help! I . . . There's . . ." She was choking over her words. "Sh . . . she's dead."

"Who is dead, miss?"

"Kat."

"Your cat is dead?"

"No!" Honey screamed. *"Kat's* dead. Get someone over here right away."

"Lady . . ."

Honey slammed down the receiver. With shaking fingers, she dialed the hospital. "Dr. T . . . Taylor." Her voice was an agonized whisper.

"One moment, please."

Honey gripped the telephone and waited two minutes before she heard Paige's voice. "Dr. Taylor."

"Paige! You . . . you've got to come home right away!"

"Honey? What's happened?"

"Kat's . . . dead."

"What?" Paige's voice was filled with disbelief. "How?"

"It . . . it looks like she tried to abort herself."

"Oh, my God! All right. I'll be there as soon as I can."

*   *   *

By the time Paige arrived at the apartment, there were two policemen, a detective,
and a medical examiner there. Honey was in
her bedroom, heavily sedated. The medical examiner was leaning over Kat's naked body. A
detective looked up as Paige entered the
bloody bathroom.

"Who are you?"

Paige was staring at the lifeless body. Her
face was pale. "I'm Dr. Taylor. I live here."

"Maybe *you* can help me. I'm Inspector
Burns. I was trying to talk to the other lady
who lives here. She's hysterical. The doctor
gave her a sedative."

Paige looked away from the awful sight
on the floor. "What . . . what do you want to
know?"

"She lived here?"

"Yes."

*I'm going to have Ken's baby. How good
can it get?*

"It looks like she tried to get rid of the kid,
and messed it up," the detective said.

Paige stood there, her mind spinning.
When she spoke, she said, "I don't believe it."

Inspector Burns studied her a moment.
"Why don't you believe it, doctor?"

"She wanted that baby." She was beginning to think clearly again. "The father didn't want it."

"The father?"

"Dr. Ken Mallory. He works at Embarcadero County Hospital. He didn't want to marry her. Look, Kat is—*was*"—it was so painful to say *was*—"a doctor. If she had wanted to have an abortion, there's no way she would try to do it herself in a bathroom." Paige shook her head. "There's something wrong."

The medical examiner rose from beside the body. "Maybe she tried it herself because she didn't want anyone else to know about the baby."

"That's not true. She told us about it."

Inspector Burns was watching Paige. "Was she alone here this evening?"

"No. She had a date with Dr. Mallory."

Ken Mallory was in bed, carefully going over the events of the evening. He replayed every step of the way, making sure there were no loose ends. *Perfect,* he decided. He lay in bed, wondering why it was taking the police so long, and even as he was thinking it, the doorbell rang. Mallory let it ring three times, then got up, put on a robe over his pajamas, and went into the living room.

He stood in front of the door. "Who's there?" He sounded sleepy.

A voice said, "Dr. Mallory?"

"Yes."

"Inspector Burns. San Francisco Police Department."

"Police Department?" There was just the right note of surprise in his voice. Mallory opened the door.

The man standing in the hall showed his badge. "May I come in?"

"Yes. What's this all about?"

"Do you know a Dr. Hunter?"

"Of course I do." A look of alarm crossed his face. "Has something happened to Kat?"

"Were you with her earlier this evening?"

"Yes. My God! Tell me what's happened! Is she all right?"

"I'm afraid I have some bad news. Dr. Hunter is dead."

"*Dead?* I can't believe it. *How?*"

"Apparently she tried to perform an abortion on herself and it went wrong."

"Oh, my God!" Mallory said. He sank into a chair. "It's my fault."

The inspector was watching him closely. "Your fault?"

"Yes. I . . . Dr. Hunter and I were going to be married. I told her I didn't think it was a good idea for her to have a baby now. I wanted to wait, and she agreed. I suggested she go to the hospital and have them take care of it, but she must have decided to . . . I . . . I can't believe it."

"What time did you leave Dr. Hunter?"

"It must have been about ten o'clock. I dropped her off at her apartment and left."

"You didn't go into the apartment?"

"No."

"Did Dr. Hunter talk about what she planned to do?"

"You mean about the . . . ? No. Not a word."

Inspector Burns pulled out a card. "If you think of anything else that might be helpful, doctor, I'd appreciate it if you gave me a call."

"Certainly. I . . . you have no idea what a shock this is."

Paige and Honey stayed up all night, talking about what had happened to Kat, going over it and over it, in shocked disbelief.

At nine o'clock, Inspector Burns came by.

"Good morning. I wanted to tell you that I spoke to Dr. Mallory last night."

"And?"

"He said they went out to dinner, and then he dropped her off and went home."

"He's lying," Paige said. She was thinking. "Wait! Did they find any traces of semen in Kat's body?"

"Yes, as a matter of fact."

"Well, then," Paige said excitedly, "that *proves* he's lying. He did take her to bed and—"

"I went to talk to him about that this morning. He says they had sex *before* they went out to dinner."

"Oh." She would not give up. "His fingerprints will be on the curette he used to kill her." Her voice was eager. "Did you find fingerprints?"

"Yes, doctor," he said patiently. "They were hers."

"That's imp— Wait! Then he wore gloves, and when he was finished, he put her prints on the curette. How does that sound?"

"Like someone's been watching too many *Murder, She Wrote* television programs."

"You don't believe Kat was murdered, do you?"

"I'm afraid I don't."

"Have they done an autopsy?"

"Yes."

"And?"

"The medical examiner is listing it as an accidental death. Dr. Mallory told me she decided not to have the baby, so apparently she—"

"Went into the bathroom and butchered herself?" Paige interrupted. "For God's sake, inspector! She was a doctor, a surgeon! There's no way in the world she would have done that to herself."

Inspector Burns said thoughtfully, "You think Mallory persuaded her to have an abortion, and tried to help her, and then left when it went wrong?"

Paige shook her head. "No. It couldn't have happened that way. Kat would never have agreed. He deliberately murdered her." She was thinking out loud. "Kat was strong. She would have had to be unconscious for him to . . . to do what he did."

"The autopsy showed no signs of any blows or anything that would have caused her to become unconscious. No bruises on her throat . . ."

"Were there any traces of sleeping pills or . . . ?"

"Nothing." He saw the expression on Paige's face. "This doesn't look to me like a murder. I think Dr. Hunter made an error in judgment, and . . . I'm sorry."

She watched him start toward the door. "Wait!" Paige said. "You have a motive."

He turned. "Not really. Mallory says she agreed to have the abortion. That doesn't leave us much, does it?"

"It leaves you with a murder," Paige said stubbornly.

"Doctor, what we *don't* have is any evidence. It's his word against the victim's, and she's dead. I'm really sorry."

Paige watched him leave.

I'm not going to let Ken Mallory get away with it, she thought despairingly.

Jason came by to see Paige. "I heard what happened," he said. "I can't believe it! How could she have done that to herself?"

"She didn't," Paige said. "She was murdered." She told Jason about her conversation with Inspector Burns. "The police aren't going to do anything about it. They think it was an accident. Jason, it's my fault that Kat is dead."

"Your fault?"

"I'm the one who persuaded her to go out with Mallory in the first place. She didn't want to. It started out as a silly joke, and then she . . . she fell in love with him. Oh, Jason!"

"You can't blame yourself for that," he said firmly.

Paige looked around in despair. "I can't live in this apartment anymore. I have to get out of here."

Jason took her in his arms. "Let's get married right away."

"It's too soon. I mean, Kat isn't even . . ."

"I know. We'll wait a week or two."

"All right."

"I love you, Paige."

"I love you, too, darling. Isn't it stupid? I feel guilty because Kat and I both fell in love, and she's dead and I'm alive."

The photograph appeared on the front page of the *San Francisco Chronicle* on Tuesday. It showed a smiling Ken Mallory with his arm around Lauren Harrison. The caption read: "Heiress to Wed Doctor."

Paige stared at it in disbelief. Kat had been dead for only two days, and Ken Mallory was announcing his engagement to another woman! All the time he had been promising to marry Kat, he had been planning to marry someone else. *That's why he killed Kat. To get her out of the way!*

Paige picked up the telephone and dialed police headquarters.

"Inspector Burns, please."

A moment later, she was talking to the inspector.

"This is Dr. Taylor."

"Yes, doctor."

"Have you seen the photograph in this morning's *Chronicle*?"

"Yes."

"Well, there's your motive!" Paige exclaimed. "Ken Mallory had to shut Kat up before Lauren Harrison found out about her. You've got to arrest Mallory." She was almost yelling into the telephone.

"Wait a minute. Calm down, doctor. We may have a motive, but I told you, we don't have a shred of evidence. You said yourself that Dr. Hunter would have had to be unconscious before Mallory could perform an abortion on her. After I spoke to you, I talked to our forensic pathologist again. There was no sign of any kind of blow that could have caused unconsciousness."

"Then he must have given her a sedative," Paige said stubbornly. "Probably chloral hydrate. It's fast-acting and—"

Inspector Burns said patiently, "Doctor, there was no trace of chloral hydrate in her body. I'm sorry—I really am—but we can't arrest a man because he's going to get married. Was there anything else?"

Everything else. "No," Paige said. She slammed down the receiver and sat there thinking. *Mallory has to have given Kat some kind of drug. The easiest place for him to have gotten it would be the hospital pharmacy.*

Fifteen minutes later, Paige was on her way to Embarcadero County Hospital.

Pete Samuels, the chief pharmacist, was behind the counter. "Good morning, Dr. Taylor. How can I help you?"

"I believe Dr. Mallory came by a few days ago and picked up some medication. He told me the name of it, but I can't remember what it was."

Samuels frowned. "I don't remember Dr. Mallory coming by here for at least a month."

"Are you sure?"

Samuels nodded. "Positive. I would have remembered. We always talk football."

Paige's heart sank. "Thank you."

He must have written a prescription at some other pharmacy. Paige knew that the law required that all prescriptions for narcotics be made out in triplicate—one copy for the patient, one to be sent to the Bureau of Controlled Substances, and the third for the pharmacy's files.

Somewhere, Paige thought, *Ken Mallory had a prescription filled. There are probably two or three hundred pharmacies in San Francisco.* There was no way she could track down the prescription. It was likely that Mallory had gotten it just before he murdered Kat. That would have been on Saturday or Sunday. *If it was Sunday, I might have a chance,* Paige thought. *Very few pharmacies are open on Sunday. That narrows it down.*

She went upstairs to the office where the assignment sheets were kept and looked up the roster for Saturday. Dr. Ken Mallory had been on call all day, so the chances were that he had had the prescription filled on Sunday. How many pharmacies were open on Sunday in San Francisco?

Paige picked up the telephone and called the state pharmaceutical board.

"This is Dr. Taylor," Paige said. "Last Sunday, a friend of mine left a prescription at a pharmacy. She asked me to pick it up for her, but I can't remember the name of the pharmacy. I wonder if you could help me."

"Well, I don't see how, doctor. If you don't know . . ."

"Most drugstores are closed on Sunday, aren't they?"

"Yes, but . . ."

"I'd appreciate it if you could give me a list of those that were open."

There was a pause. "Well, if it's important . . ."

"It's very important," Paige assured her.

"Hold on, please."

There were thirty-six stores on the list, spread all over the city. It would have been simple if she could have gone to the police for help, but Inspector Burns did not believe her. *Honey and I are going to have to do this ourselves,* Paige thought. She explained to Honey what she had in mind.

"It's a real long shot, isn't it?" Honey said. "You don't even know if he filled the prescription on Sunday."

"It's the only shot we have." *That Kat has.* "I'll check out the ones in Richmond, the Marina, North Beach, Upper Market, Mission, and Potrero, and you check out the Excelsior, Ingleside, Lake Merced, Western Addition, and Sunset areas."

"All right."

At the first pharmacy Paige went into, she showed her identification and said, "A colleague of mine, Dr. Ken Mallory, was in here Sunday for a prescription. He's out of town, and he asked me to get a refill, but I can't remember the name of it. Would you mind looking it up, please?"

"Dr. Ken Mallory? Just a moment." He came back a few minutes later. "Sorry, we didn't fill any prescriptions Sunday for a Dr. Mallory."

"Thank you."

Paige got the same response at the next four pharmacies.

Honey was having no better luck.

"We have thousands of prescriptions here, you know."

"I know, but this was last Sunday."

"Well, we have no prescriptions here from a Dr. Mallory. Sorry."

The two of them spent the day going from pharmacy to pharmacy. They were both getting discouraged. It was not until late afternoon, just before closing time, that Paige found what she was looking for in a small pharmacy in the Potrero district. The pharmacist said, "Oh, yes, here we are. Dr. Ken Mallory. I remember him. He was on his way to make a house call on a patient. I was impressed, because not many doctors do that these days."

No resident ever made house calls. "What's the prescription for?"

Paige found she was holding her breath.

"Chloral hydrate."

Paige was almost trembling with excitement. "You're sure?"

"It says so right here."

"What was the patient's name?"

He looked at the copy of the prescription. "Spyros Levathes."

"Would you mind giving me a copy of that prescription?" Paige asked.

"Not at all, doctor."

* * *

One hour later, Paige was in Inspector Burns's office. She laid the prescription on his desk.

"Here's your proof," Paige said. "On Sunday, Dr. Mallory went to a pharmacy miles away from where he lives, and had this prescription for chloral hydrate filled. He put the chloral hydrate in Kat's drink, and when she was unconscious, he butchered her to make it look like an accident."

"You're saying he put the chloral hydrate in her drink and then killed her."

"Yes."

"There's only one problem with that, Dr. Taylor. There *was* no chloral hydrate in her body."

"There has to be. Your pathologist made a mistake. Ask him to check again."

He was losing his patience. "Doctor . . ."

"Please! I know I'm right."

"You're wasting everybody's time."

Paige sat across from him, her eyes fixed on his face.

He sighed. "All right. I'll call him again. Maybe he *did* make a mistake."

* * *

Jason picked Paige up for dinner. "We're having dinner at my house," he said. "There's something I want you to see."

During the drive there, Paige brought Jason up to date on what was happening.

"They'll find the chloral hydrate in her body," Paige said. "And Ken Mallory will get what's coming to him."

"I'm so sorry about all this, Paige."

"I know." She pressed his hand against her cheek. "Thank God for you."

The car pulled up in front of Jason's home.

Paige looked out of the window and she gasped. Around the green lawn in front of the house was a new white picket fence.

She was alone in the dark apartment. Ken Mallory used the key that Kat had given him and moved quietly toward the bedroom. Paige heard his footsteps coming toward her, but before she could move, he had leaped at her, his hands tight around her throat.

"You bitch! You're trying to destroy me. Well, you aren't going to snoop around anymore." He began squeezing harder. "I outsmarted all of you, didn't I?" His fingers squeezed tighter. "No one can ever prove I killed Kat."

She tried to scream, but it was impossible to breathe. She struggled free, and was suddenly awake. She was alone in her room. Paige sat up in bed, trembling.

She stayed awake the rest of the night, waiting for Inspector Burns's phone call. It came at 10:00 A.M.

"Dr. Taylor?"

"Yes." She was holding her breath.

"I just got the *third* report from the forensic pathologist."

"And?" Her heart was pounding.

"There was no trace of chloral hydrate or any other sedative in Dr. Hunter's body. None."

That was impossible! There had to be. There was no sign of any blow or anything that would have caused her to become unconscious. No bruises on her throat. It didn't make sense. Kat had to have been unconscious when Mallory killed her. The forensic pathologist was wrong.

Paige decided to go talk to him herself.

Dr. Dolan was in an irritable mood. "I don't like to be questioned like this," he said. "I've checked it three times. I told Inspector

Burns that there was no trace of chloral hydrate in any of her organs, and there wasn't."

"But . . ."

"Is there anything else, doctor?"

Paige looked at him helplessly. Her last hope was gone. Ken Mallory was going to get away with murder. "I . . . I guess not. If you didn't find any chemicals in her body, then I don't . . ."

"I didn't say I didn't find *any* chemicals."

She looked at him a moment. "You found something?"

"Just a trace of trichloroethylene."

She frowned. "What would that do?"

He shrugged. "Nothing. It's an analgesic drug. It wouldn't put anyone to sleep."

"I see."

"Sorry I can't help you."

Paige nodded. "Thank you."

She walked down the long, antiseptic corridor of the morgue, depressed, feeling that she was missing something. She had been so sure Kat had been put to sleep with chloral hydrate.

All he found was a trace of trichloroethylene. It wouldn't put anyone to sleep. But why would trichloroethylene be in Kat's body? Kat had not been taking any medications. Paige stopped in the middle of the corridor, her mind working furiously.

*   *   *

When Paige arrived at the hospital, she went directly to the medical library on the fifth floor. It took her less than a minute to find trichloroethylene. The description read: *A colorless, clear, volatile liquid with a specific gravity of 1.47 at 59 degrees F. It is a halogenated hydrocarbon, having the chemical formula CCl CCl :CHCl.*

And there, on the last line, she found what she was looking for. *When chloral hydrate is metabolized, it produces trichloroethylene as a by-product.*

Chapter Thirty-five

"Inspector, Dr. Taylor is here to see you."

"Again?" He was tempted to turn her away. She was obsessed with the half-baked theory she had. He was going to have to put a stop to it. "Send her in."

When Paige walked into his office, Inspector Burns said, "Look, doctor, I think this has gone far enough. Dr. Dolan called to complain about—"

"I know how Ken Mallory did it!" Her voice was charged with excitement. "There was trichloroethylene in Kat's body."

He nodded. "Dr. Dolan told me that. But he said it couldn't have made her unconscious. He—"

"Chloral hydrate turns into trichloroethylene!" Paige said triumphantly. "Mallory lied when he said he didn't go back into the apartment with Kat. He put chloral hydrate in her drink. It has no taste when you mix it with alcohol, and it only takes a few minutes for it to work. Then when she was unconscious, he killed her and made it look like a bungled abortion."

"Doctor, if you'll forgive my saying so, that's a hell of a lot of speculation."

"No, it isn't. He wrote the prescription for a patient named Spyros Levathes, but he never gave it to him."

"How do you know that?"

"Because he *couldn't* have. I checked on Spyros Levathes. He has erythropoietic porphyria."

"What's that?"

"It's a genetic metabolic disorder. It causes photosensitivity and lesions, hypertension, tachycardia, and a few other unpleasant symptoms. It's the result of a defective gene."

"I still don't understand."

"Dr. Mallory didn't give his patient chloral hydrate because it would have killed him! Chloral hydrate is contraindicated for porphyria. It would have caused immediate convulsive seizures."

For the first time, Inspector Burns was

impressed. "You've really done your homework, haven't you?"

Paige pressed on. "Why would Ken Mallory go to a remote pharmacy and fill a prescription for a patient he knew he couldn't *give* it to? You've *got* to arrest him."

His fingers were drumming on his desk. "It's not that simple."

"You've got to . . ."

Inspector Burns raised a hand. "All right. I'll tell you what I'll do. I'll talk to the district attorney's office and see whether they think we have a case."

Paige knew she had gone as far as she could. "Thank you, inspector."

"I'll get back to you."

After Paige Taylor left, Inspector Burns sat there thinking about their conversation. There was no hard evidence against Dr. Mallory, only the suspicions of a persistent woman. He reviewed the few facts that he had. Dr. Mallory had been engaged to Kat Hunter. Two days after she died, he was engaged to Alex Harrison's daughter. Interesting, but not against the law.

Mallory had said that he dropped Dr. Hunter off at her front door and did not go into the apartment. Semen was found in her body, but he had a plausible explanation for that.

Then there was the matter of the chloral hydrate. Mallory had written a prescription for a drug that could have killed his patient. Was he guilty of murder? Not guilty?

Burns buzzed his secretary on the intercom. "Barbara, get me an appointment with the district attorney this afternoon."

There were four men in the office when Paige walked in: the district attorney, his assistant, a man named Warren, and Inspector Burns.

"Thank you for stopping by, Dr. Taylor," the district attorney said. "Inspector Burns has been telling me of your interest in the death of Dr. Hunter. I can appreciate that. Dr. Hunter was your roommate, and you want to see justice done."

So they're going to arrest Ken Mallory after all!

"Yes," Paige said. "There's no doubt about it. Dr. Mallory killed her. When you arrest him, he—"

"I'm afraid we can't do that."

Paige looked at him blankly. "What?"

"We can't arrest Dr. Mallory."

"But why?"

"We have no case."

"Of course you have!" Paige exclaimed. "The trichloroethylene proves that—"

"Doctor, in a court of justice, ignorance of the law is no excuse. But ignorance in medicine *is*."

"I don't understand."

"It's simple. It means that Dr. Mallory could claim he made a mistake, that he didn't know what effect chloral hydrate would have on a patient with porphyria. No one could prove he was lying. It might prove that he's a lousy doctor, but it wouldn't prove that he's guilty of murder."

Paige looked at him in frustration. "You're going to let him get away with this?"

He studied her a moment. "I'll tell you what I'm prepared to do. I've discussed this with Inspector Burns. With your permission, we're going to send someone to your apartment to pick up the glasses in the bar. If we find any traces of chloral hydrate, we'll take the next step."

"What if he rinsed them out?"

Inspector Burns said dryly, "I don't imagine he took the time to use a detergent. If he just rinsed out the glasses, we'll find what we're looking for."

* * *

479

Two hours later, Inspector Burns was on the phone with Paige.

"We did a chemical analysis of all the glasses in the bar, doctor," Burns said.

Paige steeled herself for disappointment.

"We found one with traces of chloral hydrate."

Paige closed her eyes in a silent prayer of thanks.

"And there were fingerprints on that glass. We're going to check them against Dr. Mallory's prints."

Paige felt a surge of excitement.

The inspector went on, "When he killed her—if he did kill her—he was wearing gloves, so his fingerprints wouldn't be on the curette. But he couldn't very well have served her a drink while he wore gloves, and he might not have worn them when he put the glass back on the shelf after rinsing it out."

"No," Paige said. "He couldn't, could he?"

"I have to admit that in the beginning, I didn't believe your theory was going anywhere. I think now maybe Dr. Mallory could be our man. But proving it is going to be another matter." He continued, "The district attorney is right. It would be a tricky business to bring Mallory to trial. He can still say that the prescription was for his patient. There's no law against making a medical mistake. I don't see how we—"

"Wait a minute!" Paige said excitedly. "I think I know how!"

Ken Mallory was listening to Lauren on the telephone. "Father and I found some office space that you're going to adore, darling! It's a beautiful suite in the 490 Post Building. I'm going to hire a receptionist for you, someone not too pretty."

Mallory laughed. "You don't have to worry about that, baby. There isn't anyone in the world for me but you."

"I'm dying for you to come see it. Can you get away now?"

"I'm off in a couple of hours."

"Wonderful! Why don't you pick me up at the house?"

"All right. I'll be there." Mallory replaced the telephone. *It doesn't get any better than this,* he thought. *There is a God, and She loves me.*

He heard his name called over the PA system: "Dr. Mallory . . . Room 430. . . . Dr. Mallory . . . Room 430." He sat there daydreaming, thinking about the golden future that lay ahead of him. *A beautiful suite in the 490 Post Building, filled with rich old ladies eager to throw their money at him.* He heard his name called again. "Dr. Mallory . . . Room 430." He sighed and got to his feet. *I'll be out of this goddam madhouse soon*, he thought. He headed toward Room 430.

A resident was waiting for him in the corridor, outside the room. "I'm afraid we have a problem here," he said. "This is one of Dr. Peterson's patients, but Dr. Peterson isn't here. I'm having an argument with one of the other doctors."

They stepped inside. There were three people in the room—a man in bed, a male nurse, and a doctor Mallory had not met before.

The resident said, "This is Dr. Edwards. We need your advice, Dr. Mallory."

"What's the problem?"

The resident explained. "This patient is suffering from erythropoietic porphyria, and Dr. Edwards insists on giving him a sedative."

"I don't see any problem with that."

"Thank you," Dr. Edwards said. "The man hasn't slept in forty-eight hours. I've prescribed chloral hydrate for him so he can get some rest and . . ."

Mallory was looking at him in astonishment. "Are you out of your mind? That could kill him! He'd have a convulsive seizure, tachycardia, and he'd probably die. Where in hell did you study medicine?"

The man looked at Mallory and said quietly, "I didn't." He flashed a badge. "I'm with the San Francisco Police Department, Homicide." He turned to the man in bed. "Did you get that?"

The man pulled out a tape recorder from under the pillow. "I got it."

Mallory was looking from one to the other, frowning. "I don't understand. What is this? What's going on?"

The inspector turned to Mallory. "Dr. Mallory, you're under arrest for the murder of Dr. Kate Hunter."

Chapter Thirty-six

The headline in the *San Francisco Chronicle* read, DOCTOR ARRESTED IN LOVE TRIANGLE MURDER. The story beneath it went on at length to detail the lurid facts of the case.

Mallory read the newspaper in his cell. He slammed it down.

His cellmate said, "Looks like they got you cold, pal."

"Don't you believe it," Mallory said confidently. "I've got connections, and they're going to get me the best goddam lawyer in the world. I'll be out of here in twenty-four hours. All I have to do is make one phone call."

* * *

485

The Harrisons were reading the newspaper at breakfast.

"My God!" Lauren said. "Ken! I can't believe it!"

A butler approached the breakfast table. "Excuse me, Miss Harrison. Dr. Mallory is on the telephone for you. I believe he's calling from jail."

"I'll take it." Lauren started to get up from the table.

"You'll stay here and finish your breakfast," Alex Harrison said firmly. He turned to the butler. "We don't know any Dr. Mallory."

Paige read the newspaper as she was getting dressed. Mallory was going to be punished for the terrible thing he had done, but it gave Paige no satisfaction. Nothing they did to him could ever bring Kat back.

The doorbell rang, and Paige went to open it. A stranger stood there. He was wearing a dark suit and carried a briefcase.

"Dr. Taylor?"

"Yes . . ."

"My name is Roderick Pelham. I'm an attorney with Rothman & Rothman. May I come in?"

Paige studied him, puzzled. "Yes."

He entered the apartment.

"What did you want to see me about?"

She watched him open the briefcase and take out some papers.

"You are aware, of course, that you are the principal beneficiary of John Cronin's will?"

Paige looked at him blankly. "What are you talking about? There must be some mistake."

"Oh, there's no mistake. Mr. Cronin has left you the sum of one million dollars."

Paige sank into a chair, overwhelmed, remembering.

You have to go to Europe. Do me a favor. Go to Paris . . . stay at the Crillon, have dinner at Maxim's, order a big, thick steak and a bottle of champagne, and when you eat that steak and drink that champagne, I want you to think of me.

"If you'll just sign here, we'll take care of all the necessary paperwork."

Paige looked up. "I . . . I don't know what to say. I . . . he had a family."

"According to the terms of his will, they get only the remainder of his estate, not a large amount."

"I can't accept this," Paige told him.

Pelham looked at her in surprise. "Why not?"

She had no answer. John Cronin had wanted her to have this money. "I don't know. It . . . it seems unethical, somehow. He was my patient."

"Well, I'll leave the check here with you. You can decide what you want to do with it. Just sign here."

Paige signed the paper in a daze.

"Goodbye, doctor."

She watched him leave and sat there thinking of John Cronin.

The news of Paige's inheritance was the talk of the hospital. Somehow, Paige had hoped it could be kept quiet. She still had not made up her mind about what to do with the money. *It doesn't belong to me*, Paige thought. *He has a family.*

Paige was not emotionally ready to go back to work, but her patients had to be taken care of. An operation was scheduled for that morning. Arthur Kane was waiting for Paige in the corridor. They had not spoken to each other since the incident of the reversed X-rays. Although Paige had no proof it was Kane, the tire-slashing episode had scared her.

"Hello, Paige. Let's let bygones be bygones. What do you say?"

Paige shrugged. "Fine."

"Wasn't that a terrible thing about Ken Mallory?" he asked.

"Yes," Paige said.

Kane was looking at her slyly. "Can you imagine a doctor deliberately killing a human being? It's horrible, isn't it?"

"Yes."

"By the way," he said, "congratulations. I hear that you're a millionairess."

"I can't see . . ."

"I have tickets for the theater tonight, Paige. I thought that the two of us could go."

"Thanks," Paige said. "I'm engaged to someone."

"Then I suggest you get unengaged."

She looked at him, surprised. "I beg your pardon?"

Kane moved closer to her. "I ordered an autopsy on John Cronin."

Paige found her heart beginning to beat faster. "Yes?"

"He didn't die of heart failure. Someone

gave him an overdose of insulin. I guess that particular someone never figured on an autopsy."

Paige's mouth was suddenly dry.

"You were with him when he died, weren't you?"

She hesitated. "Yes."

"I'm the only one who knows that, and I'm the only one who has the report." He patted her arm. "And my lips are sealed. Now, about those tickets tonight . . ."

Paige pulled away from him. "No!"

"Are you sure you know what you're doing?"

She took a deep breath. "Yes. Now, if you'll excuse me . . ."

And she walked away. Kane looked after her, and his face hardened. He turned and headed toward Dr. Benjamin Wallace's office.

The telephone awakened her at 1:00 A.M. at her apartment.

"You have been a naughty girl again."

It was the same raspy voice disguised in a breathy whisper, but this time Paige recognized it. *My God,* she thought, *I was right to be scared.*

The following morning, when Paige arrived at the hospital, two men were waiting for her.

"Dr. Paige Taylor?"

"Yes."

"You'll have to come with us. You're under arrest for the murder of John Cronin."

Chapter Thirty-seven

It was the final day of the trial. Alan Penn, the defense attorney, was making his summation to the jury.

"Ladies and gentlemen, you have heard a lot of testimony about Dr. Taylor's competence or incompetence. Well, Judge Young will instruct you that that's not what this trial is about. I'm sure that for every doctor who did not approve of her work, we could produce a dozen doctors who did. But that is not the issue.

"Paige Taylor is on trial for the death of John Cronin. She has admitted helping him die. She did so because he was in great pain, and he asked her to do so. That is euthanasia, and it's being accepted more and more throughout the world. In the past year, the California Supreme Court has upheld the right of a mentally competent adult to refuse or demand the withdrawal of medical treatment of any form. It is the individual who must live or die with the course of treatment chosen or rejected."

He looked into the faces of the jurors. "Euthanasia is a crime of compassion, of mercy, and I daresay it takes place in some form or another in hospitals all over the world. The prosecuting attorney is asking for a death sentence. Don't let him confuse the issue. There has never been a death sentence for euthanasia. Sixty-three percent of Americans believe euthanasia should be legal, and in eighteen states in this country, it *is* legal. The question is, do we have the right to compel helpless patients to live in pain, to force them to stay alive and suffer? The question has become complicated because of the great strides we've made in medical technology. We've turned the care of patients over to machines. Machines have no mercy. If a horse breaks a leg, we put it out of its misery by shooting it. With a human being, we condemn him or her to a half life that is hell.

"Dr. Taylor didn't decide when John Cronin would die. John Cronin decided. Make no mistake about it, what Dr. Taylor did was an act of mercy. She has taken full responsibility for that. But you can rest assured that she knew nothing about the money that was left to her. What she did, she did in a spirit of compassion. John Cronin was a man with a failing heart and an untreatable, fatal cancer that had spread through his body, causing him agony. Just ask yourself one question. Under those circumstances, would you like to go on living? Thank you." He turned, walked back to the table, and sat next to Paige.

Gus Venable rose and stood before the jury. *"Compassion? Mercy?"* He looked over at Paige, shook his head, then turned back to the jury. "Ladies and gentlemen, I have been practicing law in courtrooms for more than twenty years, and I must tell you that in all those years, I have never—never—seen a more clear-cut case of cold-blooded, deliberate murder for profit."

Paige was hanging on every word, tense and pale.

"The defense talked about euthanasia. Did Dr. Taylor do what she did out of a feeling of compassion? I don't think so. Dr. Taylor and others have testified that Mr. Cronin had only a few more days to live. Why didn't she let him live those few days? Perhaps it was because

495

Dr. Taylor was afraid Mrs. Cronin might learn about her husband changing his will, and put a stop to it.

"It's a most remarkable coincidence that immediately after Mr. Cronin changed his will and left Dr. Taylor the sum of one million dollars, she gave him an overdose of insulin and murdered him.

"Again and again, the defendant has convicted herself with her own words. She said that she was on friendly terms with John Cronin, that he liked and respected her. But you have heard witnesses testify that he hated Dr. Paige Taylor, that he called her 'that bitch,' and told her to keep her fucking hands off him."

Gus Venable glanced at the defendant again. There was a look of despair on Paige's face. He turned back to the jury. "An attorney has testified that Dr. Taylor said, about the million dollars that was left to her, 'It's unethical. He was my patient.' But she grabbed the money. She needed it. She had a drawer full of travel brochures at home—Paris, London, the Riviera. And bear in mind that she didn't go to the travel agency *after* she got the money. Oh, no. She planned those trips earlier. All she needed was the money and the opportunity, and John Cronin supplied both. A helpless, dying man she could control. She had at her mercy a man who she admitted was in enormous pain—agony, in fact, according to her own admission. When you're in that kind of pain, you can imagine how difficult it must be to think clearly. We don't know *how* Dr. Taylor persuaded John Cronin to change his will, to cut out the family he loved and to make her his main beneficiary. What we *do* know is that he summoned her to his bedside on that fatal night. What did they talk about? Could he have offered her a million dollars to put him out of his misery? It's a possibility we must face. In either case, it was cold-blooded murder.

"Ladies and gentlemen, during this trial, do you know who was the most damaging witness of all?" He pointed a dramatic finger at Paige. "The defendant herself! We've heard testimony that she gave an illegal blood transfusion and then falsified the record. She has not denied that fact. She said that she never killed a patient except John Cronin, but we've heard testimony that Dr. Barker, a physician respected by everybody, accused her of killing his patient.

"Unfortunately, ladies and gentlemen, Lawrence Barker suffered a stroke and can't be here with us today to testify against the defendant. But let me remind you of Dr. Barker's opinion of the defendant. This is Dr. Peterson, testifying about a patient Dr. Taylor was operating on."

He read from the transcript.

" 'Dr. Barker came into the operating room during the operation?'

" 'Yes.'

" 'And did Dr. Barker say anything?'

"Answer: 'He turned to Dr. Taylor and said, "You killed him." '

"This is from Nurse Berry. 'Tell me some specific things you heard Dr. Barker say to Dr. Taylor.'

"Answer: 'He said she was incompetent . . . Another time he said he wouldn't let her operate on his dog.' "

Gus Venable looked up. "Either there is some kind of conspiracy going on, where all these reputable doctors and nurses are lying about the defendant, or Dr. Taylor is a liar. Not *just* a liar, but a pathological . . ."

The rear door of the courtroom had opened and an aide hurried in. He paused in the doorway a moment, trying to make a decision. Then he moved down the aisle toward Gus Venable.

"Sir . . ."

Gus Venable turned, furious. "Can't you see I'm . . . ?"

The aide whispered in his ear.

Gus Venable looked at him, stunned. *"What?* That's wonderful!"

Judge Young leaned forward, her voice ominously quiet. "Forgive me for interrupting you two, but what exactly do you think you're doing?"

Gus Venable turned to the judge excitedly. "Your honor, I've just been informed that Dr. Lawrence Barker is outside this courtroom. He's in a wheelchair, but he's able to testify. I'd like to call him to the stand."

There was a loud buzz in the courtroom.

Alan Penn was on his feet. "Objection!" he yelled. "The prosecuting attorney is in the middle of his summation. There's no precedent for calling a new witness at this late hour. I—"

Judge Young slammed her gavel down. "Would counsel please approach the bench."

Penn and Venable moved up to the bench.

"This is highly irregular, your honor. I object . . ."

Judge Young said, "You're right about its being irregular, Mr. Penn, but you're wrong about its being without precedent. I can cite a dozen cases around the country where material witnesses were allowed to testify under special circumstances. In fact, if you're so interested in precedent, you might look up a case that took place in this courtroom five years ago. I happened to be the judge."

Alan Penn swallowed. "Does this mean you're going to allow him to testify?"

Judge Young was thoughtful. "Since Dr. Barker is a material witness to this case, and was physically unable to testify earlier, in the interest of justice, I'm going to rule that he be allowed to take the stand."

"Exception! There is no proof that the witness is competent to testify. I demand a battery of psychiatrists—"

"Mr. Penn, in this courtroom, we don't demand. We request." She turned to Gus Venable. "You may bring in your witness."

Alan Penn stood there, deflated. *It's all over,* he thought. *Our case is down the drain.*

Gus Venable turned to his aide. "Bring Dr. Barker in."

The door opened slowly, and Dr. Lawrence Barker entered the courtroom. He was in a wheelchair. His head was tilted, and one side of his face was drawn up in a slight rictus.

Everyone watched the pale and fragile figure being wheeled to the front of the courtroom. As he moved past Paige, he looked over at her.

There was no friendliness in his eyes, and

Paige remembered his last words: *Who the hell do you think you . . . ?*

When Lawrence Barker was in front of the bench, Judge Young leaned forward and said gently, "Dr. Barker, are you able to testify here today?"

When Barker spoke, his words were slurred. "I am, your honor."

"Are you fully aware of what is going on in this courtroom?"

"Yes, your honor." He looked over to where Paige was seated. "That woman is being tried for the murder of a patient."

Paige winced. *That woman!*

Judge Young made her decision. She turned to the bailiff. "Would you swear the witness in, please?"

When Dr. Barker had been sworn in, Judge Young said, "You may stay in the chair, Dr. Barker. The prosecutor will proceed, and I will allow the defense to cross-examine."

Gus Venable smiled. "Thank you, your honor." He strolled over to the wheelchair. "We won't keep you very long, doctor, and the court deeply appreciates your coming in to testify under these trying circumstances. Are you familiar with any of the testimony that has been given here over the past month?"

Dr. Barker nodded. "I've been following it

on television and in the newspapers, and it made me sick to my stomach."

Paige buried her head in her hands.

It was all Gus Venable could do to hide his feeling of triumph. "I'm sure a lot of us feel the same way, doctor," the prosecutor said piously.

"I came here because I want to see justice done."

Venable smiled. "Exactly. So do we."

Lawrence Barker took a deep breath, and when he spoke, his voice was filled with outrage. "Then how the hell could you bring Dr. Taylor to trial?"

Venable thought he had misunderstood him. "I beg your pardon?"

"This trial is a farce!"

Paige and Alan Penn exchanged a stunned look.

Gus Venable turned pale. "Dr. Barker..."

"Don't interrupt me," Barker snapped. "You've used the testimony of a lot of biased, jealous people to attack a brilliant surgeon. She—"

"Just a minute!" Venable was beginning to panic. "Isn't it true that you criticized Dr. Taylor's ability so severely that she was finally ready to quit Embarcadero Hospital?"

"Yes."

Gus Venable was starting to feel better. "Well, then," he said patronizingly, "how can you say that Paige Taylor is a brilliant doctor?"

"Because it happens to be the truth." Barker turned to look at Paige, and when he spoke again, he was talking to her as though they were the only two people in the courtroom: "Some people are born to be doctors. You were one of those rare ones. I knew from the beginning how capable you were. I was hard on you—maybe too hard—because you were good. I was tough on you because I wanted you to be tougher on yourself. I wanted you to be perfect, because in our profession, there's no room for error. None."

Paige was staring at him, mesmerized, her mind spinning. It was all happening too fast.

The courtroom was hushed.

"I wasn't about to let you quit."

Gus Venable could feel his victory slipping away. His prize witness had become his worst nightmare. "Dr. Barker—it has been testified that you accused Dr. Taylor of killing your patient Lance Kelly. How . . . ?"

"I told her that because she was the surgeon in charge. It was her ultimate responsibility. In fact, the anesthetist caused Mr. Kelly's death."

By now the court was in an uproar.

Paige sat there, stunned.

Dr. Barker went on speaking slowly, with an effort. "And as for John Cronin leaving her that money, Dr. Taylor knew nothing about it. I talked to Mr. Cronin myself. He told me that he was going to leave Dr. Taylor that money because he hated his family, and he said he was going to ask Dr. Taylor to release him from his misery. I agreed."

There was an uproar from the spectators. Gus Venable was standing there, a look of total bewilderment on his face.

Alan Penn leaped to his feet. "Your honor, I move for a dismissal!"

Judge Young was slamming her gavel down. "Quiet!" she yelled. She looked at the two attorneys. "Into my chambers."

Judge Young, Alan Penn, and Gus Venable were seated in Judge Young's chambers.

Gus Venable was in a state of shock. "I . . . I don't know what to say. He's obviously a sick man, your honor. He's confused. I want a battery of psychiatrists to examine him and—"

"You can't have it both ways, Gus. It looks like your case just went up in smoke. Let's save you any further embarrassment, shall we? I'm going to grant a dismissal on the murder charge. Any objection?"

There was a long silence. Finally, Venable nodded. "I guess not."

Judge Young said, "Good decision. I'm going to give you some advice. Never, *never* call a witness unless you know what he's going to say."

The court was in session again. Judge Young said, "Ladies and gentlemen of the jury, thank you for your time and your patience. The court is going to grant a dismissal on all charges. The defendant is free."

Paige turned to blow Jason a kiss, then hurried over to where Dr. Barker was seated. She slid down to her knees and hugged him.

"I don't know how to thank you," she whispered.

"You never should have gotten into this mess in the first place," he growled. "Damned fool thing to do. Let's get out of here and go somewhere where we can talk."

Judge Young heard. She stood up and said, "You may use my chambers if you like. That's the least we can do for you."

* * *

Paige, Jason, and Dr. Barker were in the judge's chambers, alone.

Dr. Barker said, "Sorry they wouldn't let me come here to help you sooner. You know what goddam doctors are like."

Paige was near tears. "I can't tell you how much I . . ."

"Then don't!" he said gruffly.

Paige was studying him, suddenly remembering something. "When did you speak to John Cronin?"

"*What?*"

"You heard me. When did you speak to John Cronin?"

"*When?*"

She said slowly, "You never even *met* John Cronin. You didn't know him."

There was the trace of a smile on Barker's lips. "No. But I know you."

Paige leaned over and threw her arms around him.

"Don't get sloppy," he growled. He looked over at Jason. "She gets sloppy sometimes. You'd better take good care of her, or you'll have to answer to me."

Jason said. "Don't worry, sir. I will."

Paige and Jason were married the following day. Dr. Barker was their best man.

Epilogue

Paige Curtis went into private practice and is affiliated with the prestigious North Shore Hospital. Paige used the million dollars John Cronin left her to set up a medical foundation in her father's name in Africa.

Lawrence Barker shares an office with Paige, as a surgical consultant.

Arthur Kane had his license revoked by the Medical Board of California.

Jimmy Ford fully recovered and married Betsy. They named their first daughter Paige.

Honey Taft moved to Ireland with Sean Reilly, and works as a nurse in Dublin.

Sean Reilly is a successful artist, and shows no symptoms of AIDS, as yet.

Mike Hunter was sentenced to state prison for armed robbery and is still serving time.

Alfred Turner joined a practice on Park Avenue and is enormously successful.

Benjamin Wallace was fired as administrator of Embarcadero County Hospital.

Lauren Harrison married her tennis pro.

Lou Dinetto was sentenced to fifteen years in the penitentiary for tax evasion.

Ken Mallory was sentenced to life imprisonment. One week after Dinetto arrived at the penitentiary, Mallory was found stabbed to death in his cell.

The Embarcadero Hospital is still there, awaiting the next earthquake.